MORE THAN SECOND CHANCES

ASTON FALLS BOOK 1

SARA JANE WOODLEY

Cover Design by
CANVAPRO

Nicholas & Grace art by
ARISTARH VIA DEPOSIT PHOTOS

ELEVENTH AVENUE
PUBLISHING

A THANK YOU TO MY READERS

In August 2020, I released my first book in the Legacy Inn series. I was passionate about this project, and I was hopeful that people would like my stories as much as I loved writing them. But, I never could have imagined that I would be blessed with the most amazing community of readers!

I can't begin to tell you how thankful I am for each and every one of you. I've loved every message, email, and review, and always appreciate hearing from you. Your support and kind words have been some of the *best* parts of this journey.

To my Advance Reader Team, thank you for your incredibly valuable and consistent feedback. It means so much to me to have such a wonderful group of dedicated readers.

If you'd like to connect further, drop by my Facebook Page, Instagram or Tik Tok! I like to engage with my readers and share my book inspo, new releases, and photos of my cat's antics.

Thank you again for everything you do.

Love always,

Sara Jane

1

GRACE

I'd never believed in second chances.

I didn't tell a lot of people that; Dad would've said that I was being pessimistic, or cynical, or something of the sort. But, it had been my point of view ever since I was fifteen and my mom died. When something changed, it changed forever.

Some people took comfort in the thought of a second chance. But me? I believed that second chances were simply first chances in a new context.

Like, that old pair of jeans that fit just a size too small lately. I aspired to squeeze myself back into them someday... After a few rounds of dieting and exercise. Or, the girl from elementary school who used to be my best friend until she shoved me in the mud. She'd since moved away, and I was much less prone to falling in mud now, anyway. Or, the boy from high school who broke my heart when he left town.

A boy like him didn't get a second chance.

"Gracie," a voice called, snapping me from my thoughts. "Hey, Gracie. Yoohoo!"

I turned towards the table by the window where Mrs.

Applebaum was waving me down like a ship coming to port. I glanced at the pile of dirty plates on my arm and then looked at her again. My arm was already cramping, but she was waving and smiling.

Hopefully this wouldn't take long.

I approached Mrs. Applebaum and her friend, Ms. Rodriguez. They were wearing almost identical pink flannel shirts and jeans, and Ms. Rodriguez was also sporting a lovely white cowboy hat.

"Are you ready to order?" I asked with a smile.

"Yes, dear." Mrs. Applebaum turned to the menu, lowering her glasses on her nose. "I would like—"

"Hang on, Sue," Ms. Rodriguez said. She held up a finger. "I never said I was ready to order."

Oh no... Here we go.

"What? You said the smoked salmon bagel looked good."

"But that doesn't mean I want to *order* the smoked salmon bagel."

"Then why would you say that?"

Ms. Rodriguez huffed. "I was making conversation."

"Well, hurry it up." Mrs. Applebaum rolled her eyes dramatically. "We don't have all day."

All day was exactly how long they had.

Mrs. Applebaum and Ms. Rodriguez weren't exactly known around Aston Falls for their hard work and dedicated productivity. To be fair, they'd done their time. Mrs. Applebaum and her husband opened the Sweets n' Sundaes ice cream parlor up on Center Street years ago, and Ms. Rodriguez owned the Aston Glow Inn across town.

These days, the only work these two engaged in was harmless—though occasionally intriguing—gossip about the goings on around town. Intriguing because you were never sure just how much truth was in the rumors. Often, about the amount of truth you'd find in a tabloid... or a photo on social media.

"I want to get to church before Pastor MacLean starts his sermon." Mrs. Applebaum sighed impatiently. Then her eyes went wide and she leaned across the table towards Ms. Rodriguez and me. "Speaking of church, I was talking to Jane Wendzel last week. Did you hear about her nose surgery? Apparently her snoring was so bad, she woke the neighbors. Though, if you ask me, she didn't get the surgery only to help with snoring. If you know what I mean."

Mrs. Applebaum tapped her nose twice with a mischievous gleam in her eye.

I hid my smile and kept from rolling my eyes. Whether or not Jane Wendzel was unhappy with the look of her nose, I happened to know all about her snoring. Growing up, her snuffling used to keep the girls in our grade awake at sleepovers. I'd always tried to gently roll her onto her side before the meaner kids could wake up and tease her about it.

"Oh, psh." Ms. Rodriguez swatted a hand. "That's nothing compared to what I heard last week."

I shifted from foot to foot, my arm officially aching. I tried to balance the weight of the plates across my forearm and my other hand. Mrs. Applebaum and Ms. Rodriguez were unstoppable when they got on a hot topic—I'd have to find my exit, and fast.

Ms. Rodriguez leaned towards us, her eyes darting around the cafe. "I heard that Nicholas King is coming back to town."

My arms almost gave out and the plates crashed together. I hurriedly stacked them back onto my forearm, my legs numb.

Nicholas King? There was no way.

I must've misheard.

"Now I know that you've lost it." Mrs. Applebaum looked at me and rolled her eyes as if this was a joke that we could share. "Nicholas King is in Chicago being a football star. He isn't coming back."

"But, it's true! I overheard Eleanor King at the grocery store."

Mrs. Applebaum's ears perked up and she narrowed her eyes. "Eleanor King said that?"

"The one and only," the other woman said smugly.

"That is *very* interesting news. The prodigal son returning home."

My mouth was bone dry and my body had gone cold. The plates were weighing me down, and it felt like gravity might suck me into the floor. I couldn't stand there a moment longer.

Because the boy from high school who broke my heart? He might be coming home.

"Excuse me, ladies," I croaked. "I'd better bring these plates to the kitchen. I'll be back to take your orders."

Before they could say anything, I zipped to the kitchen and placed the plates on the dishwashing station. I breathed a sigh of relief and massaged my forearms and neck.

Goodness knows that I loved Mrs. Applebaum and Ms. Rodriguez, but their chatter wasn't always well-timed. Especially when the subject of their chatter was the one man I'd rather not think about.

But I didn't have time to get into that right now.

I threw my hair into a messy bun and strode out of the kitchen. Almost immediately, I bumped into a portly man waiting next to the serving counter.

"Welcome to the Morning Bell Cafe!" I said brightly. "How can I help you?"

The man looked me up and down, his small, dark eyes

taking in my dirtied apron and stained blue jeans. Two perfectly symmetrical tufts of hair adorned his balding head above his ears, and his mustache featured a piece of dried noodle. Today's lunch probably. He had frown lines between his eyes, like he'd spent one too many days glaring at a computer screen.

"You?" he said curtly. His face tilted up a touch, watching me from down his nose—which wasn't easy given that he was about my height. "I doubt you can help, Miss. I'm here to speak to the owner—a Mr. Bell. You're clearly not the person I'm looking for."

I stepped back, shocked at the man's abrasive demeanor. I opened my mouth to respond when my dad appeared from the back office.

"Jim!" he called cheerily, striding towards us. "So lovely to meet you in person. I see that you've met my daughter, Grace."

Dad stood next to me and wrapped a friendly arm around my shoulder, kissing the top of my head. He extended a hand towards the portly man and the man sniffed before shaking it.

"Pleasure." His tone indicated that he thought the exchange was anything but.

Dad didn't seem to notice the man's condescending air. He turned to me. "Grace, Jim and I are going to my office for a moment to chat. You'll be okay working on your own for a couple of minutes?"

I rolled my eyes at my dad teasingly. "I'm 27 now, Dad. Some may say I'm a full-grown woman. I can handle the floor alone, I've done it before."

Dad laughed warmly, his green eyes sparkling. "That's my girl." Then, he turned to Jim. "Let's head to my office and see what we can work out."

Without a glance in my direction, Jim swept down the hallway, his hands clasped behind his back. Dad winked at me and disappeared into his office behind Jim, closing the door.

I frowned. What was that all about? Could Jim be the coffee machine technician? Not likely—he was dressed in a suit. Was he a bank representative? Dad had had a few bankers around lately, but he normally gave me a heads up before they came by.

Jim didn't seem like the type to work at a bank. His hair was too unkempt, his suit not quite slick enough. So who was he?

"Gracie!"

I heard the call from the front of the cafe and I shook myself off.

Better get back to work. I'd ask Dad about Jim later.

The light went off outside the front door of Morning Bell and I turned the antique wooden sign over to "Closed."

My back ached and my feet hurt, but there was still a lot of work to do before Dad and I could head home.

I turned up the volume on the radio and hummed along to a pop song as I got to work cleaning the cafe. I wiped down the tables and stacked the chairs before I grabbed a broom and began sweeping. Then, my stomach emitted a grumble that sounded remarkably like a snoring dragon.

"I heard that!" Dad called from his office. I heard his door shut, followed by thumping footsteps down the hall. He leaned against the serving counter with his eyebrows raised. "Hungry?"

"A bit." I laughed. "I didn't have dinner."

"Time flies." Dad smiled, his eyes crinkling at the sides. People said that Dad and I looked alike. I believed it was because we had the same eyes—deep green and almond-shaped when we smiled. "I'll grab you some food from the kitchen. I'm sure Tommy's cooked up something good for us."

"I sent Tommy home early. His baby's sick again."

"Again?" Dad asked, scratching his scraggly white beard. I'd have to remember to call the barber soon for him. "Poor guy. I hope it isn't too serious."

"The vet should have an answer by tomorrow." I shook my head. "That Shih Tzu is truly the love of his life. I don't know what Tommy would do without him. It's just too bad the vet bills are so expensive. Tommy mentioned that he was really thankful to have this job."

Dad's expression stalled. His mouth quirked into a sour grimace and a shadow passed over his features. But in a blink, he was smiling again.

I opened my mouth to ask if something was wrong when he suddenly winced and clutched a hand to his chest. All at once, his face went white and his breathing was ragged.

"Oof," he muttered, collapsing against the counter.

He was going to fall.

My body kicked into gear, adrenaline spiking. I dropped the broom handle and raced towards him, catching his arm and throwing it over my shoulder.

"Dad?" I asked urgently. "You okay?"

He was still clutching his chest. He didn't answer.

Somehow, I managed to lead him to a chair. I knelt in front of him and scanned his features. His eyes were squeezed shut and his mouth was a scowl. There was a sheen on his forehead and I pressed the back of my hand lightly to his head.

"You're burning up," I said, trying to keep calm but my heart was in my throat. "I'm calling Austin."

"Don't be silly." Dad swatted a hand, but the simple movement seemed to exhaust him. "I think I just pulled a muscle in my chest. I'm fine, completely fine."

"You don't look fine."

His hand was still pressed against his chest. My blood pounded in my ears.

Was it a heart attack?

Please don't be a heart attack. Please don't take my dad away from me.

Austin answered on the first ring. "Grace? You never call this late. Everything okay?"

"I don't know, Aus." My voice was strangled. "Can you come to the cafe? Dad's not looking good."

"I'm fine, son," Dad tried to shout, but his voice was weak. "No problems here."

Austin didn't hesitate. "I'll be right there."

The line went dead and I returned to Dad's side. Austin was my twin brother, and he also happened to be Aston Falls' top (and only) doctor. He was pretty much always on call, seeing as the nearest hospital was 60 miles away.

In all honesty, Austin was likely better than the doctors at any of the nearby hospitals anyway. It baffled me that he came back to Aston Falls after completing his residency in LA. He was top of his class in med school and had a number of promising offers to work anywhere in the world— Australia, the Bahamas, Switzerland. But, instead, he chose to return to our small town in the mountains of Montana.

I grabbed Dad's hand and squeezed it, my eyes trained on his pale face. He seemed so small, so weak. The last time I saw him like this was at Mom's funeral. He swore that day to be the strongest he could be for my brother and me. Now that I was older, I couldn't begin to imagine the sacrifices he made to be that person for us.

"Gracie, listen to me." Dad's face was slack now, his eyes shut and his brow unfurrowed. He almost looked like he was sleep-talking. "I've been meaning to speak with you about this for awhile, and this seems as good a time as any."

My heart slammed. He wasn't about to tell me where our life savings were kept, was he? "Talk to me about what?"

"About Jim McNeil. The man who was here earlier today." Dad's voice was faint. I squeezed his hand again and sat cross-legged on the floor next to him, just like I used to do when I was a kid.

"Dad, save your strength," I said quietly. "Austin will be here soon and you'll be good to go in no time."

"No, I have to tell you this." His voice was surprisingly gruff and I clamped my lips shut. He sighed and, when he spoke again, his words were quiet. "Jim is a representative for Ross's Burgers."

I frowned. "The multi-national burger chain?"

"Yes. Ross's Burgers is looking to expand further into Montana and they're thinking about putting a restaurant here in Aston Falls."

"So, what was he doing here?"

Dad opened his eyes to look at me. I saw a deep, profound sadness that scared me more than almost anything. "Here."

My mouth popped open. "You're saying that Ross's Burgers wants to buy Morning Bell?"

"They intend to take ownership at the start of August."

"No..." I whispered. "No way..."

"I'm so sorry, Gracie." Dad shrugged sadly and the movement broke my heart. I squeezed his hand with both of mine. "It's just been so hard. I'm not getting any younger and, since your mom passed, Morning Bell has been a lot of work."

"I'm here." My voice sounded small and far away.

Now, it was Dad's turn to take my hands in both of his. His green eyes were sincere, though his lips were pale. Typical Dad, wanting to make me feel better when he was the one in pain. "I know that, and I'm so appreciative. But, I'm getting older now, and I'm not sure how much longer I can run this place. It might be time for Morning Bell to move out of our family."

My chest felt tight. Morning Bell was a part of my life, a part of me. It was like the air, or the sunshine. It was my home, my childhood, my past. I registered what he was saying and my heart sank. "It's April now, so... we only have four months?"

"Possibly, yes. Jim and I were meeting today to review the financials. The company hasn't yet made an official offer, but we're in discussions."

A bitter taste filled my mouth and I stared at our clasped hands. Of course, I understood Dad's perspective, but it didn't make this any easier.

"Chin up, buttercup." Dad's index finger gently tilted my face. He smiled. "It's going to be okay."

"But what about you, Dad? Morning Bell's your baby. You and Mom built this cafe from nothing."

He blew a raspberry with his lips. "I'll be okay. Besides, I'm sure I'll have grandbabies in no time."

I knew he meant this as a joke and I couldn't help but roll my eyes. We were back to discussing my love life.

Great.

Dad had been on a roll lately, poking and prodding into my past relationships and dating history. Or rather, lack of dating.

Don't get me wrong, I'd been on a few dates over the years—a couple of guys from Aston Falls and one from Bozeman. But those relationships never really went anywhere. They'd all fizzled out about three months in.

I'd say that it was just lack of chemistry, or bad timing, or distance. But, in truth, I believed that *I* was the problem. I'd had a hard time trusting guys over the years. After what happened in high school—that fateful prom night—it had been easier to keep everyone at arm's length. There was no need to cross the line into being close with someone when a comfortable emotional distance felt much safer.

Maybe some people just weren't meant to fall in love, and I'd come to terms with the fact that I was one of them.

Mostly. Sometimes.

Of course, it was even harder to wrap my head around the fact that the very person who hurt me was the one person I've never been able to forget. It also didn't help that he was my brother's best friend.

Nicholas King. I wished I could turn back time and take back that night.

The front door slammed open and Austin burst into the cafe. He was wearing athletic shorts and a gray pull-over, like he was out for a jog or something. In his right hand, he held a folded wheelchair.

"Grace, what's going on?" he asked, his voice the perfect mixture of urgent and confidently-in-charge. I'd often joked that this was his ER voice, but at that moment, I understood how soothing that voice was when a loved one was in crisis.

"Hey, son." Dad waved feebly from the chair.

Austin immediately darted over to him, taking his wrist and checking his pulse. His blue eyes were urgent and alert, and his blonde hair was windswept. Though we were twins, we looked next to nothing alike. Our differing eye colors usually threw people off—where Austin had baby blues like Mom, mine were green like Dad's.

He pressed his fingers along Dad's neck and felt his forehead. "How're you doing, Dad? I'll be honest, you don't look great."

Dad sighed deeply. He'd never been good at lying to Austin. "I don't feel great either."

Austin checked Dad's pulse again and his face relaxed slightly. "Well, the good news is that it's definitely not a heart attack. But, I want you to come to my office so we can get you checked out. Would you feel comfortable moving?"

Dad nodded slightly and Austin unfolded the wheelchair. We helped Dad into the chair, and Austin led him towards the door. I felt slightly sick, my mind a heady mix of relief and confusion. Dad wasn't having a heart attack.

"So, what do you think it is?" I asked, grabbing Dad's stuff and following them out.

"I'm not sure," Austin said. "My guess is either a bad case of indigestion, or something stress-related. I'll know more after I do some tests. But I'd strongly recommend he stay off his feet for the time being."

"Oh, you kids. Don't be silly, I'm okay," Dad insisted, but he didn't move from the wheelchair. "I can't abandon Grace to run the cafe by herself."

"You're not abandoning me."

Dad shook his head sadly. His ragged breath sounded like a train rattling down the tracks. "I'll say one thing, Ross's Burgers' interest in Morning Bell is coming right on time."

2

NICHOLAS

*M*y mom always used to say that bad things happen in threes.

Growing up, I believed this to be small town superstition. Not that I would ever tell her that. It comforted her to have an explanation, an excuse for when everything went wrong.

Like the summer my dad left when I was really little, and she lost her job, and we had to move in with my grandparents in Aston Falls. It had offered Mom some comfort to know that the bad luck streak was over at three.

We'd developed a sort of ritual around our house—whenever something bad happened, we'd have ice cream in anticipation of the next bad things. At the very least, the ice cream gave us a sense of control.

I wished I had ice cream now. But, instead, I was sitting on the train rumbling towards Aston Falls. I didn't have ice cream after the first bad thing happened, or the second, or the third.

Maybe I'd cursed myself by *not* having ice cream.

I exhaled through my nose and let my eyes travel over

the scenery. The world was bright white and blue, and I had to squint every time I took off my sunglasses. The rolling hills were covered with melting snow, and jagged peaks rose in the background. Sparse black and white pine trees dotted the landscape. The sky was cloudless and the sun was shining just out of view.

But as much as I wished I could keep focused on the mellow curves and swerves of the foothills, I found myself thinking about Chicago. About the mess I left behind.

I'd rather not address the mess I was moving towards.

One mess at a time.

I massaged my right shoulder absentmindedly, and winced as a sharp pain radiated down my arm. The team doctor said that my shoulder should've been almost as good as new by now, but the healing was taking longer than I expected. After a few too many football-related injuries over the years, maybe my body had given up on trying to heal.

Ping!

My phone vibrated in my lap and I checked the text. It was from Cam, one of my teammates and closest friends in Chicago. I bit my nail and opened the message.

Hey dude, Cam's text read, *can't believe everything that's going down with Whitney. Let me know if you need anything. Coach mentioned you're headed back to your hometown for the rest of the off-season? Not a bad idea, I'll hold down the fort here. Rookie's doing well so we got things covered.*

I turned off my phone without responding and placed it back into my duffel. My stomach twisted uncomfortably and I shifted in my seat. I suddenly wished that there were more people around me, more noise and chatter. When my agent, Arnie, had booked me onto the train to Aston Falls, he didn't tell me that he'd booked the entire first class train car.

Most of the time, I enjoyed the privacy and quiet—in the

early days of my football career, traveling first class was a luxury. But these days? I missed the white noise of bustling people and murmured conversations.

"Can I get you anything else?" a lady's soft voice purred from just behind my shoulder.

I turned to see the train attendant—Cindy, according to her nametag—smiling at me.

"No, thanks." I tipped my bottle of Coke towards her. "Unless you have ice cream."

She laughed like I'd just told the world's funniest joke. "Not on the Aston Falls Express. But stick around after the ride—the restaurant car will be open this evening for diners. We might be able to get you some ice cream then."

Cindy didn't break eye contact and it suddenly occurred to me that she was flirting with me. I was too tired to muster the sparkling persona I usually used in public, so I smiled awkwardly and a silence settled between us. I'd never been entirely comfortable with the attention I received from women everywhere I went.

Luckily, at that moment, the train speakers crackled.

"Hello, valued guests of the Aston Falls Express." The conductor's grainy voice was just a touch too loud. "We'll be arriving in Aston Falls in about 10 minutes. Thank you for riding with us today, we appreciate your business."

Cindy smiled at me once more before heading to the front of the car to prepare for the train's arrival. I shifted in my seat and looked back out the window, massaging my shoulder again.

When I married Whitney, I'd thought that was it. After being in the public eye for years, I was ready to be done with dating. But now? I was 28 years old and in the middle of a messy divorce that required a team of lawyers and copious bottles of Coke to appease the knot of stress in my stomach.

Though it could've also been caused by the fact that I was injured mid-way through last season and the rookie quarterback played well, which put my position as starting quarterback in jeopardy. Or, it could be that my grandpa in Aston Falls was getting sicker by the day, and the thought of losing another person I loved broke my heart.

My stomach twisted again in dread and I pinched the bridge of my nose.

Guess my mom was right in saying that bad things happened in threes.

Aston Falls wasn't your typical small town. Of course, it did boast an adorable Center Street filled with local shops and restaurants—including a cafe with the best milkshakes you'd ever have. The high school was located on the outskirts of town, right next to the lazy, glacial river. And there were so many trees and flowers in the summertime that you could hardly believe the town was surrounded by the Rocky Mountains.

But what made Aston Falls truly unique was the fact that there was absolutely *no* easy way to get to it. The best way was by the Aston Falls Express—the beautiful and comfortable passenger train that doubled as an intimate restaurant by night.

The only alternative was the ancient dirt road that was essentially one big pothole from Helena to the streets of Aston Falls.

In the summer, when tourists flocked to Aston Falls in order to explore the mountains, raft the river, or just enjoy the simplicity of life in our small town, the train was overloaded. There was a brief period of calm in the shoulder seasons, and that was always the best time to take the train.

That was one good thing that had come from all of this —traveling to Aston Falls in April was a quiet, leisurely endeavor.

As I gathered my things in the first-class train car, I watched the few passengers disembark from cars down the line. Some walked across the platform and into the train station, while others dispersed towards the parking lot.

When the platform was less busy, I slung my duffel bag over my shoulder and exited the train. Cindy was nowhere to be found and I felt a pang of relief.

I walked across the platform towards the parking lot, and a few people stopped and waved, open-mouthed. I made sure to wave back at them with an easy smile. Despite being a pro football player for over half a decade, seeing and speaking with fans had never gotten old.

Then, I saw a couple of familiar faces through the crowd. My mom was standing by the ramp to the parking lot, waving. She was pushing my grandpa in a wheelchair, a massive tank of oxygen strapped to the side.

I picked up my pace and jogged towards them, wrapping my mom in a hug first and holding her close.

"So glad you guys are here." I laughed. Mom seemed healthy, her cheeks were rosy and her dark hair was tied back into a bun. But she looked older, softer somehow. It had been too long since I last saw her.

"Us? What about you?" Mom asked. "We saw those people waving you down."

"Guess that's what happens when you're a football star, hey Nick?" Grandpa joked.

I gave him a hug too, bending to his level. He was

wearing my jersey—the one with "King" and my number, "13."

Grandpa was my biggest fan. Ever since I'd started in the Aston Falls peewee league when I was eight, his dream had been to see me win a championship. It was the dream of everyone in our house. My playing football was the perfect distraction after my dad left—it was the thing that held us together. And, over the years, my grandparents, Mom and I worked together to achieve our goal and get me to a championship game.

Not that I'd achieved this particular goal yet. And one of my biggest regrets was that my grandma died before it could happen.

"How're you doing, Grandpa?" I asked.

He chuckled, wheezing. "Been better. But it's nothing to concern yourself with."

"Of course I'm concerned about you." I squeezed his frail hand lightly.

"No need. I'm well taken care of." Grandpa nodded at Mom and then looked back at me, his watery gray eyes faded yet bright. "So, tell me about your season. The refs really screwed you in that last game."

I forced a smile and ran my fingers through my hair. Despite knowing that my family would want to talk about *that game*, I still didn't feel prepared for the conversation. Because of that game, I'd missed half of the season, my shoulder was injured, and my career was on shaky ground.

"Ah, we have plenty of time to catch up." I stood and took the handles of Grandpa's wheelchair. "I want to hear about you first. I missed you both so, so much."

"We missed you, too." Mom kissed my cheek. "While you're here, I want you to relax and take it easy, okay? Don't worry about what everyone's saying in Chicago."

I smiled feebly and pushed Grandpa's wheelchair down the ramp to the parking lot. As we walked across the lot, I took a look around. It felt good to be back in Aston Falls. The air smelled clean and fresh, like the mountain breeze carried a restorative magic. The parking lot was filled with the sounds of laughter and cheers as people caught up with their loved ones. My stomach grumbled and I had a sudden craving for the delicious cheese scones at Morning Bell Cafe.

My hands grasped the handles of the chair, palms sweaty. Morning Bell—where Grace Bell used to work. She was my best friend's sister, but after what happened all those years ago, how could I possibly face her?

I shook my head, trying to rid myself of the unpleasant memory. "I can't remember the last time I was in Aston Falls."

"It was before you got drafted," Mom said.

She was right. I'd gone straight from the University of Florida in Gainesville to Chicago after signing my NFL contract.

"A few years, then." I took a deep breath of the small town air, letting the chill fill my lungs. "Has anything changed since I've been gone?"

Mom laughed. "It's Aston Falls, Nick. Nothing changes here."

3

GRACE

*E*verything had changed.

Since my dad collapsed at the cafe last week, I'd been trying to run Morning Bell on my own. And I was in way over my head.

Austin confirmed that Dad's collapse in the cafe was stress-induced, and he recommended that Dad take the next few months off. Dad was reluctant. But he'd always been like that—a hard worker, completely dedicated to his job. It was no surprise where Austin and I got it from.

I rolled out of bed and groggily rubbed my eyes. It was still dark outside, but I changed into my black jeans and my favorite t-shirt. Normally, I wore my blue jeans, but after spilling salad dressing on them yesterday, it was time for a wash. My black jeans were a little bit "fancier"—they weren't faded on the knees and the pockets had a mountain design on them—but I was too exhausted to care.

I shut off the light in my room, opened my door, and walked down the hallway. It was pitch black, but I knew my way around our house, and the last thing I wanted was to wake Dad.

My silver puffer jacket hung next to the front door and I put it on. Then, I slid into my favorite brown boots before tiptoeing out of the house.

Early morning was my favorite time of day in Aston Falls. The cold, fresh air felt like a smack to the face—more effective than caffeine, in my opinion. The smell of pine trees filled my senses, and I couldn't help but smile. The town was quiet, but I waved at the mailman as he passed.

I went next door to the cafe and slid the keys into the lock. Morning Bell looked almost exactly like our townhouse, except that it was painted yellow while our house was white. My parents bought both houses when they'd first arrived in Aston Falls—moving into one and transforming the other into our namesake cafe.

Once inside, I took off my puffer jacket, turned on the radio and got the coffee machine going. Then, I went to the kitchen and got to work.

I barely registered the time passing as I baked assorted pastries for the cafe. Every morning, I woke up early to bake before the cafe opened. It was one of my favorite aspects of Morning Bell these days—working in the cluttered, cozy kitchen before the world was awake. Just me, the radio, and a cup of coffee.

In no time, it was 7am—time to open shop. I pulled the last of the cheese scones from the oven and sprinkled them with basil before placing them in the display case between the cinnamon buns and the muffins.

I smoothed the front of my royal blue kitchen apron, satisfied with the results, and turned on the lights at the front of the cafe. The soothing notes of my coffee house playlist hummed through the speakers as I unlocked the front door and turned the sign over to "Open."

Within two minutes, Mayor Davis strode through the door.

"Good morning, Grace," he announced grandly, standing by the serving counter. "What's on the menu this morning?"

Robert "you can call me Bob" Davis was an Aston Falls local, through and through. It was rumored that his ancestors founded our town, and Mayor Davis had records to prove it. I'd never seen these and I didn't need to—Mayor Davis lived by a strict moral code that included never lying. He was easily the best mayor the town could hope for, though he did take his role very seriously at times... to the enjoyment of some of the more mischievous high school kids.

"We've got cinnamon buns, sesame seed bagels, bran muffins, and scones." I pointed out the pastries with a smile. "But the cheese scones are the freshest. I *just* took them out of the oven."

"Ah, the cheese scones." Mayor Davis rubbed his rather large belly and smiled. "I really shouldn't."

But, before I could close the display case, he swatted a hand.

"Oh, all right. I'll have two to go, please."

I carefully grabbed two of the cheese scones, placing them in a brown paper bag and adding a small packet of butter. Mayor Davis and I went through this exact same charade almost every morning. He pretended that he wouldn't go for the cheese scones, but he always did in the end. It was part of the reason why I prepared them last—so they'd be fresh when he arrived.

"How's your dad doing?" he asked, sniffing the scones.

"Ah, he'll be fine." I started preparing his latte. "Dad's a tough one."

"He is that. Always has been." Mayor Davis was silent for a beat and, when he spoke, his voice was nonchalant. "A little birdie told me that a rep from Ross's Burgers has been around the cafe, meeting with your dad."

"A little birdie?"

"Well, technically two."

I rolled my eyes. How Mrs. Applebaum and Ms. Rodriguez found out that Jim McNeil was a rep for Ross's Burgers, I'd never know.

"The thing is, Grace," Mayor Davis continued, "Aston Falls is special. And what makes us so special are the local businesses, the mom n' pop shops and restaurants. We need family-run cafes and diners to succeed. Bringing a big chain restaurant to Center Street will... well, it'll ruin the small town feel of the place."

I tucked a strand of hair behind my ear, unsure how to respond. The last thing I wanted was to give up Morning Bell. But, I also understood why Dad wanted to sell and get out of the game.

"I'm not sure if you know this," Mayor Davis said as I handed him his coffee. "But it's an election year coming up and we simply can't have a family-run business fail. Imagine —one of the town staples disappearing midway through election season. It would be such a dark mark on the town, not to mention an unmitigated *disaster* on the campaign trail."

His face was wrinkled into an anxious frown and I had to bite my lip to hold back my smile. Despite the gravity of the situation, I wouldn't have labeled this a "disaster." Mayor Davis was always worried about election years, even though he was well-liked across Aston Falls and had won the last several elections unopposed.

"Nothing is set in stone yet," I said gently, placing a reassuring hand on the mayor's. "Dad briefly met with Ross's Burgers. That's all."

"Well, let me know if there's anything I can do to help the two of you. Morning Bell is part of what makes Aston Falls such a great town. And your mom and dad... I know the effort they put into this place. It would be a real shame to see it change hands."

I nodded, appreciating his passion for our town. "Thank you, Mayor Davis, that's a very sweet offer. I'll definitely let you know if I think of anything."

Mayor Davis smiled and blew on the top of his latte, hazarding a quick sip. He grimaced and smacked his lips, having burned his tongue.

I wished I had another answer for our mayor. The truth was that he was right—Morning Bell was a staple of Aston Falls, and I couldn't imagine this town being without it.

But the thing I could never admit to anyone? That there was a teeny tiny, silly part of me that... kind of wanted to run this place.

Stupid, I know. It was a pipe dream if I'd ever heard of one. I was a 27 year old woman who'd never worked another job, had exactly zero business experience, and had never gone to college. That didn't make for a successful cafe owner.

But, as soon as Dad mentioned that he wanted to sell Morning Bell, it was a wake-up call for me, and a flurry of long-forgotten memories started to crop up in my mind. When I was a kid, I actually dreamed that I would own Morning Bell one day. Most girls my age wanted to be the Spice Girls or ballet dancers or actresses. Me? I wanted to run our funny, quirky, family-owned cafe. I even had a little plastic kitchen set to "serve customers"... who often happened to be my reluctant twin brother.

As many childhood dreams do, though, those hopes had faded with time. In recent years, Morning Bell was just a job, just work. I stuck around after high school to help Dad after Mom passed away, and I'd succumbed to the day-in, day-out goings on of what used to be my favorite cafe.

But, over the last week, I'd found myself rehashing those old feelings, those old hopes. Deep down, a part of me wanted nothing more than to try my hand at running our cafe. At keeping it in the family.

Running Morning Bell myself sounded like a dream, but I didn't know how to make that dream come true. I'd watched my parents run Morning Bell for years—saw it grow and flourish, and then stagnate after my mom passed away and Dad was left all alone to manage everything.

And, I knew Dad. He took a lot of pride in Morning Bell —as he should. I couldn't just walk up and ask him if I could run it myself. I had to prove myself. Prove that I could carry the Morning Bell name.

I had absolutely no clue where to start.

4

NICHOLAS

*T*he scrape of shovel on cement pierced the quiet morning air, followed by the muted *plop* of snow on snow. It was 7am and I was outside shoveling the heavy spring snow from Mom's driveway and deck.

The sky was slowly turning a lighter shade of blue. The sun would be out soon. Finally.

It'd been a long time since someone had shoveled properly, and I was hit by a familiar feeling of guilt. I should've been around to shovel before this, I should've found time to return to Aston Falls and help Mom and Grandpa. Mom mentioned that some of the neighbors had come by and shoveled occasionally over the winter, but there was only so much they could do.

That was the beauty of a small town, though—you could rely on your community. In Chicago? You never knew who your neighbors were, let alone asked them for help.

I stood straight and assessed the work I'd done, blowing warm air into my frozen hands. I rubbed them together, wishing I had a pair of gloves. It might've been the beginning of April, but the mornings still felt like the dead of winter.

I was almost at the end of the driveway now, but the moment of satisfaction didn't last long. Unwelcome thoughts started to creep back in and I bent over the shovel again. I scraped a fresh pile of snow and deposited it on the lawn.

Over the past week, it had been nearly impossible to keep my mind from wandering back to Chicago. I'd barely slept at night, instead staring at the ceiling for hours and wishing the sun would come up. All I could think about was the divorce, and what exactly went wrong between Whitney and me.

And then there was the fact that my team would likely trade me soon. And that meant that I'd be moved to yet another big city, to make yet another group of friends, and settle into yet another anonymous, gorgeous apartment. I hadn't talked to Mom or Grandpa about it. I hadn't even mentioned it to Austin Bell, my best friend. I preferred to lie low until everything was sorted out.

Helping around Mom's house offered a welcome distraction—fixing anything that was broken, improving on inefficiencies. It helped to feel useful, to feel like I was contributing. And there was the extra challenge of doing everything with my left hand to give my injured shoulder a break.

I looked back over the driveway. It was spotless, I'd cleared all of the slushy snow.

I was walking towards the deck when Mom exited the front door.

"Morning, Nick." She was carrying two steaming mugs and she held one out to me. "I made you coffee."

I smiled and walked up the porch stairs. "Thanks, Ma."

"Thank *you* for shoveling."

"I should've been here to do it long ago."

I took a long gulp of coffee, letting the bitter liquid warm my tongue and the back of my throat. I wrapped my right hand around the mug while I rubbed my injured shoulder with the other hand.

"Arm's still bugging you?" Mom asked.

I shrugged and a dull ache ripped through my body. Maybe shoveling—even with my left hand—wasn't such a good idea.

"It's alright," I lied.

"Well, I just want to say thank you. I'm so grateful to have you around these days. You've been a big help around the house, not to mention watching Grandpa while I'm at work."

"It's my pleasure, Ma. I love spending time with Grandpa. We've been watching reruns of our favorite football games." I chuckled and took another sip of coffee. "I'm surprised the neighbors haven't complained about us yelling at the TV and cheering when our teams score."

Mom smiled. "We love having you home. Ever since Grandma died... well, Grandpa's health just hasn't been the same."

I placed my hand on Mom's as a familiar sadness tore through my heart. I was very close to my grandma, she practically raised me when Mom was busy working. Her death a few years ago tore us all apart.

"Speaking of," I said quietly. "Remind me to remind you to hire a full-time nurse for Grandpa when I have to go back to Chicago."

"We're fine here, Nick. Don't worry about it."

"Fine or not, I know this is all taking a toll on you." I gestured towards the driveway. "You're working the night shift at the Inn *and* taking full-time care of Grandpa. I just want to make sure I'm taking care of you both, too. Am I not sending enough money? I can send more."

Mom shook her head. "Absolutely not. There's no need for you to be sending money in the first place."

After I'd signed my NFL contract, I'd immediately offered to buy Mom a new house. She'd refused the suggestion flat-out, no matter how many times I insisted. My priority then, as it was now, was to make sure that she and Grandpa were well looked after. But, she wouldn't even discuss it, so I also bypassed the conversation and sent money to her each month instead.

It appeared that she hadn't spent a penny of it.

"Ma," I said gently. "This is all too much for one person. In an ideal world, I would be able to stay and help out, but my hands are tied. Plus, it's not like we can't afford help."

Mom patted my cheek, her blue eyes light. "We'll think about it. I simply want to be sure that you and your future family are taken care of. Though, I suppose now, with Whitney..."

She trailed off and I kissed the palm of her hand. "You don't need to worry about any of that."

I didn't go on to tell her that Whitney and I had had no plans to start a family. But there was no point in saying that now. I was touched that, even after all these years—even with my successful football career—Mom still insisted on putting me first.

Clearly, I'd inherited my stubborn streak from her.

I swallowed the rest of my coffee. "I'd better get back to work. Almost done."

Mom took my mug and started back towards the front door. She paused. "Oh, Nick? When you're done, would you mind grabbing some sesame bagels from Morning Bell?

Grandpa was talking about them last night and I thought it'd be nice to make him lunch with his favorite bagels."

My heart leapt uncomfortably, but I smiled and nodded.

It was only a matter of time before I had to go to Morning Bell. Was Grace still working there? Austin had mentioned her a handful of times over the past few years and, as much as I wanted to ask about her, I could never broach the subject. It sounded like she'd stuck around Aston Falls—which surprised me given how smart and driven she used to be.

My stomach was a mess of anxiety as I returned to shoveling the deck. But, as the scrape of the shovel echoed through the morning air, I found myself wondering whether I packed my nicest button-down shirt.

5

GRACE

I scrambled into the kitchen and dropped dirty plates next to the dishwasher before wiping streaks of flour from the front of my shirt. The happy sounds of laughter and conversation boomed from the front of the cafe.

Back here, it felt more like a war zone.

"Are the omelettes ready, Tommy?" I asked urgently, approaching the chef. The smell of hash browns, toast, and syrup would normally make my stomach grumble, but there was no time for that.

Tommy whirled around, his hair net awry. Not that he needed it, Tommy had been bald basically his whole life.

"Not yet, just working on final touches." He chopped up some parsley, moving the knife with surprising agility and grace for someone who looked like your standard football linebacker.

"There are a couple more tables to clear, so I'll take care of those and circle back round in a minute."

"You got it!"

I dashed out of the kitchen and back into the chaos of

Morning Bell's morning rush. The rush wasn't unusual, but there were normally two of us working the floor instead of one. It felt like I was barely treading water, about to drown in absolute overwhelm. But, despite Dad's insistence this morning that I call him if things were this busy, I couldn't think about asking him for help.

One, because of his health. And two, because in some small—but annoyingly vocal—part of my mind, calling him for help was like an admission that I couldn't do this. That I didn't have a chance at running Morning Bell.

And, as foolish as my dream felt, I wasn't ready to admit that to myself yet.

Austin, bless him, had popped in and out of the cafe to help several times over the past week without me having to ask. He called it his "twinny sixth sense"—a literally decades-old reference that I was sure he was using just to get a rise out of me. But today, he couldn't come in—he was pulled away for an appointment.

I stretched my lips into an exhausted smile and approached the till, where a short line of customers were waiting to pay. Thankfully they were all locals and didn't seem impatient or rushed. I wiped my arm across my forehead, feeling way too warm. It occured to me that I might have just splattered ketchup across my face, but I was too stressed to care.

After finishing with the customers at the till, I dived back into the crowd to collect dirty plates. I jogged over to the table nearest the door, where the customers had stacked their dirty dishes on the edge of the table.

"Busy morning, hey Gracie?" Isabel Garcia asked. Her dining companion was Alan Brown, and they both taught at the Aston Falls' elementary school. "You're holding down the fort really well."

"News to me." I chuckled and they laughed with me. "How was everything today?"

"Delicious!" Alan exclaimed, dabbing his mouth with a napkin. "Truly. I swear your french toast has only gotten better."

"That was Tommy's doing—he's been adding nutmeg to the batter." Tommy would be thrilled to hear about the compliment.

"And the yogurt bowl was perfect." Isabel patted her stomach, gesturing to her half-eaten bowl. "But, I couldn't quite finish it."

I smiled. "Whenever you're ready, I'll meet you at the till."

Isabel and Alan returned to their conversation while I collected their plates. As soon as the dirty dishes were stacked on my forearm, I whipped around, ready to dart back into the kitchen.

Unfortunately, I didn't see the person entering the cafe at that exact moment. I turned directly into them and the plates of syrup and yogurt went flying. Yogurt smeared down my front as the dishes crashed to the floor.

"I'm so sorry," I exclaimed, dropping to the ground to clean the mess. "That was my bad. I didn't see you."

The person knelt with me and I heard a distinctive chuckle.

A familiar chuckle.

My head snapped up.

I was staring into the gorgeous gray eyes of Nicholas King.

My heart slammed in my chest and I shot to a stand. "What are you doing here?"

My voice was quiet and croaky. I wished it was firmer, more smooth and sure. In every dream I'd had of seeing Nicholas again, I was a lot more confident. And a lot less sweaty and covered in old yogurt.

Nicholas collected the plates and cutlery from the floor and stood in front of me. In fact, he towered over me. I forgot how tall he was. And athletic.

"My day thus far has been a bit boring. Thought I'd liven it up with a bit of yogurt." Nicholas laughed and his gray eyes sparkled.

A long-forgotten warmth spread under my cheeks, but I forced myself to ignore it. What I couldn't ignore was the fact that Nicholas King was standing in front of me... in Morning Bell. He was wearing a light gray button-down shirt that made his eyes glow positively silver, and black jeans that fit him just right. His dark hair was shorter than I remembered and lightly tousled, and his full lips were curved into a smile that could captivate a ladybug.

And the dimple. We couldn't forget about the dimple on his left cheek.

I got my mind on track, and kept my eyes squarely on his. "No, really. What are you doing here? Austin's not here."

Nicholas wiped the front of his shirt and I tried to ignore the movement of his biceps, the set of his strong jaw as he looked down.

Why? Why did he have to look *this* good after so many years?

"I'm not looking for Austin." He chuckled. "I'm looking for bagels."

My body immediately snapped to attention and I took

the plates from him. He wanted bagels? I could definitely do bagels.

"Follow me." I led him towards the serving counter, noting the long line up at the till. I glanced at him apologetically. "It could be a moment. I should probably help some of the customers in line."

Nicholas waved his hand, his face breaking into an easygoing smile. "Take your time. Go ahead and deal with them first. I'll finish cleaning up."

I tucked a strand of unruly blond hair behind my ear. I looked at the line, then back at him, then at the mess on the floor. Before I could say anything, Nicholas grabbed a cloth from the counter and strode towards the mess, gesturing with a head tilt towards the crowd of people.

Flustered, I decided to take him up on his offer. With a large exhale, I went to the till.

6

GRACE

"So? How'd it go?" Ella sat back on the raspberry pink couch in her apartment and whipped her curly brown hair into a ponytail.

I took a sip of white wine. I wasn't much of a drinker, but chatting with my best friend on a video call after a long day warranted a glass. "It was crazy. Always is."

"Cheers to that." Ella laughed and raised her own glass of wine. We held our glasses to our respective screens, yelling "cheers!"

Ella Williams was one of my best and oldest friends. She'd moved to New York City a few years ago to pursue her dream of becoming an investigative journalist, but we'd stayed close despite the distance. She was still the first person I turned to whenever I was sad or upset, the one I could always count on, no matter what.

Ella smacked her lips and placed her glass on the table next to her. Then, I heard a loud *clink* and she shot sideways across the screen.

"No!" She swore. "I spilled my drink."

I giggled as Ella wandered into the small kitchen of her

apartment. She placed a dining chair in front of her shelves and reached for a stack of dishcloths. Ella's apartment was exactly what you'd expect of an apartment in downtown NYC—cute, full of character, and absolutely tiny.

Ella was wearing a familiar green hoodie from our high school days—it had belonged to Austin before he grew out of it. When we were kids, Ella used to come by our house all the time, and Austin and I often made jokes that she was an honorary Bell sibling. We practically grew up together, even naming ourselves the "Three Musketeers."

"Sorry about that." Ella exhaled, settling back into the couch and picking up a new glass of wine. "You were telling me about the cafe. Not gonna lie, G, you look stressed."

I snorted on a mouthful of wine and winced as the drink went up my nose. "Stressed isn't the half of it."

Over the next few minutes, I told Ella all about Dad's decision to sell the cafe to Ross's Burgers, and about Jim McNeil's rather unpleasant visit. I mentioned my dad's health issues, and the four month timestamp we had left with Morning Bell.

"That's fair," Ella mused, taking a sip of her wine. "I can understand why your dad is looking to sell and get out of the game. He must be exhausted."

I winced and swirled the wine around my glass.

"You don't think so?" Ella asked, picking up on my silence.

"Oh, no, I absolutely agree." I nodded vehemently. "Dad deserves to enjoy his middle age, and his health needs to come first always. He really shouldn't be running the cafe on his own anymore..."

I trailed off into silence and bit the inside of my cheek.

"G?" Ella asked. "What are you thinking?"

I held my breath. I hadn't told anyone about my crazy,

nonsensical dream of owning and running Morning Bell. But, sitting here with my best friend and a glass of wine, I suddenly had the urge to vocalize it. Why not bite the bullet?

"Well," I started, swirling my wine more vigorously and refusing to meet Ella's screen-eyes. "I love Morning Bell with all my heart. I guess, I think it could be cool if I... you know... could run it myself?"

At this, Ella practically exploded. She threw her arms in the air and cheered. "Gracie, that is a *fantastic* idea! I always thought you'd be perfect to run Morning Bell, you just never seemed that interested."

"Oh, I was interested," I muttered shyly, shifting in my seat.

"If anyone can take over Morning Bell and breathe new life into it, Gracie, it's you. You're smart, capable, and you practically grew up in that cafe. I don't say this lightly, but I fully believe this is your calling."

I tucked a strand of hair behind my ear, blushing with Ella's praise. "Thank you, Els. I really wasn't expecting you to say that. But, honestly, me running the cafe seems so unlikely right now. I already feel like I'm in way over my head and it's only my first week at the helm. I don't know where I'd even start, and Ross's Burgers is moving in anyhow."

"So?" Ella's eyes were ginormous. "You just have to show your dad what you can do before the buyout is finalized. So that means you have..."

"Four months."

"Four months! Plenty of time to take over management of the cafe and show your dad just what you can do."

"So." I wiggled my eyebrows. "Any chance you wanna come back to Aston Falls and help me out?"

Her expression faltered. "I wish I could, but—"

"I know, I know." I cut her off with a smile. "You have work and a life in NYC. I'm sure I can find help around here. Like Austin. He's been in every once in a while to help, and that's been huge."

Ella chuckled and took another sip of wine. "How is your stinker of a brother, anyway? I haven't talked to him in a couple of days."

"Busy as ever." I tapped my fingers on my glass. "But I won't lie, I'm still surprised he decided to move back to Aston Falls after doing so well in LA. Did he ever talk to you about that?"

"I know as much as you do. He just up and left LA with no warning or explanation. Maybe he was sick of big city life."

"Maybe…" I trailed off, whipping my hair into a messy bun. "Speaking of the big city life, guess who I literally ran into this morning—Nicholas King."

Ella almost spit out her wine. She wiped her mouth, eyes wide. "*The* Nicholas King? Like the one who you—?"

"Yep, the very same."

"Wow." She bit her nail, pondering the news. "How was it seeing him again?"

I shrugged, playing nonchalant. But, in truth, my heart was doing all kinds of flips and dips. "It was fine. Kind of nice, actually. Aside from the fact that he spilled yogurt all down my front in our little run-in."

"Sounds messy."

"Definitely. But then, weirdly, he stuck around to help me clean up. It was kind of him to do seeing as it was mostly my fault. I should've been watching where I was going."

"Do you have plans to see him again?" Ella asked casually. Too casually.

It was a fair question given the Nicholas King hole I'd been in for years.

I exhaled in a laugh. "What? Like a plan to catch up over ice cream at Sweets n' Sundaes? No. I'm sure I'll see him around town. But nothing planned, of course."

Ella nodded, appeased, and took a sip of her wine. "Star quarterback Nicholas King—cleaning the floors at a cafe in small town Montana. You wouldn't expect to see that in the headlines."

I smiled and shook my head. "No, but that's Nicholas. It's the kind of chivalrous thing he used to do in high school. He always tried to do the right thing back then..."

My mind wandered and I thought back all those years ago—to the days when Nicholas was just Austin's best friend and Aston Falls High's star quarterback.

The two of them used to hang out at our house for hours after football practice, throwing the ball, eating or watching movies. I was the shy, quiet girl who faded into the background at school. Though he was a year older and could have ignored me, Nicholas always made a special effort to include me. He talked to me and laughed with me like we were good friends. We even occasionally played board games together.

It was sweet.

Ella was saying something but I barely registered her words. Seeing Nicholas today was like seeing a ghost—kind of wonderful, but also completely terrifying.

7

NICHOLAS

I twisted the screwdriver carefully, holding the screw level to the cupboard. The head of the screw was stripped, so I had to apply extra force to make sure the screwdriver didn't slip out. After a couple of painstaking turns, the screw was tight.

I leaned against the counter and opened the cupboard door once, twice. It moved smoothly, soundlessly.

"Perfect," I muttered with a smile.

I'd been fixing broken cabinets and squeaking hinges around Mom's house all morning, despite the lack of proper tools. If Mom refused to hire someone to help her around the house, the least I could do was pick up an adjustable wrench and a power drill the next time I was on Center Street.

I stifled a yawn as I slowly packed up the few tools I found in our attic. Once again, I was running on no sleep. Every time I closed my eyes, or tried to rest, my mind refused to let me be. Memories of Whitney flashed behind my eyelids as I remembered the beautiful parts of our marriage—our honeymoon in Hawaii, the parties she threw in Chicago, the time she redecorated our house.

Further reflection reminded me of the truth in those situations. That she'd booked Hawaii without even talking to me about where I wanted to go. That the parties she threw were always full of her friends and seriously lacking in mine. That when she redecorated our house, she hadn't thought to consult me about the huge painting she'd commissioned of her childhood pet, Deedee, which she'd hung over the fireplace in the living room.

She'd paid extra so that the chihuahua's eyes would follow you. It was unnerving. Especially first thing in the morning.

Still, Whitney had been my wife for the past two years. On paper, we were perfect—she was the model and aspiring actress with a killer smile and a feisty personality. I was the pro football player leading Chicago to a hopeful championship.

I grabbed myself another cup of coffee and let the bitter, smoky taste overwhelm my senses. I'd always preferred black coffee, and Whitney, with her love for green tea, never understood why.

My phone vibrated on the kitchen counter, but I didn't bother picking it up. It was likely one of the many Chicago news networks covering our apparently "high-profile" split. It could've also been one of my coaches or my agent telling me that I'd been replaced by the rookie quarterback.

In all honesty, the kid was good. He reminded me of myself when I was his age. But now? With my various injuries and years of body-breaking experience, I was beginning to understand what my coach always said—that you're only young once and, if done right, once is enough.

I stood and rubbed my shoulder before heading to the

fridge. Grandpa was sleeping upstairs, but I decided to get started on lunch for us. I opened the fridge door and saw the bagels on the highest shelf.

The sesame bagels.

A buzz of warmth spread through my body at the thought of Grace's smile when she'd handed me the bag, her wild blonde hair shoved into a bun.

Grace hadn't changed since high school. She had the same pert, upturned nose, striking green eyes and perfectly bowed lips. She was shorter than I remembered, but that was likely just time taking a toll on my memory. She still moved like a dancer, gliding this way and that without realizing how graceful she was. Her red shirt was streaked with flour, and her black jeans with the mountain peaks on the pockets fit her perfectly.

I rubbed the back of my neck as I remembered spilling yogurt on her. I still felt terrible. I should've been paying more attention, but I was nervous to see her again. Helping her clean the mess was the least I could do.

There was something comforting about Grace, something about her that reminded me of home. Maybe it was because she was quirky and hilarious as ever. Cute, too.

But, I had to keep my distance. For the both of us.

My phone vibrated again, pulling me from my thoughts, and I checked the screen reflexively.

Three missed calls, eighteen texts, and various emails from Arnie. As I stared at the screen, another text came through and I saw the message preview.

Nicholas, call me back NOW!!! The text read. *It's urgent. Chicago's impressed with the rookie. They're thinking of trading—*

I placed my phone on the counter, screen down, without

opening the message. I suddenly felt way too hot and I took off my hoodie.

Was I surprised that I was being traded? Not at all, this was the news I'd been expecting. But I couldn't say I felt excited by the prospect. To be fair, being traded wasn't necessarily a bad thing—Chicago was a great team and I'd loved playing for them, but with my impending divorce, maybe a new start was what I needed.

I bit my nail and picked up my phone again, intending to call my agent back. But I couldn't seem to dial the number. I stared at the screen for a long moment, my fingers poised.

Then, there was a knock at the front door.

I left my phone on the counter and strode to the front of the house. When I opened the door, a familiar, smiling face was staring back at me.

"Hey bro," Austin said. "It's been awhile."

Austin and I went to the living room and he plopped onto a couch like he used to do in high school. Meanwhile, I looked through the fridge in the kitchen and grabbed two glass bottles of Coke, popping the tops off easily.

"When'd you get back?" Austin asked, untucking his white button-down work shirt. "I had to hear about your big return from your mom. Your *mom*."

I laughed. "Yeah, sorry. I didn't want to make a big deal out of it."

"As your oldest friend, I think I should get a say in making that call."

"I thought Ella Williams was your oldest friend."

Austin chuckled and took the proffered Coke. "I said *your* oldest friend. Almost thirteen years."

I rolled my eyes and fell onto the other sofa. "Cheers to that."

The bottles clinked together and I took a long pull of the sweet drink.

I'd known Austin Bell since elementary school, but we became close friends in high school when we were on the football team together. I'd made varsity my freshman year and climbed the ranks quickly. By my sophomore year—when Austin joined as a freshman—I was the youngest starting quarterback in the school's history.

Austin and I worked well together. He was a talented football player and I had no doubt that he could've gone pro, or at least played college ball. But, he'd stopped playing after his junior year of high school. Even then, Austin's dream was to go to med school, and he chose to dedicate his time to keeping his grades up and volunteering at the county hospital to ensure that would happen.

Austin swallowed his drink and hiccuped inadvertently. "I heard things are pretty nuts in Chicago. How's everything with Whitney?"

The drink turned sour in my stomach. "The short answer?"

"If there's such a thing."

"You don't want to know."

Austin shook his head and took another long swig of his drink. "But, you're here now. When did you get in?"

Austin's voice was light and happy, and I tried to pull myself together. It was impossible to feel sorry for yourself around Austin-the-eternal-optimist.

"Been here for about ten days now, I guess."

"Seriously?" Austin threw a pillow at my head. "You didn't think to come visit?"

I reflexively lifted my right arm to protect myself and a

sharp pain shot down my shoulder. I winced and lowered my arm slowly.

Austin frowned. "How's the shoulder?"

"Been better." I rolled my shoulder a couple of times until the pain slowly eased. Not wanting to get into it, I returned to our conversation. "It's been hectic since I've been back. You know, with Grandpa being sick and everything."

Austin ran a hand through his sandy blond hair, his brow furrowed. "I wish I could do more to help, but he needs a specialist and his doctor in Bozeman is one of the best I know. I've no doubt that she'll get your gramps back on track in no time."

I smiled hopefully. On the kitchen counter, my phone buzzed again.

Austin glanced towards the phone and back at me, his blue eyes sharp. "What's going on? Your phone's been going off nonstop."

I stood from the couch and approached the counter. I checked the screen and saw that it was yet another message from *Chicago Today*.

"Literally nothing," I said, exasperated. I returned to the couch, eager to change the subject. "By the way, I saw Grace a couple days ago."

Austin's eyebrows shot up into his hairline. "Really? You must've gone to Morning Bell. She never leaves that place."

He laughed and I chuckled with him. But an uneasy feeling gripped my stomach. It was a good thing Austin never found out exactly what happened between Grace and I on prom night. It would've changed everything.

8

GRACE

$\mathcal{T}$he kitchen bell dinged and I raced to the back, my arms loaded with dirty dishes. I deposited the plates by the dishwasher and whirled over to the pass, where Tommy was lining up four mouth-watering plates of food.

"What've you got for me, Tommy?" I asked in a rush.

"Two omelettes, one fried egg special and one french toast." Tommy pointed at each plate in turn and then whipped back towards the grill. "Next up, a granola bowl and a grilled cheese with fries."

"You're a dream," I said, picking up the plates and running back out of the kitchen.

I delivered the food to the table nearest the window. "Here we are. Can I get y'all anything else?"

The family of four shook their heads in unison, already diving into the food. It was for the best that they didn't need anything, as I was distracted by what was happening at the serving counter. A small line-up was forming at the till—customers wanting to pay for their meals. At the other end of the counter, Dad was cleaning glassware. I watched as he assessed the line-up and my blood pressure spiked.

As frazzled and flustered as I felt, I had to at least make it *look* like I had things under control. That was the only way to show Dad that I could handle more managerial tasks around the cafe.

So, I threw back my shoulders and smiled wide as I approached the counter, trying to ignore my sweating palms. I clicked a few buttons on the cash register, noticing that Dad's ears were perked in my direction.

"Thank you for waiting, Mr. Lee." I smiled brightly. "How was everything today?"

"Fantastic, Grace," Mr. Lee answered with a wide smile. He peeked over his shoulder and, thankfully, lowered his voice. I hoped that Dad couldn't hear his next words. "Though, it seems that you're rather run off your feet. Do you have any additional staff?"

This time, my smile was forced. So much for it looking like I had things under control. "Not today, unfortunately. It's just Dad and me, but with his health, I don't want him working the floor."

Mr. Lee nodded sagely. "I see."

He paid his bill and I tended to the other customers in the line quickly. I was about to run back onto the floor to collect dirty dishes when Dad approached me.

"Gracie," he said seriously. "Mr. Lee's right. You need help. I know you don't want me working here because of the stress, and I appreciate your concern, honey. But please, you need to hire someone."

My mind whirred. I knew that if we hired another cafe worker, we'd barely be breaking even. And in order to show that I could run Morning Bell effectively, I needed to demonstrate that the cafe was turning a profit. "I can handle it, Dad. I've got this."

Dad opened and closed his mouth a couple of times, frowning. Then, he lifted an apron from behind the counter. "That's it. I'm coming back to work." His breath was slightly shaky. "I can help you."

I grabbed his hand. "No. Dad, please. You need to rest and get off your feet."

"I'm fine."

"You're not," I said, my eyes stinging. "You're not fine right now and I need you to be fine. So, please, go home. We can talk about this later, but I'll handle this rush for now." I blinked away the tears and took a deep breath. "Besides, Austin will be here in no time."

Dad's eyes narrowed and he assessed me skeptically. "Will he?"

"Yes," I said, knowing full well that it was a bald-faced lie. Austin was caught up in appointments all morning. But with the stress of the rush, I couldn't also bear the stress of Dad being stressed. "I have it under control, Dad. Austin and I will take care of this."

Dad continued to stare at me and then, very reluctantly, nodded his head. "All right. But if you need help, you come and get me right away. I mean it, Grace."

I bowed my head solemnly. "I will."

He didn't know that I had my fingers crossed behind my back.

When Dad finally left the premises, I exhaled a breath of relief. But the relief didn't last long. We were still in the middle of a morning rush and customers were waiting.

I dashed towards the coffee machine to start making

lattes. I ground the coffee beans and the smoky smell offered me a sliver of comfort. But, as soon as I inserted the portafilter and clicked the button to brew the espresso shots, it was clear that something was wrong.

The machine was silent. Too silent.

And then I remembered—the coffee machine technician. He'd never arrived, and neither Dad nor I followed up. And now? The machine was broken.

My ears rang and waves of hot and cold traveled across my body. My hands shook and I dropped them by my side. There was a line of ten people waiting for coffees, and the machine was broken. On top of everything else.

If I wasn't panicking, I would've probably started laughing.

The bell dinged from the kitchen and I walked to the back on auto-pilot. I could barely pay attention to where I was going or what I was doing.

I had to figure out a way to make coffees. Fast.

Tommy saw me and his eyes went wide. "Everything okay, Gracie? You look a bit... peaky."

"Just the usual, Tommy." I laughed, the noise slightly hysterical.

I left the kitchen with the plates of food but, when I approached the floor, I stopped dead.

Nicholas King was at the serving counter, talking to a frenzied Mrs. Applebaum, who was clearly ecstatic to see Aston Falls' biggest celebrity. He was wearing a black beanie pulled low over his forehead and a black hoodie with a white checkmark on the front. He was smiling kindly and his gray eyes were bright and alert as he glanced around the cafe. Even at this hour of the morning, he looked good. Really good.

I realized that I was holding my breath and I snapped

myself out of it. I knew I should be thinking about the crowded cafe, the broken coffee machine, or my dad. Instead, I was thinking that I must look like a disaster right now. I was wearing an old pink t-shirt with a ridiculous pun on the front and my usual work jeans. My hair was greasy and pulled back into a messy bun, and I wasn't even wearing makeup.

Now, more than ever, I wished Austin was here. He could run interference if nothing else.

I ducked my head and tried to blow past Nicholas, hoping he somehow wouldn't see me.

But, no such luck.

"Hey, Ace!" He called, using his old nickname for me. He waved, like he wasn't basically standing right next to me, and then excused himself from speaking to Mrs. Applebaum. "I was hoping to see you."

I turned to him, pasting a smile on my face. His eyes traveled up and down my body. I tried to pop a hip out, look somewhat cool despite carrying plates full of food. "You found me."

Nicholas chuckled as his eyes returned to mine. "Lucky I did. It's busy here, I'm surprised you're not lost in the crowd."

I rolled my eyes, surprised to hear the same teasing reference from our high school days. "I'm not *that* short, Nicholas."

He half-smiled. "Maybe. Maybe not."

His silver eyes gazed intently into mine and I couldn't look away. My heart did a weird leaping thing and my breath hitched. For a moment, just a moment, the cafe felt quiet. The world felt quiet.

Then, I shook my head. "I don't really have time for this right now. I have to drop off this food."

"I can see that." Nicholas smiled and my heart did that thing again. "Maybe we can have a quick conversation, when you get a chance?"

I pursed my lips. "That probably won't happen for a while. I've got food to run in the kitchen, a stack of dirty dishes to get through, and a line-up of people to help. And the coffee machine's broken, so I have to figure out how—"

"Hang on." Nicholas held up a finger. "The coffee machine's broken?"

I shrugged. "Yeah."

Nicholas took off his beanie and strode behind the serving counter. Before I could stop him, he was running his fingers over the machine. He turned back towards me, his jaw set. "Where are your tools?"

"Back office."

"Great." Nicholas disappeared down the hallway towards Dad's office.

I took a step to go after him and then remembered that I was carrying stacks of food. I paused for a second, debating my next move. I really shouldn't allow Nicholas—who was basically a virtual stranger now—to go rifling through the back office. But, I also didn't have time to take a break, let alone chase him around.

Nicholas returned with the cafe's bag of tools, and shot me a wink and a confident smile. The same smile I'd see on TV when he scored a touchdown, his jersey, number 13, sparkling across the screen.

If Nicholas wanted to fix the coffee machine, I certainly wasn't going to stop him. I turned on my heel and served the food to the waiting customers, wondering just how long Nicholas King would be hanging around my cafe.

9

NICHOLAS

$\mathcal{I}$ wiped a clean dishcloth over the last table as Grace turned the wooden door sign over to "Closed."

"We did it!" She collapsed onto a chair and untied her bun. Her long blonde hair cascaded down her back and I smelled the slightest whiff of her coconut shampoo.

"We did." I sat on the chair next to hers.

She smiled at me shyly, and then breathed out a long sigh. She closed her eyes and her eyelashes fluttered on her cheeks, her rosy lips slightly parted. She began to massage her temples.

It'd been a long day for us both.

I came into Morning Bell this morning intending to speak to Grace about what had happened last week. I hadn't been able to get the yogurt incident out of my head and I wanted to apologize for running into her. But the moment I saw her with her arms loaded with plates, her hair awry and chocolate sauce on her cheek, I knew I had to help.

The coffee machine was a quick fix, and I wound up helping wash dishes, clear plates and run drinks. I'd received a few interested stares from our diners, and a number of people pulled me aside to ask me about playoffs or life in Chicago. But, having to get back to work was the perfect excuse to cut those conversations short when they got too personal.

I'd never intended to stay for more than a few minutes, but the day whizzed by. And, if I was completely honest, I was exhausted. There were times when I wasn't even this tired after football practice. Running around the cafe, trying to keep up with Grace, was a constant challenge. But, wonderfully, my mind was kept off the chaos back home. Over the past several hours, I hadn't had a single passing thought about Whitney, or football, or my future.

It was a new record for me.

"Welcome to the life of a Morning Bell employee," Grace muttered, pulling me back to the moment.

"All I can say is..." I blew out slowly. "Hectic."

She turned to me, her eyes wide and deadly serious. Her expression was a perfect—and hilarious—contrast to the shirt she was wearing, featuring the words "You're Brew-tiful" and an animated cup of coffee with a winking face. "I appreciate you helping out today, Nicholas. Having you here made things so much easier. So... Thank you."

Her words were hesitant but I could tell they were sincere. I bowed my head. "I was happy to help, honestly. It was kind of fun."

Grace's eyebrows shot up and she giggled. "Fun?"

"Yeah." I smiled. "I feel tired but happy. Like I did something good, something meaningful."

I stretched my arms above my head and realized that, miraculously, my shoulder didn't even hurt.

The door to the cafe swung open and an older gentleman I knew well walked in. Mr. Bell looked almost exactly the same as when I'd last seen him ten years ago. Except that he'd put on a couple of extra pounds and he had significantly less hair.

He saw me sitting next to Grace and did a double take, eyes wide.

"Nicholas King?" He shook his head and his face broke into a wide smile. "What are you doing here? How long are you in town for? How are you?"

I stood to give Mr. Bell a firm handshake. I wasn't sure which question to answer first so I settled with, "It's great to see you, too, Mr. Bell."

"Steve." Mr. Bell slapped my shoulder, and I was grateful he got my left side. "You know that you can call me Steve."

I laughed. "Steve, then."

He stepped back and looked at me like he couldn't quite believe what he was seeing. "It's been too long. What brings you to Morning Bell?"

"He came by this morning," Grace piped in. "He fixed the coffee machine."

Mr. Bell's face turned white. "The coffee machine broke? What happened?"

"It's okay, Dad. Nicholas got it running again and the customers barely noticed the delay. It's a good thing he came in when he did."

Mr. Bell nodded at me. "Lucky number 13."

I refrained from rolling my eyes. Seemed everyone in Aston Falls liked to refer to me by my jersey number.

"That's very kind of you," Mr. Bell continued. "But you didn't have to stick around for the rest of the day. Austin was here to help Grace."

I frowned. "Austin?"

Mr. Bell narrowed his eyes and whirled to face Grace. "You said he was coming in today."

Grace cleared her throat and looked everywhere but at her dad. If she could whistle, I had no doubt that she'd be in the middle of a tune.

I'd clearly stepped into sensitive territory and my mind raced. How could I fix this? "Yeah, right, Austin... He did pop by to help, but, seeing that I was here, he left."

It wasn't a complete lie—Austin did drop by this afternoon between appointments to say that the rest of his day was booked up. He'd seemed concerned and asked Grace if he should cancel his appointments. But, once he saw me in an apron, he'd relaxed.

"Well," Mr. Bell said to me, his mouth stretching into a smile. "I've always trusted you more than Austin, anyway. You're practically family, after all."

Grace snorted and I chuckled too, shooting her a side-long glance. She met my eyes but quickly looked away. After Austin and I became friends in high school, I often went to the Bells' house to give my grandparents a break. Austin and I would play ball in the yard, or I'd play board games with Grace. Given that I was a hungry teenage boy with a penchant for football, Mr. and Mrs. Bell used to joke that I might eat them out of house and home, but there was nothing they could do about it—I was practically family.

"In all honesty, it was my pleasure helping out today," I said sincerely. "I've been looking for things to do this off-season, and this was a perfect way to pass the time."

At this, Mr. Bell's face suddenly lit up. He looked between Grace and me, practically glowing. "Gracie, we've been looking for help around the cafe. Why doesn't Nicholas help you?"

You could've heard a pin drop, the cafe was so silent. Grace's mouth was open, her cheeks pink. "I don't think that's such a good idea."

"Why not?" Mr. Bell asked excitedly. He turned his piercing green eyes on me. "You think it's a good idea, don't you, Nicholas?"

I sputtered as I stared between Grace, who was now glaring at her father, and Mr. Bell, whose entire face was red with glee.

"I think Nicholas, Chicago's *star football player*, might have better things to do," Grace said between gritted teeth.

"It's the off-season! What else is Nicholas gonna do? Right?"

He looked at me so earnestly, so eagerly, that the very thought of saying no felt wrong. It would've been like taking a puppy away from an excitable toddler.

"Right," I confirmed feebly, ignoring the voice in the back of my head screaming at me that I should focus on my off-season workout regime.

"Fantastic," Mr. Bell said proudly, hands on his hips. "It's a plan. Now, if you'll excuse me, I'm going to the kitchen to speak with Tommy about the Ross's Burgers deal. But, I'll be back shortly to help you guys clean up."

"Don't you dare," Grace said, her normally light and melodic voice sharp.

Mr. Bell shot Grace a rebellious glance before he disappeared around the corner.

"Ross's Burgers?" I asked, looking at Grace.

She visibly deflated. "Long story."

My phone buzzed in my back pocket. I took it out, frowned at the screen and rejected the call.

"What's that about?" Grace nodded towards my phone.

"Also a long story."

Grace half-smiled at me, her emerald eyes dancing. "I'll tell you mine if you tell me yours."

I chuckled, but she watched me closely. She leaned

forward, her expression open and curious. I could never say no to her when she looked at me like that.

"All right," I said, and then my smile disappeared as I looked at my hands. "I don't know if you've heard, but I'm kind of in the middle of a messy divorce with my wife— soon to be ex-wife—Whitney."

Grace nodded slowly. "Whitney Cade. The model."

"That's her. For almost two years, we were happily married. We argued about regular things married people argue about, but we were generally happy. And then, suddenly, she's throwing me out of our house in Chicago and saying I don't love her enough. I don't exactly know where it all went wrong." I picked at my nails, frowning. "But, I guess, maybe that's the problem."

Grace lifted her hand, almost like she wanted to pat me on the back or something. But instead, she folded both hands under her thighs. "I'm really sorry, Nicholas. I've heard rumors around town, but I never expected it to be so bad."

I chuckled dryly. "My mom has this expression—that bad things happen in threes. When it comes to my relation-ship, I guess she was right. Married for two, together for three, and now, getting divorced."

Grace bit the inside of her cheek. "Bad things come in threes... That sounds like small-town wisdom if I ever heard it. But, it doesn't mean it's wrong."

"True." I took a deep breath. "Everything was so much worse when I was in Chicago. Don't get me wrong, I came back to Aston Falls mostly for my grandpa and to see my mom. But I also came to escape the media. They're going *crazy* over my split with Whitney."

"And didn't you separate your shoulder this season, too?"

I looked at Grace, a cheeky smile crossing my lips. "You followed my games?"

She froze, her mouth open, and a light blush colored on her cheeks. But, the next second, she laughed and rolled her eyes, pointing to the small TV in the top corner of the cafe. "Don't get too big a head, Nicholas. Dad bought that TV specifically for your games, that's the only time it's on. He had to buy it, otherwise the cafe was completely dead during your games. He always makes jokes that he's added it to your tab."

I chuckled along with her. "Well, don't worry, that might not be the case for much longer. I'm not sure how much longer I'll be playing."

I clamped my lips shut. Why did I say that? I hadn't told anyone my doubts about the future. I hadn't spoken to my mom, or Grandpa, or Austin about it. My agent knew that I'd be traded, obviously, but not even *he* knew the full story.

Grace tilted her head. "What do you mean? You think you'll be retiring soon or something?"

I'd already said too much, I might as well spill my guts. I bit my lip and frowned at my hands. "I'm not sure, Ace. I do know that I likely won't be playing with Chicago next season —they're looking to trade me. But, I've just been injured so much over the years. My body's been through the wringer."

I massaged my shoulder, tabulating the injuries in my head. Ankle sprains and torn ligaments in my knees, back problems and countless dislocations. Not to mention the concussions and almost chronic shoulder injuries. There were days when getting out of bed was almost excruciating. And, the aching pain in my left knee always informed me when it was about to rain.

"You always go all in," Grace said quietly. "Even in high school. Your mindset has always been all or nothing."

Her mouth was quirked into a little smile and her eyes were sincere. My heart rate slowed and I found myself falling into the deep green of her gaze.

She had the most striking eyes. It was the first thing I'd ever noticed about her. When Grace's eyes were on you, the rest of the world fell away. She had an indescribable way of making you feel like you were at the center of it all, making you feel seen. Like you had her undivided attention.

Even now that I was constantly in the public eye, always in the spotlight, I'd never felt like anyone truly *saw me* the way Grace did.

Then, she blinked a couple of times and looked away, taking off her apron. My heart started up again and I ran my fingers through my hair. "Anyway Ace, I'd better get home, Mom's headed to work soon and I need to watch Grandpa. But, thanks for letting me spend time here today."

Grace chuckled and went to the serving counter, her long blonde hair swinging behind her. "You were a big help. And, honestly, disregard everything my dad said. You absolutely do *not* have to work here, I'm sure you have much better things to do."

"I don't, actually," I said slowly. "I genuinely enjoyed myself today."

I felt as surprised as Grace looked by the sincerity of my words.

"I think I might kind of love to work here this off-season," I mused. "I've been trying for so long to get my mind off everything happening in Chicago. And for some inexplicable reason, Morning Bell seems to be the answer. But, only if you're fine with it, of course."

I could hardly believe what I was saying, but something about it felt right. Deep in my gut, I actually *wanted* to work at Morning Bell. And I always trusted my gut—it was what brought me to this stage of my football career.

Grace leaned against the counter, her brows furrowed in thought. She looked me up and down, then she took a deep breath and squeezed her eyes shut. "Yeah. I mean, Dad's right, I guess I do need the help. And the last thing I have time for is to run interviews. So... here we are."

A slow smile spread across my face. "Here we are."

"The pay isn't much."

"I wouldn't dream of letting you pay me."

Grace paused for a moment longer, then her face broke into a lovely smile. She nodded once, curtly, and disappeared into the kitchen to grab the broom.

I took off my apron and threw on my black hoodie, feeling happier than I had in days. It was bizarre to feel excited by the prospect of work, but something about working at Morning Bell filled me with a small sense of purpose. Some direction in the midst of everything falling apart.

But then, reality kicked in and my smile was slowly replaced by a grimace.

We'd be working together. Grace and me. Me and Grace.

After everything we'd been through—all of our history —was this a good idea? Or were we entering dangerous territory?

Grace came back around the corner and I felt a need to ask her, to check how she was feeling after what had happened between us. But, my question died in my throat.

I came to Aston Falls with the express intention of staying away from trouble, of avoiding hurting people— hurting her. If I brought up our past now, was there a chance I was resurfacing something that I should leave alone?

It seemed like Grace was doing well these days—she was

taking control of the cafe while her dad was out of commission, she was clearly loved by the people of Aston Falls, and she was kind and gorgeous as ever. For all I knew, she might've even had a boyfriend.

I watched Grace as she swept the floor and hummed along softly with the radio, swaying across the cafe gracefully. I was hit with a pang of completely uncalled-for jealousy at the thought that Grace might have a man in her life.

Back it up Nicholas, that's none of your business.

I shook myself off and placed the cloth in the sink.

There was no sense in rehashing the past. What was done was done.

10

GRACE

"It's not really that simple." I kicked a pebble on the middle of the path.

"What's so complicated?" my friend JJ asked, swinging her arms wide. "It's dating. You can meet guys literally anywhere."

"Easy for you to say. You met your fiancé on the first day of freshman year."

"Yes, but if I didn't have Ted, I'd be all over the dating websites, and the blind dating, and the speed dating and the what-have-yous." JJ smiled, exposing the adorable gap between her front teeth. "There are so many options out there for you single people."

"What if I don't want options?" I sighed and kicked the pebble again. "What if I want one option—one guy—forever? Preferably someone who gives me foot massages after long days at work."

JJ slung an arm around my shoulder. "Sorry friend, but men like that simply *don't* exist."

I chuckled as JJ let go of me and ran ahead, skipping and sliding in the mud just off the path.

JJ Sutton, whose first name was actually Jessica Jade—though you didn't call her that unless you wanted a face full of snowball—had been a close friend of mine since high school. She'd fallen in with Ella and I after she moved here from Bozeman. She'd met Ted on her first day at our school and that was it. They'd been inseparable ever since.

"Come on, Gracie!" She shouted, gesturing for me to follow her. "It's Moaning Monday, let's get that heart rate going."

I jogged after JJ, but she was far ahead on the path already. For someone who worked at an ice cream parlor, JJ sure had a lot of energy. Though surely the treats at Sweets n' Sundaes were at least partly responsible for her enthusiasm.

Not that I blamed her. I was a sucker for ice cream myself. Rocky Road had always been my flavor of choice, though I'd started ordering Bubblegum after Mom died. Sure, I didn't particularly like the flavor, but it reminded me of her.

So now, after a bad day at work or a bad date, when a normal, well-adjusted person would eat cookie dough and watch cheesy comedy movies, I usually sat on the couch with bubblegum ice cream and watched old home movies so I could see Mom's smile again.

JJ disappeared down the path and I slowed to a walk. Next to me, the sun peeked through the bare branches of the aspen trees. Small, slushy snow banks bordered the trail and, just a few feet away, the river flowed lazily. I peered at the glistening surface as it flowed in the opposite direction.

It was a quiet and calm afternoon in Aston Falls. Morning Bell was closed on Mondays, so it was my one and only day off.

Not that I'd taken many Mondays off recently—I'd

started using the day to sneak into the cafe and catch up on work in the back office. Like today, I'd spent the morning looking at our finances—worse than I'd expected—and brainstorming ways to save Morning Bell from being bought out.

As I reviewed the paperwork, though, I always came back to one big, looming question—how on earth had Dad done this alone all these years? I had enormous amounts of respect for him, and my heart sank at the possibility that I might not be able to fill his shoes.

This afternoon, when JJ had knocked on the cafe door and insisted that I join her for a walk, she wouldn't accept any excuse. She'd simply shoved my jacket into my hands and physically pushed me out the door.

And now that I was here, strolling the riverfront, I was pretty grateful. The pathway along the Aston River was cleared of snow and well-maintained. Aside from a few walkers and joggers, the world felt serene and peaceful. I took a deep breath and the smell of pine and cottonwood relaxed me. A soft breeze brushed my cheeks, but I loved the chill.

My pocket started vibrating and I reached for my phone.

It was a video call from Ella.

"Hey JJ!" I shouted, hoping she wasn't out of ear shot. "Ella's calling. Come chat!"

I clicked the "Accept" button and Ella's face appeared on the screen. Her brown hair was done into a bun on top of her head and she was wearing large black glasses. She smiled wide when she saw my face.

"Grace! You look like less of a zombie today!"

Had to love good friends and their unfailing honesty.

"Hello to you, too, Els." I rolled my eyes, but I couldn't hide my smile. "How're you doing?"

Ella opened her mouth to answer when JJ suddenly attacked me from behind.

"Hey, girl!" she screeched and her voice echoed over the water. "How's life in NYC?"

Ella laughed and caught us up. She'd had interviews with a couple of different journals and newspapers, but she wasn't sure she'd found one that felt right for her. At the moment, Ella was a freelance journalist, sending her articles to different magazines and newspapers. She seemed interested in getting hired full-time, but if she was going to be tied down anywhere, she wanted to know it was a good place.

"Anyway, enough about me." She sat back on her pink couch and grabbed an open take-out box of Chinese food. "Gracie, tell us about the cafe. What's happening? You've been running it for a couple weeks now, are you feeling more comfortable with it?"

"Define comfortable." I shook my head. "It's a *lot* of work, but thankfully, I should be getting help soon."

I clamped my lips shut.

Why, oh why, did I have to say that?

Unfortunately, Ella and JJ heard me. They looked at me, their expressions curious.

"That's great!" JJ beamed. "Who's going to be helping you?"

My stomach twisted into a knot and I looked at my hands. "Well... I'm not sure you'll approve."

Ella put down her take-out box and rested her chin in her hands. "Spill it, Gracie."

I took a deep breath and told Ella and JJ the whole story with Nicholas. I described our accidental reunion at the cafe, and then explained what happened last night, when Nicholas agreed to help me in the cafe.

"Why would he do that?" Ella asked. "What does he get out of it?"

"He said that working in the cafe takes his mind off Chicago."

JJ frowned. "What's happening in Chicago?"

I shrugged. "Don't ask. Basically, he wants something to occupy him during the day when he isn't busy with his grandpa. Apparently, working at Morning Bell is a good way to fill time."

JJ bit her lip and stared at the ground. Ella was silent for so long I wondered whether the screen was frozen. But then, she moved, knocked over her take-out box, and grunted in annoyance. We were silent the entire time she cleaned the mess.

"Someone say *something*," I eventually begged, staring between my two friends.

Ella cleared her throat. "Look, Gracie. I'm really glad that you've found someone to help you. But, are you sure that spending time with Nicholas is a good idea after what happened in high school?"

I forced a laugh. "What happened in high school is in the past. It's not like anyone died, or was physically hurt."

"Well, no." Ella frowned. "But what he did broke your heart."

"Which is exactly *why* this is a good idea," I said, finding strength in my words. "After what he did, I could never fall for him again. Nicholas King is off limits. He's completely off my radar."

JJ nodded. "Plus, he's married."

"Really?" Ella tilted her head. "I heard he was getting a divorce."

They both looked at me expectantly, eyes wide like I had the answers to all of life's questions.

"He's in the middle of a divorce, but—"

JJ and Ella spoke at once, shooting questions back and forth and insisting that this was a terrible idea.

"Guys!" I held up a hand, hoping to silence my friends. Surprisingly, it worked. "It doesn't matter what his marital status is, Nicholas and I are *never* getting together. It's not like I could ever trust him again after what he did. Besides, he's headed to Chicago, or wherever he gets traded when football starts up again. This is just a temporary fix until my dad can come back to work or we sell to Ross's Burgers. That's it."

Ella and JJ both stared at me with their eyebrows raised.

"What I felt for Nicholas King is lost to the past. Now, he's just my brother's best friend—and, I suppose, my coworker, whenever he comes in for his first shift. But, that's all he'll ever be. End of story."

But, even as I said the words, I felt a long-forgotten glow of warmth deep in my belly. Nicholas's confident smile flashed in my mind, his dimple cuter than ever. I remembered the moment his eyes met mine at the cafe and the world stopped.

A warm blush rose to my cheeks and I rubbed my face to try and hide it. The rapid beating of my heart meant nothing. It was just a remnant of a feeling from my high school days.

11

NICHOLAS

The football was comfortingly familiar in my hands. I wound my left arm back and launched the ball through the air, a clean throw. It arced against the backdrop of the clear blue sky.

On the other side of the park, Austin kicked up a mess of slush as he dived for the ball. He caught it midair and landed gracefully on his feet.

"Woo!" he cheered, holding the football above his head. "Nice throw, 13."

"Awesome catch!"

"Can't believe you throw like *that* with your left arm."

I laughed. "Well, it seemed logical to start practicing with my other arm after dislocating my good shoulder a few times."

Austin and I walked towards the trees on the outskirts of the Aston River park. Austin grabbed a bottle of water while I chugged Gatorade. The park wasn't too busy today—there were a few joggers and walkers passing through from the river pathway, and the shouts and laughter of excited children on the playground echoed through the air. It was a pleasant Monday afternoon, so the kids probably came straight from Aston Falls elementary to enjoy the nice weather.

I clasped my hands behind my head and turned my face towards the sun. The rays were warm—the first hint of the coming summer.

Austin screwed the lid back onto his water bottle. "So, how're things going with the divorce?"

I peeked at him and then dropped my hands, exhaling. "It's tough, honestly. My lawyers are in constant discussion with Whitney's. And, on top of that, I'm still getting at least three calls a day from various news desks or tabloids wanting an 'inside scoop' on our split." I shook my head and took another long pull of Gatorade. "Don't they know that I don't want this—my failed marriage, one of the worst times of my life—splashed across the pages of a magazine?"

"I don't think they see things that way." Austin frowned. "Sorry, Nick, I was hoping things might've calmed down for you by now. You've been here, what, a couple weeks now?"

I nodded somberly. "Want to know the craziest part? I found out yesterday that Whitney's dating someone."

I felt a pang deep in my heart as I said the words aloud for the first time. Whitney, my wife—my almost ex-wife—was already dating. My lawyers had called last night to say that she'd met some famous basketball player and that they'd been seen together around Chicago.

It was hard enough to wrap my head around the fact that Whitney and I were no longer a couple. She'd been in my life for so long, but somewhere along the way, things had fallen apart. Over the last year, I'd found myself dreading going home after football practices, and Whitney would spend almost entire nights out.

In the final months of our marriage, I'd set up appointments with couples' counselors and sought advice from friends in successful marriages. But, despite my best efforts, Whitney wasn't interested in trying to fight for our relationship.

And now, she was dating someone new.

It was hard not to feel like I'd done something wrong. Like I'd failed, badly.

My lawyers had insisted that I allow them to use the information against her in court. But, I told them to scrap the idea. As much as it stung to see her move on with someone new, what could I do? We were getting divorced, and though a part of me still loved her, I'd known this day would come. I just didn't know it would come so soon.

"You're kidding," Austin said, his eyes flashing blue. "Whitney's *already* dating?"

"Apparently. Magazines in Chicago have published articles about it. This morning, I broke my own rule and checked the news. There are photos of her and this basketball player on dates around the city." I chuckled dryly. "I'm surprised that you haven't heard about it from the Aston Falls rumor mill."

Austin shook his head and smiled. "I never listen to the rumors around here. The gossips would happily create an entire imaginary world just to keep themselves occupied."

I laughed and picked up the football, passing it from one hand to the other. "What a world that would be."

"How does it feel being back after so many years? Last time you were here was like..." Austin scratched his clean-shaven jawline. "High school? College?"

"Something like that." I chuckled.

It *had* been a long time since I'd been back to Aston Falls. I'd come back briefly during college for my grandma's funeral, but hadn't spent any time around town or seen any of my friends. The summers when I was in college in Florida, I couldn't fathom returning and facing Grace. So, I'd signed myself up for extra training and odd jobs around Gainesville until the summer football regimes started up. I'd liked Florida—it was perpetually warm and sunny, and after Grandma died, my mom and Grandpa had always come out to see me.

By the time I'd signed with Chicago, coming back didn't feel like an option.

"It's nice to be here," I said, surprising myself to know that I meant it. "I've missed spending time at the house with Grandpa and Mom, but I'm finding it hard to keep from spiralling. I'm barely sleeping at night because all I can think about is what's happening back home. But, I think I may have a solution."

"What's that?"

"You know how I was working with Grace at Morning Bell yesterday? Well, I've offered to help her out more often... like, whenever she needs me."

Austin's eyebrows shot up. "Seriously? You're planning on working with Grace?"

My mouth stretched into a hesitant smile. "I guess so. If that's what she wants."

The truth was that I had serious reservations about our arrangement. When I came to Aston Falls, I'd resolved to stay out of Grace's way, give her the space she needed in our small town. But, it seemed that my resolution was falling apart. Fast.

I knew that we'd run into each other eventually, and I didn't know what to expect when that happened. I figured that I would have to face her, face what happened between us on prom night. It wouldn't be easy, but it was time to put it to rest—for the both of us. I could only pray that she could find some way to forgive me.

So, imagine my surprise when bumping into her in Morning Bell turned out to be one of the best things to happen to me lately. Because of that accidental moment, I'd returned to the cafe. And every time I'd been back, I'd had a blissful reprieve from the anxiety of my life back home.

There was something about Morning Bell—about Grace —that put me at ease. I'd welcomed the vacation from my own thoughts.

The more I thought about it, though, the more guilty I felt. I should call it off, I should tell her that I couldn't help her. It was the only way to make sure that neither of us got hurt again.

But, leaving her alone with all of that work? I couldn't do that to her either. Yesterday's rush had been eye opening for me. Grace was doing everything by herself. She was carrying the entire weight of Morning Bell right now due to Mr. Bell's health, and she'd admitted that she couldn't really afford to hire anyone to help her.

Could I really abandon her with that burden when I had the time and energy to help?

"Honestly?" Austin's voice pulled me from my thoughts. He fiddled with his Fitbit and then sighed. "It's kind of reassuring to hear that you'll be helping my sister. I haven't been able to give her a hand in days. I'm glad that you'll be there, looking out for her, making sure she takes breaks and doesn't wear herself out."

I smiled weakly. "That's what I'm here for."

"So, when do you start?"

"Soon, probably."

"Good man. But, I do have one condition." Austin's face was serious, but his eyes twinkled mischievously. "I know how it is when two people work closely together under romantic kitchen lights, the intimate smells of chicken and waffles wafting all around..."

I snorted. "What are you saying?"

"That you'd better not fall in love with her or anything. Grace may be my twin, but she is *much* smarter than me. She can do better than the likes of you."

"Agreed. Besides, doesn't she have a boyfriend or something?"

I was fishing. It was stupid, I shouldn't have been wondering about Grace's relationship status in the first place. It was only because she was my coworker now and I was curious.

Right?

"There've been a couple guys over the years, but nothing serious. She doesn't seem to want to settle down." Austin jokingly widened his eyes and held up his hands. "Just don't wanna see you get your heart broken."

I laughed. "I can promise you that I will not fall for Grace. Not that she would fall for me, either—have you tasted the cheese scones she bakes? Or seen how she's absolutely killing it at Morning Bell? A girl like that has it together."

Austin punched my arm lightly and grabbed the football from my hands. We ran back onto the field and Austin wound up for a throw. But, my mind wandered back to Grace and our agreement.

I'd told her that I would help her in the cafe and I was a man of my word. I'd just have to make sure that we didn't get too close. The last thing I wanted to do was hurt her again or let her down. Even after all these years, Grace had a special place in my heart. She always would.

Partly because she was my best friend's sister, and partly

because, before everything happened, we were good friends too.

After all, I only had a couple of months before I had to go back to Chicago—or wherever the trade would take me. What could possibly happen?

I heard a loud, tinkling laugh towards the riverfront and I reflexively swiveled to face the sound. Grace was walking the riverfront pathway with her friend from high school, JJ Sutton. She was holding her phone and clutching her belly from laughing so hard.

I couldn't help but smile as I watched her. She'd always had the most contagious laugh.

12

GRACE

*T*uesdays were relatively quiet for Morning Bell. We usually got a flurry of customers through the morning, followed by a rush around 11am. Most of them, like Mrs. Applebaum and Ms. Rodriguez, were old regulars from when Mom and Dad first opened Morning Bell.

Some days, I believed that they only chose Morning Bell for the memories, for the fact that this was where they'd always gone.

Over the years, we'd lost quite a few regulars to our competitors in Aston Falls, and even outside of town. Sure, they might come in every once in a while, but they certainly didn't visit Morning Bell as often as they'd used to. Dad blamed it on the better prices at Joe's Espresso, but I didn't think that was the whole story.

I pressed a button on the cash register and, with a jarring *ding*, the drawer jerkily slid open. I frowned at the old thing. It might be time for an upgrade—if and when we got the chance to make such improvements at Morning Bell.

I manually slid the cash drawer the rest of the way open and counted the money, putting some aside for

Tommy's tips. But, as I gathered the cash on the counter and took stock of the debit and credit card payments, I was hit by a wave of disappointment. While it had been a quiet day compared to other days of the week, Morning Bell certainly wasn't dead. And yet, looking at the money we'd brought in today, it was barely enough to cover expenses.

My shoulders drooped as I stared at the money on the counter. I had a mild headache and realized I hadn't had water today. I filled a glass and chugged the whole thing, before filling it again and drinking the rest. But, the headache wouldn't go away.

With a frustrated sigh, I filed the money away and grabbed a dishcloth from the sink. I wiped down the tables a little harder than necessary, trying to find comfort in the regular, circular motion.

I was wiping a table by the door when I noticed a sheet of paper taped to the window outside. I stood for a moment, watching the paper blow in the breeze. Then, I exited the cafe and took the paper from the window.

My eyebrows shot up when I saw the familiar handwriting.

It was a note from Nicholas.

Hey Ace, he wrote, *sorry I can't help at the cafe today—Mom is working an early shift and I have to watch Grandpa. But, I was hoping to speak with you about something. It looks busy in the cafe, so I'm hoping that we can chat after the cafe closes?*

If you're not too exhausted/trampled by tall people, meet me at our spot by the riverfront. I'll be waiting.

The bottom of the note featured his trademark signature with the blocky "N". I remembered him perfecting the signature in high school and proudly showing it to me at our kitchen counter. I'd taken basic calligraphy so I was giving him tips on how to make the letters "pop." It looked like some of those lessons stuck.

I smiled despite myself and my insides warmed. Did he really remember our spot?

I bit my lip as I went back inside to finish closing the cafe. Should I meet with Nicholas? Or should I go home and pretend I never saw his note? I hadn't yet seen him outside of the cafe and I didn't want to risk any of my old feelings coming back. Especially seeing as he was leaving in a couple of months.

After all, he was part of the reason I'd had a hard time trusting the men I'd dated. Was it really a good idea to meet with him alone?

My mind weighed the options as I finished the rest of my evening duties. A persistent thought reminded me that I was older and wiser now. I'd made mistakes, but I'd learned a lot. And I meant what I said to Ella and JJ—I couldn't fathom ever trusting Nicholas in a romantic capacity after what happened on prom night.

That night had changed everything for me. But the events of the night still confused me to this day.

I turned out the lights in the kitchen and slid into my puffer jacket. I changed out of my work shoes and into my brown boots. Then, I let my hair loose, letting it hang long down my back.

I wanted answers. And there was only one person who could give them to me.

13

NICHOLAS

*T*his was a bad idea. This was a collosally stupid idea.

The words were on repeat in my head as I perched on the teeter totter of a children's playground in the darkness with two ice cream cones that were beginning to melt down my fingers. Having removed my gloves, my hands were frozen and neither were free to check the time. I wasn't sure how long I'd been waiting.

I also wasn't sure whether Grace would even show up.

I'd gone by the cafe earlier hoping to speak with her about our arrangement. I'd wanted to hammer out the details of my helping her at Morning Bell. I figured that, if we had a set schedule and strict boundaries, we'd be more comfortable working together.

But, seeing the rush in the cafe, I'd decided to write her a note. I'd taped the note onto the window, and now, I was wondering whether it had flown into the breeze. Or, maybe another person found the note and threw it away. Or, maybe Grace saw the note and opted not to come.

Which left me sitting alone in a dark playground with two melting ice cream cones. Great.

Soon, my fingers were numb and my ice cream was running swiftly down the side of my cone. That'd teach me to take a couple of licks.

I slurped up the remnants and scrambled awkwardly to a stand.

Guess Grace wasn't coming.

"Hey."

Her voice was smooth like warm honey. I whirled around to see Grace approaching on the path from town, illuminated by the street lanterns. She smiled wide, her blonde hair tumbling around her shoulders.

"Hey." My heart thumped in my chest. I held out her ice cream cone. "This is for you."

Grace's eyes lit up and she took the cone. She licked the ice cream and moaned. "Rocky Road. My favorite."

I laughed, my body warm all of a sudden. When we were kids, Grace always used to order Rocky Road ice cream. After her mom died, she'd switched to Bubblegum. I was pleased that I'd remembered her favorite flavor.

"I'm happy you came," I said sincerely. "I wasn't sure you would."

She shrugged and took a seat on the other end of the teeter totter. "I thought about it."

"What made up your mind?"

Her brow furrowed for a second, like she was thinking hard about her answer. Then, she glanced at her cone before looking back at me, her eyes glowing playfully. "I sensed that you might bring ice cream."

I chuckled. "Am I that transparent?"

"One hundred percent." She took another lick of ice cream. "How's your grandpa?"

"Good." I bounced off the ground, feeling the teeter totter rise and fall with our combined weight. "Well, he's doing alright. He's still on oxygen, but the doctor said that he's beginning to stabilize. How was your shift?"

Grace was silent for a long moment. She slurped her ice cream in a decidedly unladylike fashion and I could see her blush through the darkness. I snorted and she chuckled.

"It was..." Her smile faded and she sighed. "In all honesty, it was busy but disappointing."

"I'm sorry to hear that," I said quietly. "That's frustrating."

"That's the price you pay for losing your regular customers, I guess. I wonder how Ross's Burgers will handle that."

I tilted my head. "What do they have to do with this?"

"Ross's Burgers wants to buy out Morning Bell." Grace stared at the ice cream cone in her hands. "Dad's in negotiations with them to take possession over the summer. So, we only have about three months left."

The sadness in her voice broke my heart. "Your dad wants to sell Morning Bell? The cafe's a staple of Aston Falls, it's been here as long as your family. He can't do that."

"He can. And he wants to. He doesn't want to run it anymore."

I frowned. "Is that what *you* want?"

"No." Grace's answer was firm. "I love Morning Bell. It's a part of who I am. My dream would be to take it over from Dad, to run it myself."

"Why can't you do it?"

"Oh, a number of reasons. Starting with the fact that I have absolutely no idea what I'm doing or how to run a business."

"Well, you've been running it for a couple weeks so far and it hasn't tanked."

Grace laughed dryly. "That's a miracle if I ever heard one."

I shook my head. "Miracles have nothing to do with it. Don't discount yourself, Ace. You have so much to offer Morning Bell, and I'm sure that if you talked to your dad, he'd love for you to run it."

"Maybe. I guess I just feel that I need to prove it to him first. Or, maybe I need to prove it to myself..." she trailed off, her words a whisper. Then, she shifted awkwardly. "Sorry, I don't know why I told you that. It doesn't matter."

"Of course it does," I said, strangely touched that she'd shared something so personal with me. "I completely get it. But proving something to yourself doesn't mean you have to exhaust yourself in the process. Besides, one of the first big business decisions you made was a brilliant one."

Grace blinked a couple of times. "What business decision was that?"

I winked. "Hiring me, of course."

Grace hiccuped in a laugh. "About that... to be clear, I don't expect you to be around Morning Bell all the time or anything. You don't have to spend any time at the cafe if it doesn't work for you."

"I know I don't have to. But I want to."

Grace's eyes met mine and she nodded gratefully. She took another lick of her ice cream.

"All right," I said, getting down to business. "What exactly do we have to do to keep Morning Bell from being bought out?"

"Good question. I've spent a lot of time thinking about this," Grace said, getting down to business. "When my parents were running the cafe, Morning Bell was booming.

Then, after my mom passed and everything fell on my dad... Well, from what I've seen in Morning Bell's financial records, it's been in a steady decline for years. And that's no fault of Dad's. He was dealing with tragedy, raising two children, and running an entire business all by himself. I actually think he did remarkably well."

There was a clear note of reverence in Grace's voice. It was obvious how much she loved and respected her dad. I couldn't imagine how hard this whole thing was for her.

"So, as I see it," she continued. "We need to get Morning Bell flourishing again. The first step is hiring someone to work the floor with me at the cafe. Which, if you're happy to come in every once in a while, solves that problem." Grace frowned, her expression pensive. "I'd also like to figure out a way to keep our regular customers. And, of course, I want to grow our customer base. But, I don't know how to go about doing all that."

"I'm sure I can help with that." I nodded enthusiastically.

"No offense, Nicholas, but this isn't really in your wheelhouse."

"So?" I asked, a small bloom of excitement rising in my chest. "I need something to keep me occupied, something to do during the day when I'm not with Grandpa. It'll keep my mind off the divorce, and the way my football career's going."

Ice cream dribbled down my fingers and I hurriedly tried to slurp it up. Grace laughed and stood from the teeter totter, reaching into her back pocket. She handed me a couple of napkins.

"Stashed them away from the cafe," she said, answering my unasked question. "But that's all I have so you better finish your ice cream before it melts all over you."

"Yes ma'am." I stood in front of her and took a gigantic bite of ice cream. The cold, sweet substance shocked my mouth and gave me an instant brain freeze. I squeezed my eyes shut and grimaced, trying to swallow the offending ice cream as fast as possible.

Grace burst into laughter. "How was that?"

I made a show of swallowing the ice cream, and then I smacked my lips. "Painful, but delicious."

Grace giggled and then her eyes dropped to the front of my jacket. She frowned and reached towards me, firmly pressing two fingers to my chest to brush off a drop of ice cream.

The gesture, for being so innocent, felt strangely intimate.

She wiped her hand with a napkin and her eyes met mine again. Even in the relative darkness, her eyes glowed and twinkled. My heart slammed in my chest, and I almost forgot where we were. The feeling of the ice cream dripping down my fingers faded into nothing.

Then, there was the squelch of slushy snow as someone walked the pathway near us, and the spell was broken. Grace looked away and I cleared my throat before taking another lick of my ice cream.

It was too easy to fall into old patterns with her. Now that we were officially working together, I had to remember to keep things professional.

14

GRACE

"Did you hear about Mr. Kirkpatrick and Sheila Barnes?" Ms. Rodriguez stage-whispered to Mrs. Applebaum as I picked up her plate. "The talk around town is that they planned to run away together."

Mrs. Applebaum tutted and sipped her tea. "Poor Mrs. Kirkpatrick. She found out the night before they intended to leave and divorced him on the spot." She shook her head. "You think you can trust someone."

I stacked their dirty dishes in my arms and turned away quietly, hoping to remain invisible. Mrs. Applebaum and Ms. Rodriguez had been here all morning, drinking tea and sharing stories. As much as I appreciated them being here and not at Joe's Espresso, I was doing my best to avoid being involved in their conversations.

It was necessary given that I was the only one working the floor on this busy Friday.

With the plates carefully balanced, I took a step away.

"Gracie, what do you think?" Ms. Rodriguez asked from over my shoulder.

Oh, no.

I turned, smiling weakly. "Me?"

"Yes, dear." Mrs. Applebaum nodded impatiently. "What do you think about the situation with the Kirkpatricks and Sheila Barnes?"

"I think..." I frowned. "I think that people aren't always what they appear to be."

Mrs. Applebaum and Ms. Rodriguez stared at me blankly. I smiled feebly again and hoped they'd release me soon. I had a couple of urgent orders to send out to our suppliers before noon, but I hadn't had a spare moment all morning. It was quickly approaching twelve and the pressure was on.

Austin said he might be able to come by and help, but he could only come this afternoon. And Nicholas? Well, I'd asked him to start tomorrow.

Given that Friday could be just as busy as Saturday, that wasn't my brightest idea.

A hand lightly touched my wrist, keeping me in place. "You know, Gracie, you're completely right," Mrs. Applebaum mused. "Take Nicholas King. He's a big shot now, a celebrity, a star football player known across the country. But, he's humble and sweet as ever. The fame hasn't gone to his head one bit, and that's certainly not what you'd expect of a man of his caliber. But, I suppose that's what happens when you come from a good, strong community."

"Like Aston Falls?" I asked innocently.

"Exactly," Ms. Rodriguez agreed, misinterpreting my sarcasm. "Without Aston Falls, really, Nicholas King wouldn't be who he is today. He's successful and famous *because* of our small town and wonderful community."

Mrs. Applebaum and Ms. Rodriguez smiled at each other proudly, like their combined efforts had propelled

Nicholas to stardom. I refrained from rolling my eyes. Of course, they would try to take the credit for his hard work and dedication.

Nicholas was just in a league all his own.

"And, speaking of whom." Ms. Rodriguez's expression immediately changed from gleeful pride to obviously flirtatious. She waved at a point behind me. "Yoohoo! Nicholas!"

I whirled around to see Nicholas coming through the front door of the cafe. He was wearing a leather jacket over a casual blue button-down shirt and black jeans. His dark hair was windswept and his cheeks were slightly pink.

He smiled brightly and walked over. Ms. Rodriguez pursed her lips sultrily and Mrs. Applebaum hurriedly fixed her hair. Now, I couldn't help but roll my eyes and smile at the two older ladies. They truly knew no shame.

Not that I blamed them. Even I couldn't help but notice how gorgeous Nicholas looked today.

"Good morning." He nodded courteously. "What kinds of trouble are you lovely ladies getting into?"

Mrs. Applebaum giggled. "Just here for some tea and treats."

"And we were hoping to spot the star of Aston Falls," Ms. Rodriguez said, her voice a couple octaves higher than normal.

Nicholas laughed. "Well, when you see them, please let me know." Before the ladies could respond, he turned to me. "I was walking by and saw the rush. Thought I'd come in to help."

I giggled, the noise breathier than I would've liked. I couldn't tear my eyes away from him. "You're not meant to start until tomorrow."

Nicholas's gaze was intense. "Why wait?"

He took off his leather jacket and ran his fingers through

his hair as he glanced around. My eyes dropped to the sliver of tanned, washboard abs as his shirt rose at the bottom. My mouth went dry and, for once, both Mrs. Applebaum and Ms. Rodriguez sat frozen and silent.

Nicholas took the plates from my arms and strode towards the kitchen. My body came back to life and I excused myself from the older ladies, following Nicholas. He grabbed an apron from below the serving counter, tying it around his waist.

He even managed to make the boring, old royal blue "Morning Bell" apron look like the hottest thing in GQ.

"Are you sure about this?" I asked, my voice uneven. Apparently, seeing his midsection was enough to completely throw me.

"Absolutely." He smiled and then placed a strong arm around my shoulder. "Anything for Austin's sis."

His masculine smell of sawdust and clean laundry was enough to make my legs weak. He squeezed me close for a moment, the move playful, but I found myself wanting to melt into him. His side was firm and strong, and his arm wrapped around me comfortably. If I wanted to, I was sure I could fall asleep in his arms. Just like this.

Too soon, he let me go and started bustling around the coffee machine. His eyes scanned the tables, searching for ways he could help.

I forced my breath to return to normal as I leaned against the counter, ignoring the weakness in my legs. It was nothing, just exhaustion.

I exhaled in a laugh, trying to sound as casual as possible. "It's not every day that you see a pro quarterback playing server."

Nicholas's gray stare was enough to make my knees

weak all over again. "My coach used to say that we have to make every day count. I want to make today count."

He smiled a half-smile and I almost forgot where we were or what we were doing.

I must really need some sleep. Get it together, Grace!

Nicholas nodded towards the back of the cafe. "I've got it under control here, why don't you go to the office and get those orders out. I'm assuming you haven't had time yet today?"

"How did you...?" I trailed off, shaking my head. I couldn't remember telling him that I had orders to send out today. The man's memory was better than I thought.

"Go on." He smiled that confident smile. "I've got this."

Before I could say anything, he dived into the crowd, moving swiftly and easily among the tables. I watched him for a moment as he took orders and cleared plates. Then, I kicked myself into gear and went to the back office.

It was a bizarre thing to feel grateful for the man I thought I'd spend the rest of my life avoiding.

I stretched my arms above my head and yawned loudly, feeling my back and neck release after hours spent bent over the desk.

Hours?

My eyes went wide and I checked the time. 3pm.

I'd been holed up in the back office for a little over three hours.

I scrambled to my feet and gathered the stack of papers I'd been working through. After barely managing to get all of our orders done before noon, I'd noticed a stack of work that I'd been meaning to get to—connecting with our suppliers, putting together next week's schedule, and perusing information booklets about marketing for the cafe.

At first, I'd popped my head out to check the floor a couple of times to be sure that Nicholas and Tommy were doing okay. Nicholas assured me that he could handle it, and the devilish sparkle in his eye and his self-assured smile appeased me.

I hadn't expected to leave him alone for this long, though. I'd gotten lost in a deep dive of work, including drawing up a schedule that had tentative blocks of time for Nicholas.

I hurriedly threw my apron over my jeans and left the office. When I got to the front of the cafe, a table was occupied—rare for this time of day. The high-pitched sounds of a child's laughter were quickly followed by a rumbling chuckle I knew well.

Nicholas was sitting at the table with a woman and her child. He was playing paper football with the boy while his mom watched, her face gleeful and relaxed. Nicholas threw the paper football and the boy caught it midair, exploding into another fit of giggles. Nicholas laughed too, patting the child lightly on the arm.

My heart skipped a beat and I smiled to myself. I'd never seen Nicholas around children, but the way he was making the boy laugh, the way he engaged with him, gave me a funny feeling. Nicholas was going to be a great dad one day. I was sure of it.

Imagine—a little boy and girl running around on the lawn. He'd reach for the boy and toss him onto his shoulders. The girl would giggle as he picked her up, too. Then, they'd come inside where I'd have dinner ready—

Wait. No.

Was I just imagining a life—*kids*—with Nicholas King?

Nope, had to backpedal right out of that particular daydream.

Right then, Nicholas's gray eyes found me and he smiled, waving me over.

"Ace, I want you to meet Mrs. Abernathy and her son, Nolan." Nicholas smiled at the small family. "This is Grace Bell. She and her family have owned Morning Bell, our town's beloved cafe, for years. She's currently running the cafe while her father recovers from a health scare."

Mrs. Abernathy's brown eyes were kind. "This is a true gem you have here."

My cheeks warmed and I smiled, flattered. "Are you from Aston Falls?"

"No, we're visiting from out of town. But, we do come to Aston Falls often—it's a beautiful train ride in and Nolan's favorite ice cream is from Sweets n' Sundaes."

"They do have the best Rocky Road."

Nolan turned towards me with wonder in his eyes. He smiled, revealing two missing front teeth. "That's my favorite, too!"

Mrs. Abernathy glanced around. "In all the months we've been coming to Aston Falls, I've never dropped by this little cafe. It's cozy and the food is amazing! My compliments to the chef. And, seeing as we used to live in New Orleans, we certainly know good food."

Mrs. Abernathy, Nicholas and I fell into easy conversation while Nolan played with the paper football. My cheeks hurt from smiling and laughing, and I felt more at ease than I had in a long time.

It reminded me why I used to love Morning Bell. There was nothing like chatting with the people who came through—hearing their life stories.

"My friends and I are always looking for nice cafes and

restaurants in the area, and I'll be sure to recommend this place for our next meeting," Mrs. Abernathy said. "I'm surprised that I haven't heard of it sooner. The only reason we came in today was because Nolan noticed Nicholas King through the window." She laughed. "I thought I was having a stroke. I never expected to see Chicago's star quarterback here in Aston Falls."

Nolan smiled up at Nicholas. "I want to be a quarterback someday. With the number 13, just like you."

"You can do it, little dude." Nicholas ruffled the child's hair. "With that arm? No problem."

The four of us laughed and Mrs. Abernathy wrapped her little boy in her arms. Nicholas looked at me, eyes dancing, and we shared a secret smile before he gave Nolan a high-five.

My heart fluttered seeing Nicholas's smile. Thinking he was cute was one thing—with his strong jawline, dark brows and slate gray eyes, Nicholas looked like he could grace the cover of any magazine. Even in high school, whenever I was with him, everyone else was invisible, lost in the shade of Nicholas's sunlight. Not that I minded. When he turned those sparkling eyes on me, it didn't matter whether I was on earth or in heaven.

But, seeing this side of him was another thing entirely. He was caring, kind, generous. Despite the fame and fortune, he was happy to sit with a couple of customers and joke and play. There was no reason for him to do this, but he was doing it anyway.

All or nothing, as usual. After all these years, how could it be that he still had this sweet side to him?

A pleasant warmth spread under my cheeks and I felt my heart give way just a tiny bit. But, I snapped myself to attention. I couldn't forget what happened in high school. I couldn't wilfully ignore our past.

Besides, this was the reality of my relationship with Nicholas—amazing one minute, gone the next.

Best to not get attached.

15

NICHOLAS

Working at Morning Bell proved to be a saving grace. Not only was I blissfully occupied during the day but, by the time I returned home at night to watch Grandpa, I was too tired to even think about Chicago. Or Whitney and her new boyfriend.

I could hardly believe it was May. Grace and I had been working together for a few weeks now, and time passed quickly. I found myself really enjoying working at Morning Bell. It was fun to be in the middle of the rush, with the pressure on and the stakes high. It was almost like throwing the ball into the endzone with seconds left on the clock, knowing that the fate of the game rested on my shoulders.

The hype around my working at the cafe had also, thankfully, died out. At first, there was some awkwardness as every diner in the cafe wanted to talk about my career, and Chicago, and stardom. But, after a few days, the talk of the town moved onto the next subject and people started to treat me as normal. Like any other local in Aston Falls.

I was loving the feeling of familiarity and stability.

Grace and I had also done well with keeping our

distance. We talked to each other as professionals or as friends would. We asked for help when needed, and we worked off each other extremely well. Sometimes, I almost believed that she could read my mind, see what I needed before I was even aware of it. And I always did my best to return the favor.

There was just something about Grace. She made me laugh with her dry wit and humor, even when I wasn't in a good mood. And she was so goofy, it was hard not to want to spend all my time with her.

She was also extraordinarily gorgeous, though I tried not to dwell on that. I did notice the looks she got from the men passing through Morning Bell, and I did my best to tame the little green beast that threatened to rear its head without my permission.

But, I did find myself staring at her sometimes—the curve of her chin, her high cheekbones, the way her emerald eyes crinkled at the sides when she smiled. She reminded me of a butterfly, or a perfect rose. Something beautiful but so rare.

I was trying especially hard not to think about her beauty as she locked the door of the cafe after another shift. She'd let her hair down and it swished down her back. She sighed with her eyes closed, as she did after every shift. Like it was a ritual.

I picked up a dishcloth and wiped down the tables, keeping my gaze averted away from her.

"Music?" she asked.

I smiled. "Absolutely."

This was another ritual. As soon as the last guest left, Grace sent Tommy home and the two of us cleaned the front of the cafe. We always turned on the radio and played classic rock, pop, or R&B.

Grace turned the radio dial to the classic rock station and a song from our childhood pumped through the speakers. She hummed as she refilled the napkin holders on the serving counter.

I closed my eyes and bathed in the sounds that felt like home. I was aware of a rumble in my stomach—I was hungry. But other than that? I felt totally and completely at peace.

Until the high pitched ring of my phone blasted through the air.

Grace looked up from the napkin holders, bewildered. I muttered an apology and grabbed my phone from my back pocket. "Sorry, got to take this. My agent said that he has big news for me so I told him to call after 9pm. Seems he didn't want to wait a minute longer."

Grace chuckled and returned to her task while I accepted the call.

"Hey Arnie, what's up?" I asked, my voice sounding exhausted even to my own ears. With a grimace, I realized why—I always sounded exhausted in Chicago.

"NICK!" Arnie boomed down the line. "Finally! Where've you been, kid? It's been too long. Anyway, glad I got ahold of you out there in podunk nowhere. I have some *excellent* news. As you know, Chicago is looking to trade you. Well, good ol' Arnie has your back, don't you worry. I've been scoping out other teams to see where you might fit, and guess what."

There was the slightest pause, a rarity in any conversation with Arnie. "Wha—"

"Pittsburgh is looking for a quarterback. Pittsburgh! Can you believe it? Their starting quarterback is leaving—contract dispute—and, you know Pittsburgh, they won't cave. So, they're looking for a new one. They're interested in you, Nick. I have a call with them next week to hammer out the details, but if we can get the money right, it's a great shot."

My heart picked up speed. "Pittsburgh, Arnie? Are you serious? They're a championship—"

"They're a championship team, I KNOW!" Arnie boomed again excitedly and I had to hold the phone away from my ear. "I'm working on this deal for you, Nick. We're going to figure this out. You're going to the big leagues, kiddo."

"Amazing," I said, feeling weightless. "Thank you, Arn. Keep in touch and let me know if you need anything from me."

"Will do, kid. Ciao!"

The line went dead and I stared at my phone, a wash of emotions racing through my body. Pittsburgh wanted *me*?

The team had been on my wishlist for a while. They were perennial favorites and they'd won a number of championships over the years. Their current players were good—really good—and I knew they were in the running for the championship again next year. If I was on their team, that meant that the dream I'd shared with my grandparents and mom might finally come true!

"What was that about?" Grace's melodic voice asked from behind me.

I ran my fingers through my hair. I couldn't keep the smile off my face. "Ace, you won't believe it! Pittsburgh is interested in trading for me."

Grace's eyes went wide. "Pittsburgh? Didn't they *just* win a championship, like, two years ago?"

I nodded, my body buzzing. "They did."

Grace dropped the napkin holder and spun in a circle,

her arms wide. She reached across the counter to give me an enthusiastic high-five. "That's so exciting!"

She was practically bursting with giddiness, and her excitement meant so much to me. It occurred to me that I was happy to be celebrating this moment with Grace.

"Grandpa will be so excited," I said with a smile. "This is everything he's wanted."

Grace brought a hand to her chest. "I'm so happy for you."

On cloud nine, I returned to work. I was picking up one of the ketchup bottles to refill it when something in my injured shoulder twisted funny.

I winced in pain and dropped the bottle. Ketchup exploded onto the floor like a crime scene.

"You okay, Nicholas?"

"All good," I reassured Grace, even as discomfort pricked my skin. How could I have forgotten about my injured shoulder? "Just handling the ketchup like I did the ball during the playoffs."

Grace chuckled and examined the mess on the floor. She frowned. "This is a real mess."

"Don't worry about it," I said hurriedly, embarrassed. "I'll clean it up."

Grace looked at me, her emerald eyes sparkling. "You better not."

To my surprise, Grace gingerly stepped into the ketchup, getting it all over her work shoes. She slid from side to side, spreading ketchup around in a circle. Then, she took a running leap through the ketchup, surfing through it. She laughed as she slipped back and forth, swinging from one side to the other.

"Ace." I chuckled. "What are you doing? You're making an even bigger mess."

Grace giggled and continued sliding, attempting a half-turn. "Sometimes, the mess is worth it."

She ran through the ketchup again. "Come on, Nicholas, don't be such a stick in the mud. Come join me!"

I watched her for a moment, speechless. Could I really do such a thing?

But, within minutes, I was also sliding across the floor without a care in the world. It turned out that it was a lot of fun surfing through spilled ketchup. Grace and I cheered as we slid from one end of the room to the other, tracking ketchup around the cafe. We competed to see who could make the bigger mess, and we joked about pushing each other into the ketchup. Grace laughed so hard she almost toppled over, which made me laugh all the more.

I would've never done something like this in Chicago. Chicago Nicholas was too buttoned-up, too sleek and stern. Just like everyone else in the city. We all cared so much about what people thought, how we were perceived. Whitney would've turned up her sweet little nose—she didn't do "silly." But here? I loved the freedom, the ability to do what you wanted when you wanted. There were no rules, and it was liberating.

I spun on my heel and skated backwards through the ketchup. Then, I heard a scuffle behind me, followed by a high-pitched squeal.

I whipped around in time to see Grace losing her balance. She teetered and slipped sideways, eyes panicked.

I reacted instinctively and flew towards her. My arms circled around her midsection, pressing her body firmly to mine and cradling her head. Her eyes were shut and her hands gripped the back of my neck, holding onto me almost as tightly as I was holding onto her. She felt so small in my arms, and in that moment, a part of me fiercely wanted nothing more than to protect her.

When I opened my eyes, she was wrapped in my arms, her breath in short bursts on my cheek. She gazed at me and I was stunned again by how beautiful she was. Slowly, I raised her to a stand, my arms still clasped around her and her hands locked behind my neck.

My heart was racing, my skin tingling where her skin met mine. She smelled like cinnamon and nutmeg, and I felt almost lightheaded with her in my arms. Her heart beat against my chest and I realized that the last thing I wanted to do was let her go.

"Good catch," she whispered, her eyes locked on mine.

I smiled, strangely breathless from being this close to her. "Guess football training does come in handy."

16

GRACE

I trailed my fingers through the Aston River, watching small waves break around my hand. The cold shot up my arm, and my reflection in the water's surface was smiling. It was the middle of May and the river level was high, lazily pawing at its embankments.

The water dripped down my hand as I rose to a stand and took a deep breath of fresh air. The smell of blossoming flowers and green grass hinted at the arrival of summer. Though it was early evening, the air was warm and I was only wearing a long-sleeved shirt.

I skipped back to the riverfront pathway and continued my walk towards the park. My heart felt light and happy. It was a Monday afternoon, and I'd decided to take a walk after a busy "day off" spent in the back office of the cafe.

Busy. Not hectic.

Work had been much more pleasant lately and I was starting to enjoy Morning Bell again, instead of it being my main source of stress. Since Nicholas started at the cafe a month ago, we'd fallen into a wonderful groove, working together seamlessly. Despite having a career in professional football and never having done customer service, Nicholas had picked up the cafe work easily. He could scope out the floor and see what customers needed, and his handiwork around the cafe was helpful when a lightbulb went out or the cash register stopped working.

All in all, he'd been a huge help to Morning Bell, and I found myself smiling every day that he worked.

I wandered to a bench by the river and pulled out my phone. I'd been meaning to talk to Ella for the past couple of weeks, but hadn't had the chance. I dialed her number and waited for the video call to connect.

A moment later, her face appeared on the screen. Her brow was furrowed and her expression was dark. Her hair was in a messy bun and her eyes were slightly puffy.

"Hey Els," I said, frowning in concern. "You okay?"

Ella rubbed her eyes and a smile crossed her lips. It might've been a bad connection, but even from here, the smile looked forced. "Absolutely, why do you ask?"

"You seem... upset. You look like you've been crying."

Ella sighed. "That's what I get for sticking with friends from childhood. You really aren't afraid to tell me when I look bad."

"I'm not saying you look bad." I chuckled despite myself. "You just look sad or something."

"I didn't sleep last night." Ella rubbed her eyes again and smiled. "That's all it is. Anyway, what's up, Gracie? How're things at the cafe?"

I shot her a quizzical look, but her eyes were clear and she was smiling expectantly.

Over the next few minutes, I caught her up on everything at the cafe. I described the craze of the morning rushes and the ebbs and flows of the afternoons. I told her about Tommy and his Shih Tzu, and I went on to detail the more manageable workload I'd had recently.

"I finally feel like I'm starting to get a hold of this, Els," I said and a wave of pride washed through me. "I feel like I can do this, maybe. Like I can manage Morning Bell."

"Of course you can, hun." Ella shook her head. "That was never up for debate."

"And, it's even better because Dad's started handing off some of the more complex work, the management stuff that can't wait any longer."

Ella smiled brightly. "That's awesome news. I'm so, so happy for you."

"Thank you." I beamed. "Of course, there's no way I could do this alone. Nicholas has been a huge help around the cafe. He's whip-smart and very capable. Not to mention he's extremely good with the customers. He's charmed people from far and wide."

Ella looked at me slyly. "Gracie, you're blushing."

My eyes went wide. "Am not!"

I pressed my cool fingers to my cheeks and... I supposed they were a little warm. But that could've easily been the sun. I might've just been sunburnt from the spring rays.

"You are," Ella taunted.

"I have no reason to blush," I said, ignoring the warmth in my face. "Nicholas and I are just coworkers. Maybe friends. Friends who sometimes slide in ketchup."

"What?"

"But we're nothing more than that. We haven't talked about what happened on prom night and I wouldn't bring it up with him anyway. What's done is done. The past is in the past, and our present is a different story. Besides, he's leaving to go back to Chicago—or Pittsburgh—in about a month."

"Him leaving doesn't sound all that different to me," Ella muttered.

I laughed off her comment. Sure, his current behavior confused me. Sure, I thought he was gorgeous, and his kindness and generosity threw me off sometimes. But the damage was done. There was no getting away from that.

Just then, a couple of strong hands gripped my shoulders, shaking me from my thoughts.

"Hey, Els!" A familiar voice shouted directly next to my right ear.

"Ouch," I mumbled, covering my ears and handing my phone to my annoying twin brother.

"Sorry, sis." Austin laughed, taking the phone. "I had a feeling you were talking about something important. My twinny sixth sense was tingling."

I rolled my eyes. "No such thing!"

"Or." Austin ignored me as he spoke to my phone screen. "Maybe it's just that I heard a particularly loud and obnoxious voice from across the park. Though that could just be my 'spectacular doctor's ears.'"

"You know Tina didn't mean it like that," Ella quipped back without pause. "I should've known you were close by. With how big your head is, you might as well be here in New York."

"You wish," Austin sang with a smile, pacing with my phone. "How're things in NYC, anyway?"

While Austin and Ella fell into their usual sarcastic banter, I rolled my eyes and sat back on the bench.

My mind wandered back to how things were going with Nicholas. Despite what I'd said to Ella, there was one moment I hadn't been able to get out of my head—when I'd slipped in the ketchup and Nicholas somehow, miraculously, managed to catch me.

I remembered the feeling of his strong arms locked around me, his taut body pressed against me. I remembered barely being able to breathe as his silver eyes locked on mine. I remembered the way my body responded, my heart fluttering, to feel so safe, so protected in his arms.

A part of me berated myself for thinking these thoughts, for reliving these memories. But, there was another part of me—a voice that seemed to be gaining strength every day— that knew that I would've done anything to be back in the arms of Nicholas King.

17

GRACE

The next week, I made the executive decision to shut Morning Bell early on a Wednesday. It was often our quietest day, so I sent Nicholas and Tommy home, and then placed a sign in the window announcing that the cafe was closed from 3pm onwards.

Once the cafe was empty, I locked the door and went to the back office to get started on the managerial work. While Dad handled the negotiations with Ross's Burgers, I was doing my absolute best to stay on top of the cafe's operations.

And that meant grinding through some unpleasant, though necessary, paperwork.

I brewed a cup of black coffee, and then changed into my coziest gray sweatpants and a pink hoodie. I whipped my hair into a bun, and then settled, cross-legged, into the huge plush office chair.

I was just getting into the work when I heard a loud knock on Morning Bell's front door.

"There's a sign for a reason," I mumbled as I padded in my fluffy socks to the front of the cafe.

In the afternoon light, I saw Nicholas waiting just outside. I froze, reflexively covering my sloppy attire with my arms. I debated running to the back office, changing into my regular clothes, and returning, but he was already peering through the windows.

Then, he caught sight of me. His smile widened and he waved.

I forced a tight-lipped smile, ground my teeth. Why, oh why, did he always see me at my worst?

I self-consciously played with my hair, trying to tame the wild tendrils, as I approached the door. Then, I took a deep breath, unlocked the door and threw it open.

"What's up, King?" I blurted oh-so-casually, and then immediately regretted my awkward greeting.

He looked me up and down with an adorable half-smile on his face. "You look…" his eyes met mine, the gray depths moving like waves. "Cozy."

I blushed despite myself and tried to ignore the fact that he looked gorgeous, as usual, in black slacks and a blazer. I decided to take the angle of easy nonchalance, and I crossed my arms, leaning against the doorframe. "I've got work to do. You need something?"

"Can you take the evening off?"

I laughed dryly, gesturing towards the back office. "You know I can't. I have a stack of work to do."

"But, what if I can help you?" he asked, his eyes light. In fact, he was practically bursting with excitement. "What if I have a plan to help?"

My eyebrows shot up. "You're going to help me with paperwork?"

"It's something else," he said. "Something better than paperwork. You won't regret it."

I pressed my lips together skeptically. The work needed

to be done, but what did he have planned? I couldn't ignore the spark of curiosity. A spark that became a full-blown fire as I noticed his muscles were taut and tense with giddiness. His cheeks were flushed and his smile was practically blinding.

He looked like a kid on Christmas morning, about to open a long-awaited present.

"Alright..." I said slowly. "But, I have to get some work done tonight so this can't take too long."

"It won't," Nicholas responded quickly. Then, he stepped out of the doorway and pointed at my house next door. "Here's what you need to do."

About a half hour later, I was sitting in Nicholas's old Jeep from high school, holding the grab handles for dear life as we careened along the gravel road north of Aston Falls. The road was filled with potholes and jagged bumps. Due to the freeze of winter and the melting snow, the road was a certifiable mess.

"Now, are you going to tell me where we're going?" My voice was jumbled as we bumped through a large pothole.

Nicholas smiled, looking cool and calm as ever. "Not yet."

I picked at the strap of my bathing suit top restlessly, wondering for the thousandth time what Nicholas had up his sleeve.

Yep. It was barely summer and I was wearing a bathing suit.

After convincing me to join him on this grand adventure, Nicholas had instructed me to head home and change into my bathing suit. I snuck into my house, avoiding Dad's prying questions, and changed quickly before running back outside.

It had been a sort of deja vu to approach his Jeep, parked like it was by the rosebush in front of our house. When we were younger, Nicholas used to drive Austin and I to school sometimes. I used to wait for the days that Austin was sick, or that he had to go to school earlier than usual. Those rare days meant that I had Nicholas to myself for the entire ride to school.

Those were my favorite days.

As much as I tried to find out what Nicholas had planned for this evening, his lips were sealed. For the entire ride, all he'd done was smile mysteriously and say, "we'll see."

I was getting a bit impatient.

Eventually, we turned right onto an even more bumpy stretch of road. I frowned as we hurdled along the gravel. I knew of only one place on this road. And, surely, Nicholas wasn't suggesting...

Nicholas parked in front of "Sam's Sled Tours (And Paddleboards, too!)"

Without a word of explanation, Nicholas undid his seatbelt and hopped out of the Jeep. He opened the trunk and grabbed his black backpack. "You coming, Ace?"

I fumbled with my seatbelt. "Why are we here, Nicholas? I'm confused."

"Come with me and find out."

I hesitantly undid my seatbelt and stepped out of the car. Sam's Sled Tours was located in a large red farmhouse with white trim. On warm summer evenings, Sam often opened the barn doors and hosted local vendors and musical acts for the town to enjoy after paddleboarding.

But winter was when Sam really shined.

Sam McCurdy moved to Aston Falls from Canada a few years ago. He'd opened his sled tour shop on the outskirts of town, and no one knew what to expect at the time. Aston Falls welcomed tourists in the summer, but was significantly less busy in the winter. And, our town wasn't exactly populated enough to sustain him if he was giving sled tours to locals only.

To our surprise, Sam prevailed. In fact, his sled tour business grew exponentially over the years. Now, tourists traveled from around the world for his sled tours. I believed that Aston Falls could thank Sam for its booming winter tourist season.

"Are we going on a sled tour?" I asked Nicholas slowly. We were verging on summer now, surely the conditions would no longer be good.

"Oh, no," Nicholas answered with a laugh. "The snow's melting, there's no way we could do a sled tour."

I narrowed my eyes. "We can't be here to paddleboard... It's far too early in the season."

"I don't know about that." Nicholas's eyes twinkled as he gestured for me to follow him into Sam's shop. His hand lingered behind him for a moment, almost like he wanted to take mine. But then, he dropped it.

I found myself wishing that I'd slipped my hand into his.

No, Grace. Holding hands with Nicholas King is not part of the plan.

The bell over the door dinged as Nicholas and I strolled into Sam's. The room smelled like campfire smoke and bug spray. Like summer. Various camping items were crowded around the room, as well as wetsuits and warm blankets. The shop felt chaotic but cozy.

"Hey there, folks," Sam boomed from behind the counter. He was a jolly man with a white beard and a balding head. He ambled towards us, a smile on his face. "You must be the Kings."

Nicholas and I looked at each other, and my cheeks turned bright red. "Nope. No. He's Nicholas King and I'm Grace Bell."

"Oh!" Sam exclaimed. "My mistake. Pleasure to meet you both, Nicholas and Grace. I'm Sam."

With his joyful manner and the familiarity of using our first names, I warmed up to Sam immediately. He waved for us to join him at the counter.

"I have your reservation ready to go." His eyes sparkled. "It should be a beautiful evening on the water. The weather's cooler than usual, so I took the liberty of grabbing a couple of brand new wetsuits for the two of you. Wouldn't want you getting cold out there and spoiling a good time."

He guffawed good-naturedly and I couldn't help but smile with him. "Thank you, Sam."

"My pleasure. I love having kids like you come by for a tour or a float. Makes me feel young by extension." Sam then asked whether the two of us had gone paddleboarding before—I shook my head while Nicholas nodded—and then he went on to explain the basics behind the activity.

He directed us to the back of the shop—where Nicholas changed into his trunks and we got into our wetsuits—and then gave us our gear. My stomach flip-flopped nervously as Sam confirmed that we understood what to do on the water. Then, he slung a cooler bag over his shoulder and gestured for us to follow him. We left the comforting warmth of the shop and exited through the barn doors. A lovely side path brought us to a long stretch of beach along a slow-moving section of the Aston River.

"Now," Sam instructed. "The paddleboards are technically lent by the hour, but given that you're my first customers of the season and I don't have anything else lined up today, feel free to take them out as long as you'd like. I'd recommend paddling up that-a-way—a family of great horned owls makes its home around the corner. Do you have any other questions at this point?"

Nicholas and I looked at each other and shook our heads. My mouth was dry and my heart was in my throat, but I tried to put on a brave face.

Sam smiled wide. "Wonderful. In that case, I'll pass this bag to you." He gave Nicholas the cooler bag, and I gazed up at Nicholas in confusion. His face gave nothing away. "And I wish you both a happy paddle! I appreciate your business and I hope you have a great time."

With a salute, Sam disappeared up the path, leaving Nicholas and I alone with the paddleboards, paddles, and cooler bag. Not to mention the mess of nerves in my stomach.

"Now what?" I asked.

Nicholas's eyes sparkled as bright as the reflection of the afternoon sun on the river. "Now, we get on the water."

18

GRACE

$\mathcal{M}$y board sliced through the calm surface of the water as I glided across the Aston River. My breath caught and I was mesmerized by the sight of the waves breaking on either side of my board.

It had taken several painstaking minutes for me to feel comfortable on the water. There were many flopped attempts at paddling and several narrow misses falling off. But, now that I had paddling somewhat under control, I felt a lot better.

"Come on, slowpoke!" I called over my shoulder. "I thought you said you'd done this before!"

"Are you sure you want to challenge me, Ace?" Nicholas growled playfully behind me.

"I live for challenge."

Nicholas chuckled. "You got it!"

I turned my head and saw that he was rapidly approaching, his board sailing towards me. I whipped back around and plunged my paddle into the depths of the river, propelling myself forward.

The constant, rhythmic splashes of his paddle grew louder.

He was gaining on me.

Nicholas overtook me, pulling up next to me and splashing me with cool river water.

"No!" I screeched, laughing, as I tried to splash him back. But, instead, my paddle caught in the water and my board whipped sideways, almost sending me flying.

"Woah!" Nicholas chuckled. "You better be careful or you'll wind up in the Aston River."

I regained my balance, my heart racing. My toes were frozen due to an influx of cold water through the wetsuit boots. I tried to keep my composure, posed with a hand on my hip.

"Is that a threat?" I responded smoothly.

"A threat?" Nicholas's eyes were wide and innocent. "I could never. I'm a gentleman, Ace, you know this."

"Since when?"

Nicholas shot me a look and, feeling bold, I blew him a cheeky kiss.

He burst into laughter and then gestured for me to follow him. He paddled with his left arm, heading towards the family of owls that Sam had pointed out.

I went after him, trying not to notice how the wetsuit hugged his perfectly sculpted body. Through the tight fabric, I could see his arm muscles working, moving, as he dragged the paddle through the water. His broad shoulders were strong and firm. His legs were hip-distanced on the board, grounded like tree trunks. And, just a little further up, those incredible abs...

I stared at my board, my cheeks flaming red. I was definitely *not* checking out Nicholas King.

We paddled for a while, enjoying the peace and quiet of

the river. My mind was silent, any anxieties about the cafe blissfully absent. I closed my eyes and took a deep breath, letting my shoulders relax for the first time in what felt like a long time.

Soon, golden hour was upon us and the sun was beginning to set behind the mountain peaks. The sky turned into a kaleidoscope of colors, and I turned my face upwards to take in the sight.

"Break time," Nicholas said from beside me.

I faced him and he was watching me with a half-smile, his eyes curious. It almost felt like he'd caught me in a vulnerable moment and I self-consciously tucked my hair behind my ear.

Nicholas approached my board and I tensed, gripping my paddle with white knuckles. "Don't worry." He laughed. "I'm not about to throw you overboard or anything."

My body relaxed as he carefully knelt on his board and pulled a cord from the front of the cooler bag. Using the cord, he tied our boards together on the slow-moving river.

Nicholas sat back with his shins crossed, looking the picture of effortless confidence. "Thirsty?"

As soon as he asked, I realized just how dry my mouth was. I sat cross-legged on my board. "Am I."

Nicholas pulled an enormous thermos out of the cooler, along with two mugs with dogs on them.

"Which pug mug do you want?" he asked so seriously that I couldn't help but snort with laughter.

I held a hand in front of my mouth in embarrassment. "The blue one."

He handed me the mug before twisting open the top of the thermos. He poured steaming hot liquid into my mug and I smelled the unmistakably rich scent of hot cocoa. I eagerly took a sip and the sweet liquid warmed my mouth and throat. I closed my eyes and enjoyed the delicious drink, moaning with delight.

"This is perfect," I said as Nicholas took a sip from his own mug.

He smiled. "Glad you like it."

"So, why'd you bring me here, Nicholas?" I gestured at the river, currently yellow with the setting sun. "I can't seem to make any connection between Morning Bell and paddleboarding."

"We're not here for paddleboarding." Nicholas chuckled at my confused expression and backtracked quickly. "I mean, we are. But, we really came here to see Sam."

"Sam?" I tilted my head. "What about him?"

"Well, what did you think of him? Of how he treated us?"

I remembered the warmth I felt for the elderly man, the sweet way he engaged with us. "He was kind and personable. Very friendly."

"Exactly." Nicholas's eyes lit up like I'd solved a math equation. "Friendly. He treated us like friends instead of customers. He even gave us wetsuits on the house. That's the secret to keeping your regular customers. You don't treat them like customers..."

"You treat them like friends," I murmured, finishing his sentence.

His words tugged at childhood memories, bringing them to the light. Was that why I used to love Morning Bell? Because our customers felt more like friends? It'd been a long, long time since I—or my dad—viewed our patrons that way. Years of stress and hard work had taken a toll on our perspective towards our beloved cafe.

"That's why people came to Morning Bell when we were growing up," Nicholas continued, reading my mind. "Your mom and dad were a dynamite pair, they were friends with everyone. If you can bring that back to Morning Bell, you'll be golden."

I took another sip of cocoa, wrapping my fingers around the mug. "I see your point," I muttered. "Morning Bell used to feel more like home than like work. I wish I could recreate that feeling, that magic. Our cafe was the locals' spot, a place to gather and feel at home. If we don't have that, then why keep the cafe? If we don't have that, Ross's Burgers might as well buy us out."

Nicholas's eyes were intent on me. Usually, I would've felt self-conscious under such a directed stare. I would've wondered what was wrong with my hair, or whether I had food on my face, or whether my wetsuit was on backwards. But, with him, it felt like he was simply paying attention. He wasn't internally criticizing my every move and word, he was listening.

It was incredibly comforting.

I found myself blushing and I stared into my mug. "You know, Nicholas. You're a lot smarter than people give you credit for."

I snuck a peek at his face and he was smiling, his eyebrows raised. "Does that surprise you, Ace?"

"Yes." I winked.

Nicholas's eyes danced. "Well, if it helps, a lot about you surprises me, too."

He leaned across his board and teasingly shoved his shoulder against mine. Unfortunately, I wasn't expecting this and my body rocked unevenly on the water. I almost dropped the mug in my rush to hold onto the edges of my board, but I didn't want to lose his mug in the depths of the Aston River.

I flailed sideways and careened towards the water.

But, right before I hit the surface, strong, muscled arms caught me, holding me in mid-air. Nicholas's wetsuit-clad torso was wrapped around mine, keeping me from falling.

"Ace, you really do seem eager to go for a swim this cold evening." Nicholas's husky voice murmured in my ear, his breath was warm and sweet on my cheek. He took my mug and placed it safely on his board.

"I'm not afraid of the cold," I whispered, suddenly finding it hard to breathe.

His expression turned serious, his eyes gazing into mine. "But, I'm afraid of losing you."

Those words sent delicious chills down my spine and I froze. He didn't mean—? He couldn't mean—?

He seemed to realize how that sounded too, because he blinked a couple times and stuttered. "In the water. Don't want to lose you in the water."

I forced a smile, but my body was buzzing with electricity being this close to him. His eyes traveled over my face and my gaze lingered on his lips. I got the almost indescribable urge to kiss him. Just a little peck, just to feel his lips on mine again. The lips I'd tried my hardest to forget.

I felt weightless in his arms. He didn't seem to want to let me go, and the feeling was mutual.

Then, the hoot of an owl pierced the air and we sprang apart, back to our respective boards. I felt flustered, my face red and my heart skipping.

What just happened?

Nicholas cleared his throat. "We should probably head back. Sun's set already."

I gathered myself on my board, my stomach filled with butterflies. I tried to focus on the world around us as it turned a lovely shade of muted blue.

"Right. You're right," I muttered faintly.

Nicholas was silent as he clipped the cooler back onto his board. Together, we paddled towards Sam's shop, the only noise coming from the splashes of our paddles in the water.

My heart refused to slow until long after we'd reached the shore.

19

NICHOLAS

"So, any news on Pittsburgh?" Austin asked as he pressed his fingers along my collarbone.

I winced as he touched a sore spot near the bump that had appeared right after my shoulder separation. According to my doctor in Chicago, my shoulder blade had moved downwards and I needed physiotherapy. Austin agreed to help me in exchange for a couple of beers.

"Nothing yet." I shook my head. "Arnie's been working with them to hammer out the details."

"That's awesome. Pittsburgh would be amazing, especially if you're able to keep your number. Talk about a dream come true."

My smile didn't quite reach my eyes. "It would be."

Even to my ears, my voice was flat.

What was wrong with me these days? I couldn't muster any enthusiasm at the thought of moving to Pittsburgh... or anywhere else. I'd been blaming it on my exhaustion after working long hours at the cafe, but the truth was that I simply hadn't put a lot of thought into the move. Here in Aston Falls, the future seemed so far away, so intangible.

"Gracie told me that you took her paddleboarding last week." Austin lifted my arm and rotated my shoulder. "How'd that go?"

Now, I smiled for real. The mere thought of Grace made me chuckle these days. "It was really fun. We spent a couple of hours on the water, paddling around. We stayed until the sunset and had hot cocoa on our boards. At one point, Grace almost fell off. It was pretty hilarious."

I shook my head at the memory. I remembered her wide eyes, her mouth forming a perfect "o." The way she grasped her pug mug, even though it would've made much more sense to grab the board to steady herself.

Austin was silent for a moment, his eyebrows raised in amusement. "I meant, how'd it go for your shoulder?"

Heat rose to my face and I rubbed the back of my neck to hide it. "Right. The shoulder was okay. I've been wanting to get back out paddleboarding for a while, so it's good to know I can use my left arm. I barely did anything with my right."

"Good." Austin got back to work on my injury. "Don't forget that you do *want* to use your injured arm so the muscles don't atrophy. You just don't want to push it too far."

"I think working at Morning Bell is the perfect balance." I nodded seriously. "Somehow, my shoulder never hurts there."

Austin rotated my shoulder again. "It was nice of you to let Grace come along on your paddleboarding adventure. I worry about her sometimes. She needs to get out of the cafe and have fun. Try new things. Variety is the spice of life, and all that."

I burst into laughter. "It's been awhile since I heard those words of wisdom."

"It's a good motto. That's what I miss most about LA—

life was so fast-paced, so dynamic. The city changed my life."

"Well, why'd you leave?"

Austin dropped my arm to my side and signaled that I could put my jacket back on. His face was troubled, his eyes faraway. "I didn't have a choice."

I frowned as I chewed on his words. Austin had never been forthcoming about why he'd left LA. This was the most information I'd ever been able to get out of him. "What do you mean?"

Austin bit the inside of his cheek and took notes on his notepad. He must not have heard me, so I opened my mouth to repeat my question.

"Anyway," he said brightly before I could ask. The lid of his pen snapped on. "I hope my sister's not annoying you yet."

His eyes were clear and bright, his mouth turned up in a genuine smile. The cloud that had passed over his features appeared to be long gone. I chuckled despite my lingering curiosity. Someday, I'd find out why Austin left LA. "No, Grace isn't annoying me."

There was a loud knock at the door and Becca, the receptionist, peered into the room without waiting for an acknowledgement. To be fair, even if I'd been doing naked cartwheels around the room, it wouldn't have mattered. Becca's eyes were riveted to her cell phone. She barely looked up to make sure that Austin was actually *there*.

"Hey doc," she said, smacking her gum. "There's a call on line 1 for you."

Austin frowned. "Know who it is?"

Becca raised a thin, penciled eyebrow and met Austin's gaze for a split second. "Didn't say."

"Okay. Thanks, Bec," Austin said through a forced smile.

Becca slammed the door shut behind her and Austin rubbed his temples. "That girl. If she wasn't so smart…"

"You'd what?" I asked, amused. "Fire her?"

Austin shook his head. We both knew that he wouldn't do such a thing without just cause and several warnings first. "Of course not. She's just a kid, finishing her sopho- more year at Aston Falls High. But she has the worst phone manner. Probably because she's always on *her* phone, and never bothers to answer the office phone."

I laughed. "Isn't that part of the receptionist's job description?"

"I just need to figure out a way to train her on her phone etiquette…" Austin trailed off, and then, with a start, remembered that someone was waiting for him on line 1. He strode towards the phone in the corner of the room and picked up the receiver. "Doctor Austin Bell speaking. How can I help?"

Even from where I was standing, I could hear the hooting laughter down the phone line. Immediately, Austin's face relaxed and he took a seat, slumping in his chair.

"Oh, hey weirdo." Austin chuckled, rolling his eyes in my direction. Then, he raised his eyebrows at the response on the line. "Yeah, you're 100% the weirdest person I've ever met."

It was immediately apparent who he was speaking to— Ella Williams. His oldest friend and the girl I was sure he'd had a crush on in high school. Despite his numerous, vehe- ment denials.

While Austin and Ella carried on with their banter, my mind spiraled back to Grace, as it so often did these days. The truth was that I didn't know what to think or how to feel. When I closed my eyes now, instead of thinking of the stress of Chicago, I found myself thinking of her. Of having her in my arms on the paddleboards.

I remembered the feeling of her hands on the back of my neck, my arms wrapped tight around her slim body. Even though she'd been wearing a full neoprene wetsuit, she still smelled like cinnamon and nutmeg.

And the look in her eyes. The way her full lips were so close to mine...

My brain had completely shut off and all I was aware of was her. If that owl hadn't interrupted us, I would've kissed her right then and there.

Was I crazy for feeling this way? Clearly. I was in the middle of a bad divorce, and it was way too soon for me to fall for *anyone*. But Grace? She was the last person I should have feelings for. I was headed to Pittsburgh soon, and there was no way I was going to risk hurting her again. I had to be careful.

And yet, I couldn't fight the confusion that nagged at me. Not even Whitney made me feel the way I felt around Grace. Like I wanted to spend all my time with her. Like I couldn't get enough of her. Like, even when we were apart, I was looking for her.

The feeling was foreign and yet uncomfortably familiar. It reminded me of how I felt for her in high school, back before everything fell apart between us. But, we weren't in high school anymore. We were adults, and I needed to remember to do the right thing by her, always.

I simply couldn't risk falling for Grace Bell again. No matter how much my heart said otherwise.

20

NICHOLAS

I opened my eyes, pulled from the depths of a black, dreamless sleep. I felt disoriented, wondering where I was and what I was doing here. A bright ray of sunlight shone through my window, lighting up my room. My childhood room.

And then I remembered. I was in Aston Falls.

I rolled over in bed and the entire left side of my body was numb. I doubted I'd moved in my sleep last night. Since starting work at Morning Bell, I was sleeping a lot better, often drifting off into a deep sleep and not waking until morning. It had been awhile since I'd slept so soundly.

My joints creaked and groaned as I stretched. My knees ached, as did my shoulder. This, however, was not unusual. My body had taken one too many beatings over the years. I was definitely feeling it this morning.

I slipped into my gray sweatpants and a white V-neck t-shirt before making my way downstairs. It was a beautiful early June day—we were officially coming into summer.

I couldn't wait. Summer in Aston Falls was by far my favorite season.

Not that I would be staying for much of the summer. I had to return to Chicago by mid-July at the latest.

I walked down the stairs slowly, working through the aches and pains. When I reached the bottom step, I heard laughter in the kitchen. It was likely Mom and Mrs. Kirkpatrick, her good friend who was currently going through a divorce.

With an enormous yawn, I turned the corner and stopped dead in my tracks, mouth wide open. Mom wasn't speaking with Mrs. Kirkpatrick.

"Ace?" I tilted my head, surprised to see her sitting at my kitchen counter. I wondered for a moment whether I was dreaming.

"Hey, sleepyhead." She pulled up a stool for me and patted the seat. "It's 10am. You sure had a good sleep in today."

I looked between Mom and Grace, both smiling at me cryptically. Like they were up to something.

"I guess," I said suspiciously, squinting at her as I took a seat. I turned my face away, knowing that I hadn't brushed my teeth yet. I patted down my hair and hoped that it wasn't too crazy. "What are you doing here?"

"Just having a chat with your mom." Grace and Mom shared a playful glance. I noticed the light shade of pink in Mom's cheeks. "We were talking about your awesome Pittsburgh news."

"Nothing's set in stone, yet."

Arnie had been in talks with Pittsburgh's General Manager for a few weeks now, trying to help them broker a deal with Chicago. Things were looking good... as good as they could be for someone about to be traded. But, there was no way I was going to let myself feel too excited. Deals like this fell through all the time.

"Grace also had a wonderful thought." Mom sipped her coffee, her eyes a little too innocent. "She's got a plan for you guys today."

I frowned at Grace. "A plan?"

Grace nodded, but didn't elaborate further. I noticed that she was wearing a pair of dark shorts and a tight sky blue sweater with a hood. She looked... athletic.

She was dressed like her twin brother. But much cuter.

"I'm going to check on Grandpa." Mom cleared her throat. "But you two have fun."

I scratched the light layer of scruff on my chin. "You have work tonight, right? I should be back to watch Grandpa by then."

"No, the Inn gave me the day off. Grace is right—it's nice having Mondays free." She placed a friendly hand on Grace's shoulder, kissed me on the cheek, and disappeared down the hallway towards Grandpa's room.

I swiveled back towards Grace. Her eyes sparkled in the sunlight and her mouth was curved into a cute, though mysterious, half-smile. I smiled with her. Ever since we went paddleboarding together, I'd discovered a secret, favorite hobby of mine—making Grace smile.

"Okay, Ace," I said, my tone stern. "What's all this about?"

She handed me a full cup of black coffee, her gaze locked on mine. "Get dressed and you'll find out soon enough."

My Jeep rumbled to a stop and I put it in park. Grace was sitting in the passenger seat, having given me directions towards the location of her mysterious plans.

I opened the driver's side door, but instead of hopping out of the car, Grace reached across the dashboard and turned up the volume on the car radio. "One sec," she said with a small smile. "This is one of my favorite songs."

I raised my eyebrows in surprise. "You like *Journey On* by Eddy Class?"

"Absolutely. His style reminds me of Queen."

I smiled. "This song is one of my favorites, too."

Grace and I sat in silence as the music played out. As soon as the final strum of the guitar rang over the Jeep's speakers, Grace nodded curtly. "Great. Now, let's get going!"

With that, Grace launched herself out of the passenger side of my Jeep. I chuckled to myself as I stepped out onto the pavement. We were parked at the trailhead of one of Aston Falls' most popular hikes. It was a relatively short one, but the views at the end of the trail were spectacular. In the summer, the trail was usually packed full of locals and tourists alike, shepherding back and forth to the viewpoint.

To be fair, my memory of the view itself was foggy, but I remembered feeling an overwhelming sense of peace at the end of this trail—when it wasn't too busy, of course.

Grace grabbed a duffel bag from the back of my Jeep and walked purposefully towards the start of the trail. Amused, I watched her blonde ponytail swing back and forth, the movement of her hips as she strode forward confidently.

"We're going hiking?" I asked as I followed her.

Grace reached the starting point of the trail and turned towards me, her hair whipping over her shoulder. She bent to open the backpack, pulling out a range of items. "Our little paddleboarding excursion gave me an idea for the cafe. I want Morning Bell to be more involved in the community. And what better way to do that than to *serve* the community?"

Grace held out a pair of shears and a linen bag.

"So..." I ventured. "You're going to serve the community by murdering me on a hiking trail?"

Grace's eyes widened and then she doubled over with laughter. "No! We're going to walk the trail and clean it up. The trees and bushes are probably overgrown after the winter. It's as good a time as any to start maintaining it for the summer."

This didn't surprise me. Grace had a big heart, she always found some way to help others. It was why the people in town loved her so much.

I chuckled as I took the shears. "Good to hear."

"Besides. I thought you could do with a day out of town."

"I have been getting a bit cabin feverish." I shrugged. While there were parts of the big city that I did not miss— like the fast, unforgiving pace—I'd been feeling cooped up in Aston Falls lately. How did Grace know that this was exactly what I needed?

"The only thing we might have to look out for are bears." Grace glanced towards the woods nervously.

"I'll protect you."

The words came out of my mouth before I could think about how they'd sound. I pressed my lips together. First, I said that I didn't want to "lose her" when we were paddleboarding. And now this?

I was close to crossing a line here and I knew it. Why did I always put my foot in my mouth around Grace?

Luckily, she just smiled and picked up the duffel bag. She went to sling it onto her back, but I held out my hand. She looked at me, confused, before I grabbed the strap and placed it over my shoulder.

Together, we walked the full length of the trail. I used the shears to cut back wayward branches while Grace picked up rubbish and moved bigger rocks or fallen tree branches out of the path. We chatted comfortably, and Grace had me keeled over laughing a few times with her dry wit. Even at the cafe, when there were terrible rushes and we were both flat-out busy, things always felt easier and more fun when she was around. Like her very presence dispelled all obstacles.

It was fitting that she was walking the trail to do just that.

While we talked about everything and anything that came to mind, there was one topic we never, ever touched on—prom night. It had been on my mind a lot lately, and I wanted to bring it up with her. Given how comfortable Grace and I were together, it was hard to have this one daunting, obvious thing between us. But, the last thing I wanted to do was bring up our past too soon.

A couple of hours later, we reached the end of the trail. I stretched my back, grateful that my aches and pains weren't too bad.

"Almost there," Grace murmured.

I followed Grace up a small path before scrambling up the final rock face. We reached the top at the same time and my breath caught in my chest.

The view was better than I could've remembered. We were looking at almost a full panorama, with gorgeous snow-laden peaks in every direction. Below, a wide, lush valley stretched from one mountain base to another, and a couple of turquoise rivers snaked through. The sky was perfectly blue and the sun heated my face. The air smelled fresh—like a warm day after spring rain.

I barely wanted to blink. "Wow."

"Pretty okay." I could hear the smile in Grace's voice.

I bumped my shoulder against hers jokingly. "Just okay?"

"It'll do."

With a snappy response at the ready, I turned to her, but my voice died in my throat. Her eyes were closed and her face was turned towards the sun. Her cheeks were tinged pink from the exercise, and her lips wore the faintest smile. My eyes traced the curve of her nose and full pout, and then dropped down to her slim hips, the length of her toned legs.

Grace wasn't wearing any makeup. She wasn't dressed in fancy clothes, or bathed in glitter and jewelry. She was wearing hiking gear, her hair pulled back into a ponytail. And she was by far the most beautiful woman I'd ever seen.

"Grace..." My voice was husky. I couldn't look away from her.

Her eyes popped open and she looked at me. Without thinking, I reached out to touch her arm, pull her close, do something. But then, her shoulders tensed and her eyes went wide.

"Did you hear that?" she whispered, the color draining from her face.

"Hear what?"

Then, I heard it.

There was a distinct rustle in the bushes. The crash of a branch. The stomp of a heavy foot.

I instinctively shot in front of Grace, pulling her behind me to shield her.

Someone—something—was coming up the trail we'd just cleared. And, at this time of year, I doubted it was human.

21

GRACE

*M*y breath came in short, quiet bursts as I instinctively pressed my body against Nicholas's back. In any other circumstance, I might've been happy to be in this position—so close that I could smell the spicy scent of his shampoo mixed with clean laundry, his arm muscles taut and strong as they circled back around me.

But, as it was, adrenaline shot through my veins and my heart raced a million miles a minute. The footsteps were getting closer, and every snap of a branch sent horrible chills up and down my spine.

I looked at my duffel bag on the ground steps away. I'd packed the bear spray, just in case. I didn't actually think I'd need it this time of year.

Despite the numbness in my legs, I placed my hands lightly on Nicholas's shoulders and stood on my tiptoes to whisper in his ear. His back and shoulders were firm and steady under my fingers. "There's bear spray in the bag. Let's shuffle over and I can grab it."

Goosebumps rose on Nicholas's skin—undoubtedly

from the fear. He broke his gaze from the bushes and glanced at the duffel bag.

"Okay," he whispered. "On the count of three. One..."

The footsteps were close. I could hear the crunch of dirt, the squelch of mud. My heart leaped sickeningly in my chest.

"Two..."

I heard a grunt, a guttural growl. My breath caught.

"Three."

I held onto Nicholas's strong torso as we launched sideways towards the bag.

But it was too late, a shadow was approaching the end of the trail. They'd have a clear view of us soon. Nicholas held me firmly behind him as the shadow emerged.

And it was...

Mayor Bob Davis.

I exhaled in a breathy laugh and Mayor Davis's gaze shot towards us. But, upon seeing that it was just Nicholas and me, he beamed.

"Well, I wasn't expecting to have company on the trail so early in the season," Mayor Davis boomed, walking the path towards us.

Nicholas chuckled as he reached down towards the mayor with his left hand, helping him scramble up the rock face. "Same here. We thought you were a bear."

Mayor Davis guffawed with good-natured laughter. "What gave it away?"

I couldn't help but smile, my lips pressed together, as I took in Mayor Davis's outfit. He was dressed like a real outdoorsman—with dark khaki shorts boasting a million pockets, a linen shirt with the sleeves rolled up, and a fly fishing vest. His gray hat with a mosquito net completed the outfit.

"I came here for a morning stroll after a particularly frustrating call with the county commissioner." Mayor Davis grabbed a bottle of water from his fanny pack. "The man won't listen to my proposition about building a paved roadway to Aston Falls! The nerve. After all these years, you'd think he'd at least listen to what I had to say. We used to play golf together..."

Mayor Davis grumbled under his breath, and Nicholas and I listened politely. His war with the county commissioner about the road to Aston Falls was practically legendary around our town. Poor Mayor Davis never seemed to make any headway, though.

If I was being honest, I agreed with the commissioner's stance. A paved road leading to and from Aston Falls would likely put the train out of commission.

Except for the train's restaurant, maybe. The Express Restaurant was a favorite around our town. After completing all of its trips for the day, the train opened its dining car to the general public and it was basically required to have dinner on the train while in Aston Falls.

Nicholas's pinky brushed mine and a pleasant warmth shot up my arm. I stole a glance at his profile as he nodded at the mayor, his brow furrowed in concentration. We were still standing close together, his body partly shielding mine.

I let my eyes roam the sharp corners of his cheekbones and jawline, which was covered with neat, dark scruff. My gaze dropped to the muscles in his arms and shoulders as he scratched his jaw. His dark hair was thick, and just long enough to run your fingers through...

Not that I ever would.

That weird moment on our paddleboards last week—when I thought he might kiss me—was just a fluke. I'd almost fallen into the river, he was just trying to save me.

And the only reason I wanted to kiss him was because he had.

I wasn't thinking straight. I wasn't thinking at all.

Even though, these days, that moment seemed to be the only thing I could think about.

"What're the two of you doing here, anyhow?" the mayor asked and I was wrenched from my thoughts.

"We were..." I trailed off into silence, dazed by the memory of Nicholas's lips so close to mine.

Nicholas shot me an amused glance. He turned back to the mayor. "We got a headstart on maintaining the trail for the season."

Mayor Davis's eyebrows shot up. "I thought the path was looking pretty clear after the winter we've had." He glanced between the two of us. "What a kind, community-oriented thing for the two of you to do. The townspeople will be *thrilled*."

While I thought "thrilled" was a bit of a strong senti-ment, I appreciated Mayor Davis's praise. I bowed my head, my cheeks warm. Nicholas, too, smiled gratefully.

Mayor Davis strolled away to take photos of the scenery and Nicholas shot me a look, his expression unreadable. I bit my lip and held his gaze a moment too long, almost getting locked into the slate gray of his eyes.

I blinked a few times and grabbed the duffel. I couldn't let myself get caught up in Nicholas, but I also wasn't ready for our day to end. I thought fast. "Given our near-death experience. I have an idea for what we can do after this."

Nicholas faced me, tall and strong, and I had an almost overpowering urge to run my fingers down his arms and chest. I clasped my hands tight behind my back. I had to remember that Nicholas King was the one who'd left me. He'd hurt me, and that pain had reverberated through all of my subsequent relationships. I needed to keep myself in line.

Yet, the look in his eyes made my heart race. "What's that?"

I took a breath to steady myself. "Let's get back to the Jeep and I'll show you."

22

GRACE

*W*e pulled up outside of Morning Bell and Nicholas cut the engine. He looked at me, brows furrowed. "Your idea was to come to Morning Bell?"

"Yup," I said simply, undoing my seatbelt and hopping out. Nicholas didn't move. I placed my hands on my hips. "You coming?"

Nicholas narrowed his eyes, smiled, and followed me out of the car. I unlocked the door of Morning Bell and we walked inside. The sky was getting darker by the second; the sun had just set, which made for a beautiful drive home after our hike.

"Okay, Nicholas." I rubbed my hands together. "You grab the blender, I'll grab the ice cream and strawberries."

His eyes widened. "You're kidding. We're not actually going to..."

"Oh yes, we are."

Nicholas immediately went behind the serving counter to grab the blender.

Sweets n' Sundaes might've had the best homemade ice cream in town, but they used to share the title of "Best Milkshake" with Morning Bell. Our crowning glory was our strawberry milkshake, which, when I was a kid, used to draw people from far and wide. After Mom died, Dad removed the shakes from our menu, saying they took too long to make. Eventually, the buzz around the shakes dissipated and the steady flow of milkshake-craving customers eased to a trickle.

Now? Morning Bell's strawberry shake was a thing of the past, an off-menu item only enjoyed by our oldest and most loyal customers.

And tonight, by Nicholas and myself.

While Nicholas set up the blender on the counter, I grabbed the ingredients from the kitchen. We worked together to add the ice cream, strawberry syrup, and frozen strawberries, then blended the mixture slowly while adding milk. Soon, we had thick, creamy, sugary goodness.

"And voila," I said, grabbing a couple of tall glasses from behind the counter. "The one-of-a-kind, world-famous Morning Bell Strawberry Shake. Trademark pending."

"Ace." Nicholas smirked. "You've always been smart, but this might be one of your brightest ideas."

He held up a hand for a high-five and I clapped my palm against his with a giggle. Instead of pulling away, though, our palms rested together, our fingers interlacing easily. Like it was instinct. Nicholas stepped closer to me at the same time that I leaned back against the counter. His eyes were locked on mine, and warmth exploded under my skin.

He was so close, it was making me lightheaded.

"Let's go to the roof!" I blurted.

Nicholas looked bewildered, like he'd been snapped out of a trance. He dropped my hand. "The roof?"

"Yeah, I haven't been to the rooftop patio in awhile and it's a nice night. We could drink our milkshakes there."

I regretted my suggestion almost immediately. I wanted to go somewhere where we could put space between us. Morning Bell's rooftop patio seemed like an obvious choice, given that it was outside and spacious. But it was also very private and more than a little chilly, especially with our cold milkshakes.

I opened my mouth to suggest something else when Nicholas smiled. "Sounds great."

With an ounce of reluctance, I put on my puffer jacket and grabbed one more item before we climbed the stairs to the patio. We got onto the roof and my anxieties eased in the cool evening air. The sky was dark and a lone star shone overhead. I turned on the fairy lights and took a seat, gesturing for Nicholas to sit a few feet away. A comfortable distance.

I pulled the last ingredient from my jacket pocket and sprinkled it into my milkshake before stirring with my metal straw.

Nicholas stared at me incredulously. "You're adding pepper to a strawberry shake?"

"That's right." I grinned and offered it to him. He held out his shake and I sprinkled some pepper on top. "It's our secret ingredient. Pepper makes the strawberry flavor pop, and it adds an exotic twist no one's ever been able to pinpoint. But, you have to promise not to tell anyone."

Nicholas crossed his heart. "It'll be our secret."

His words send a delicious thrill down my spine. I liked the idea of sharing a secret with Nicholas.

Another secret.

My stomach curdled and a bad taste filled my mouth. I felt the words coming without any power to stop them.

"Nicholas, what happened that night?"

As always with Nicholas, my brain wasn't functioning at capacity.

He froze, his mouth to his glass. A blur of emotions crossed his face—confusion followed by horror followed by resignation. He put down his milkshake and shook his head, pain crossing his features. "Prom night."

I nodded jerkily, my chest tight. My palms were clammy and my mouth was dry. I couldn't believe it—I'd finally asked him the question that had been at the forefront of my mind for years.

Nicholas was silent for a moment and it was like a trigger. All of a sudden, I was rambling. "When my mom passed away at the start of junior year, I thought I was going to die. I was angry and devastated and out of my mind with grief. I didn't think I'd ever escape. Then, at the end of the year, Austin basically forced me to go to prom. Said it was time to 'get back to normal.' Somehow, I was surviving. Somehow, I was doing okay. So, I said yes."

"Austin can be extremely convincing," Nicholas said, his eyes turned towards the ground. He'd shoved his hands deep into his pockets, his milkshake on the bench next to him.

"Yeah. So, I went with him, Ella, and JJ. And then, I saw you." My voice was quiet and I stared towards the lights on Center Street. I remembered how he looked that night—his dark hair swept over his forehead, his handsome face rounder and less rugged than the face of the man I was sitting with tonight. He wore a black tuxedo and it was clear that every girl at prom was swooning over him.

And when he'd turned his gray eyes on me? Well, I knew my heart was his.

"You looked beautiful," Nicholas whispered and my heart splintered with the memory.

"You asked me to dance," I continued. I needed to finish what I'd started. "And we went for a walk outside the gym, and I finally, finally, told you how I felt. I told you about the crush I'd had on you. And it wasn't just that you were gorgeous or going to play professional football. I liked you for your weird jokes and awesome stories, for the board games we played together, for the way you listened when I talked... I meant what I said that night."

In my peripheral vision, I saw Nicholas shake his head slowly. "So did I, Grace."

His use of my full name made my heart skip. "You told me you felt the same, and it was everything I wanted. It was everything I'd dreamed of for so long. And, after a year of grief and pain, I thought that maybe, somehow, I could find a way to be okay."

What I didn't say—what I couldn't bring myself to say— was that I'd had my first kiss that night. When Nicholas's lips met mine, it was like the earth shook, the moon moved, the world tilted on its axis. It was a bond strengthened, a promise fulfilled. I'd never been kissed like that in my life.

Using every ounce of courage I had, I looked at him. Nicholas's shoulders were slumped and he was shaking his head.

"And then, you left me." My voice shook and I shut my eyes. "I tried calling you, went by your house. But, you were gone. You left for college in Florida without a word of explanation or a goodbye. And you never told me why."

23

NICHOLAS

The night air felt thick and heavy, pushing my shoulders towards the ground. My heart raced and my stomach churned uncomfortably. Finally, Grace and I were talking about this... on her terms. I could explain to her what exactly had happened that night.

The night that changed everything and sent me into a spiral of shame and regret.

"Grace," I started, my voice low. "I'm so sorry. I can't even begin to tell you how sorry I am."

Grace was silent and I dared a look at her profile. She was staring towards Center Street, her hands clasped and her knuckles white. The edge of her mouth was curved down and her eyes were glassy.

"What happened that day was complicated," I said. "And I handled it poorly. Very poorly."

Now, Grace looked at me dead on. Her eyes were teary, angry. I wished I could hug her, make it all go away. "What's complicated, Nicholas? That you never said goodbye after telling me you wanted to be with me? Or that you never bothered to give me an explanation in the ten years since?"

My heart broke and I shook my head. It was time I told her the truth. It was the least I could do to fix what had happened between us.

I took a deep breath and dived into my story.

"When I said that I liked you and wanted us to be together, Grace, I meant it." My voice was a stranger's, raw and vulnerable. "That was all I'd wanted for so long. And then, we kissed and I'll tell you right now, I've never had a kiss like that in my life. Things between us felt *right*, I knew it in my gut. As sure as I know when to throw a pass during a game."

Grace was completely silent next to me. That kiss was like a dream, a beautiful, untouchable memory. I soldiered on.

"Right after our conversation, do you remember what happened?"

She bit her lip, thinking, and then shook her head.

"I went back into the prom to tell Austin how I felt about you. He was my best friend and you were his sister. He had to be the first—well, the second—to know that I was crazy about you. I was scared out of my mind, but it was the right thing to do. And I told you I would come back to see you—"

"Outside. At the bench by the football field," Grace whispered, her face going slack.

I nodded solemnly. "I never showed up and I'm sorry. I found Austin at the dance and marched up to him, ready to tell him about us. But then, he cut me off. He said that he was so thankful that I was around to help you after your mom died. He said that he could barely keep it together himself, but that he was so appreciative of how good of a friend I was to you both. He said that other guys might've tried to take advantage... you know, tried to date you or something."

I remembered every moment of that conversation with Austin. And I remembered the way my stomach lurched sickeningly at this proposition.

I took a deep breath of the cool air. "I was shocked and horrified. That wasn't my intention, that wasn't what I was doing at all. I'd had a crush on you forever, but I couldn't handle the thought that I was taking advantage of you."

Grace's eyes were wide. "You weren't taking advantage of me. I never had that impression."

"Well, you said so yourself, Grace. You were grieving, you were in pain. I couldn't bear the thought that I might cause you more pain. Especially because I was leaving."

"For Florida," Grace whispered. "You weren't meant to leave until the end of summer."

"But that was the thing. I *had* to leave you, I had to go for my family. But, leaving you after everything that happened with your mom? I couldn't do it. I couldn't handle the thought of hurting you. So, I left early. I genuinely thought at the time that it was the right thing to do—disappear before we fell for each other for real. Because, the truth is, if we'd started dating and I fell for you, leaving you would've destroyed me. And I didn't want you to feel any of that pain."

Grace wasn't breathing. Her expression was unreadable. "But why not tell me that?"

Her voice was small and my heart ached all the more. I squeezed my eyes shut. "I couldn't. I didn't have the words to say and I didn't know how to explain it to you. I picked up the phone so, so many times to call you, but I couldn't. I was young and I didn't handle it well. Eventually, weeks had gone by and it was fall. You were starting your senior year and I was at college. I guess I hoped you'd forgotten about me, that you were better off without me."

"Well." Grace shook her head. "That wasn't very well thought out, Nicholas."

I chuckled dryly. "You can call it like it is. I was an idiot."

Grace was silent, but I swore I saw the hint of a smile cross her lips.

I bit the inside of my cheek and leaned back on my seat. "How I treated you is the worst thing I've ever done. I was a coward and I can't tell you how ashamed I am. Since that day, I've made every effort to be kind and compassionate to everyone I meet. I guess I was looking for some way to atone... not that any of it ever felt like enough. As the years went on, it was like my shame and regret festered, creating a chasm between us that felt impossible to overcome."

"Is that why you never came home?"

"I couldn't risk coming back into your life and hurting you again, so I stayed away. I was a loyal husband to Whitney, I supported my teammates, and I treated my fans well. It was the least I could do."

There was an echoing silence and I squeezed my eyes shut. I didn't expect Grace to understand or forgive me, but I wanted her to know the truth.

"Every once in a while, right before I fell asleep, I'd think of you," I said quietly. "And I'd wake up sometimes thinking about you, too. It was like you lingered at the back of my mind, visiting me in my dreams when I most needed you."

24

GRACE

*N*icholas's voice faded into the night as his gaze met mine. In the dim fairy lights, his eyes still shone bright, piercing into my soul.

My entire body was shaking, vibrating. Waves of warmth traveled over my skin and my mind was a chaotic mess. It felt so good to have answers, finally, after all these years. Never in my wildest dreams had I imagined that this was the reason Nicholas had left so suddenly—he truly believed he did it for me.

And knowing that Austin, my ridiculous twin, had a hand in this? I'd have to remember to punch him in the arm later.

But, as it stood, I felt an incredible, powerful wave of revelation. I couldn't yet wrap my head around the extent of Nicholas's perspective and motivations, but there was one thing I *did* understand to my very core.

Nicholas King used to be crazy about me. He'd wanted to be with me.

And I'd wanted to be with him.

Suddenly, I felt like I was in high school again. Swaying

with Nicholas at the dance, going for a walk outside together to our bench, our conversation turning serious. I remembered the way my purple dress felt—the long skirt flowing around my ankles, and the tightness around the chest because it was strapless. I remembered the mild scent of Nicholas's oaky cologne. And the way his arms circled around me, pulling me close...

My breath caught as I realized that Nicholas and I were leaning slowly towards each other. Like a magnetic force was pushing us together.

I swallowed hard. "Do you remember the kiss?"

Nicholas's eyes dropped to my lips for a second. "How could I ever forget? We were holding hands, just like this."

He reached forward and tentatively grabbed my hand, lacing his fingers through mine. Despite his hand being much bigger than mine, our palms fit together perfectly.

"Right." A whisper of a smile crossed my lips as I shifted onto the bench he was sitting on. "And I was leaning into you like this."

I ever so slightly leaned into him.

"Do you remember what you said?" Nicholas's voice was a husky rumble and butterflies exploded in my stomach.

"I was so nervous. I think I was rambling about what a beautiful night it was. Kind of like this one. I always ramble when I'm nervous."

Nicholas placed a finger under my chin and tilted my face up so I had no choice but to get lost in his eyes. "Are you nervous now?"

My heart skipped a beat and my cheeks felt warm. A glow radiated from my core through my limbs. He was so close to me, his body firm against my side. His thigh pressed against mine and his hand encompassed mine. He smelled like clean laundry mixed with a hint of that same oaky cologne. It was intoxicating.

He was intoxicating.

I was swept away in him, and I couldn't tell you whether I answered the question, whether I was even breathing. In that moment, Nicholas was my world. He took over my senses.

Then, his lips met mine, gently, softly, and I sighed with something close to relief.

He pulled back a moment, eyes searching for permission, which I happily gave. This time, when he kissed me, there was nothing gentle about it. I melted into him completely.

There was no fighting destiny. And there wasn't a shred of doubt in my mind that this kiss was meant to be.

25

GRACE

*W*hen I woke up the next morning, my body was buzzing and my lips tingled with the memory of my kiss with Nicholas. I still couldn't believe it— Nicholas King kissed me last night. And not just one kiss, but many kisses, culminating with him walking me to my door like a true gentleman and pressing his lips tenderly to my forehead.

I was on cloud nine. I couldn't be any happier than I was at this very moment.

Then, I heard a soft tap.

And another.

What was that?

With a frown, I sat up in bed, looking for the source of the noise.

Tap.

I glanced at my window in surprise. The morning sun was shining bright and crisp through the windowpane, blinding me.

Tap tap.

Someone was throwing rocks at my window.

Cautiously, I approached the window, my blanket in front of me. As though my duvet would offer any sort of protection against an intruder.

I peeked outside, and my heart skipped. Nicholas was standing on the lawn of our house, throwing pebbles at my bedroom window. Upon seeing me, he waved. He looked amazing in blue jeans and a white t-shirt that hugged his sculpted chest just right. His eyes glowed, and his smile was enough to make my stomach flip.

Then, I remembered that I'd literally just rolled out of bed.

I peered into the mirror and winced. I had a serious case of bedhead and one side of my face was red from where I'd been sleeping on it. I debated crawling around my room to find a suitable shirt, a hairbrush, and maybe a touch of makeup. Surely, Nicholas's ex-wife Whitney never looked this disheveled when she woke up in the morning.

Tap.

Another pebble hit my window and I knew I had to make a decision fast.

I hastily tugged my fingers through my hair, and tapped my cheeks to even out the redness. Then, I opened the window and smiled breezily, hoping I looked calm and cool instead of a bedraggled mess.

"Good morning, 13," I called, my voice more flirtatious than intended.

I couldn't help it, the guy brought it out in me.

"Hey beautiful," Nicholas said and I almost melted on the spot. "Feel like doing something fun today?"

I tilted my head. "Well, Morning Bell is closed. So, I could be talked into it."

"Oh, could you?" He winked. "Get dressed and meet me downstairs. I want to take you on a date."

"A date?"

"A first date. Well, another first date."

My heart skipped a beat and I smiled coyly. "I suppose I could make time in my schedule."

"Ace." Nicholas's eyes smouldered. "I'd wait forever for a second chance with you."

I bit my lip to hold back a beaming smile, and I shut my window. I pressed my back against the cool bedroom wall and slid to the floor, just like the girls did in those cheesy rom coms, which were, in fact, a guilty pleasure of mine.

A second chance. That was what we were doing, right? I was giving Nicholas King—I was giving us—a second chance.

It was completely out of my comfort zone. And yet... I'd never wanted to take a risk so badly.

I hopped up and did a quick happy dance around my room—the rom coms really did have that right—and then I opened my closet wide. It had been awhile since I'd dressed in anything but work attire.

But what better reason could there be for dressing up than a date with Nicholas King?

26

GRACE

I stepped through the front door of our house and I was pleasantly surprised to see Nicholas's reaction. First, his eyes met mine, twinkling. Then, they dropped down my body slowly, like he was drinking me in, and his jaw went slack. He ran his fingers through his hair—a move I loved so much—and he smiled almost bashfully.

"Grace, you look…" He shook his head. "Spectacular."

"Spectacular, you say?" I laughed. "I think that's better than beautiful."

"You always look beautiful."

He took my hand and pulled me towards him, then wrapped his arms around me. I gasped as he suddenly dipped me, and he silenced me with a kiss.

I knew I looked good, I just didn't know I looked *that* good.

My blonde hair was done in a half-ponytail and I'd put on a touch of mascara and concealer. I was wearing my cute jean jacket over a light blue sundress that cinched at the waist and fell elegantly down my legs. It wasn't my fanciest dress, but it was one of my favorites. Mom always used to say that you could never go wrong with a good sundress. Apparently, she was right.

He extended his hand and I placed my palm in his. Together, we strolled Center Street, so close together we essentially formed a wall. Austin was out of town for the week, so there was no concern about seeing him on our date. Nicholas and I fell into easy conversation. Now that we'd addressed the big "prom night" question, I felt closer to him than ever. We joked and laughed, and I kept my arm wrapped around his the entire time. My heart felt light and happy with him.

As we walked Center Street, it became clear that Nicholas had a particular destination in mind.

"The carnival?" I asked.

"Of course." Nicholas's smile could've lit any room. "I'm not letting my girl miss the legendarily epic, unbelievably fantastic RiverSpring Carnival."

My body buzzed with excitement.

His girl. I was *his* girl.

Nothing had ever felt so right.

The RiverSpring Carnival was the reason Morning Bell was closed today. Everyone in Aston Falls was headed to the park by the river to celebrate one of our biggest town traditions.

It'd been years since I'd been to RiverSpring, but I had awesome memories of the celebrations. When we were kids, Austin, Ella, and I used to go together, and when Nicholas joined our group in high school, he always came too. We'd play games along the midway, ride on the ferris wheel, and eat cotton candy until we felt sick. It truly was one of the highlights of my childhood.

And I couldn't be more thrilled to be reliving those days with Nicholas by my side.

Together, we explored the lengths of the carnival. We shot darts at balloons and tossed rings at cola bottles. Every time I won a game, I was rewarded by Nicholas's strong arms wrapping around me and swinging me around. My hands rested on his broad chest, firm beneath my fingers. Talk about motivation.

For lunch, we had slightly over-salted popcorn and hot dogs with lemonade. The cotton candy tasted as sweet as I remembered, and the deep fried oreos almost burned my tongue. Not that that stopped me.

We took a horse-drawn carriage ride along the riverfront, pressed close together. And we went on the carousel, the circular motion giving me the giggles. We went to the pedal boat launching area, and we lazily floated along the glacial Aston River, splashing water at each other and laughing so hard we almost flipped.

It was the perfect introduction to what was sure to be a life-changing summer. And we finished off our amazing day with a sunset ride on the ferris wheel.

It was exactly what I would've expected for a first date with Nicholas King—mind-blowing in every way.

By nightfall, we wandered away from the carnival, Nicholas's arm over my shoulder and my fingers intertwined with his. We were quiet, but it was comfortable, easy. We didn't need to speak. All I knew was that time passed differently when I was with Nicholas. It was elastic and didn't abide by any rules—every minute I spent with him felt slow and delicious, but as it came time for us to separate, it always felt way too soon.

I didn't want our date to end. And, as if on cue, my stomach grumbled loudly.

"Whoops." I chuckled, embarrassed by my rather vocal organs.

Nicholas burst into laughter. "Whoops?"

"Yeah, wasn't expecting that." My cheeks were warm. "I guess I am pretty hungry."

Nicholas turned to me and grabbed both my hands. His hair was slightly ruffled from the ride on the ferris wheel, and I ran my fingers through it. It was soft and thick, just as I imagined. I let my hand linger on his cheek for a moment, getting lost in his eyes.

"How would you feel about a classic Aston Falls dining experience?" Nicholas kissed my palm.

"I think I would enjoy that."

"Follow me, Ace."

Together, Nicholas and I walked to the train station. By some stroke of luck, the Express Restaurant had a last-minute cancellation and they could take Nicholas and me. We were seated in a quiet corner of the dining car with views over the twilight mountains in the distance.

Nicholas opened his menu, drumming his fingers on the table. All I could do was stare at him, a ridiculous smile on my face. I felt breathless, my body light and tingling. I couldn't remember the last time I'd been so happy.

I wanted it to last forever.

27

NICHOLAS

*D*inner at the Express Restaurant was as good, if not better, than I remembered. Though, this could've been because I was having dinner with Grace Bell. The sounds of other diners faded as Grace and I laughed and joked and spoke comfortably. Too soon, the waiter informed us that the restaurant was closing for the night. I could hardly believe how quickly the time had passed.

Grace and I left the Express Restaurant and I wasn't ready for our night to end just yet. With a smile, I grabbed Grace's hand and we returned to Center Street. The River-Spring Carnival was beginning to wind down—the final performance of the evening would be taking place soon.

But, instead of turning towards the carnival, I led Grace back to our playground. The place was deserted—most of the children of Aston Falls were in bed, dreaming of cotton candy and ferris wheel rides.

"Push me?" Grace asked as she sat on one of the swings.

I remembered the words of one of Grace's favorite movies. "As you wish."

I gave her a tender kiss on the side of her neck and she

moaned softly. Then, I placed my hands gently on her hips and gave her a little push. She giggled as she swung forward, kicking her legs out in front of her. I loved the sound of her laugh, the way it bubbled from her chest. I pushed her again and she swung a little higher. We fell into a comfortable rhythm—I'd push her forward and she'd kick her legs towards the sky.

It occurred to me that I could do this forever. Come to this playground with Grace, eat ice cream on the teeter totter, hear her laugh as I pushed her on the swing. Maybe, someday, I'd be pushing a little someone else on the swing —our child.

I jerked in surprise at the thought. Having kids had always seemed like such a distant, intangible concept, I'd barely considered it at all. Even with Whitney, we seemed to have an unspoken agreement that we wouldn't have kids. Wouldn't even discuss it.

But the thought of having a child with Grace? I was filled with the glow of warmth and possibility.

"How did this become our spot again?" Grace's question pulled me from my happy daydream. She squealed as I swung her high.

"Don't you remember?" I pushed her again. "It was all because of Austin."

"That's right." I could hear the smile in Grace's voice. "He was supposed to meet us here."

"And then didn't because his girlfriend of the day had some sort of emergency."

"Not that he bothered telling us that." Grace shook her head. "He just never showed up."

I chuckled, thinking back to that day. I'd only known Austin and Grace a few months then. My crush on Grace was already pretty strong, so when Austin didn't come to the playground as promised, I took the opportunity to get to know Grace better.

"It was spring," Grace said dreamily. "I remember because you picked a dandelion and put it in my hair."

I laughed. "You hated that."

"Only because there was a ladybug on the petals," Grace huffed, as she always used to do whenever I brought up this exchange.

"Which I promptly and carefully relocated to another dandelion."

"That's right. I guess I still did make a fuss. I'd never had a boy give me a flower before." Then, she chuckled. "If I'm being honest, I liked it."

"Thought you did." My hands lingered by her hips for a moment while I pushed her. "That's why I kept finding dandelions for you."

Grace swung upwards again and I stepped backwards, out of the way of her pendulum movement. She began to slow, dragging her feet along the rocks. I pulled something out of my back pocket— a keychain I'd found at the carnival today, carved into a sweet, smiling dandelion. The object was small and smooth in my palm and I held it behind my back as Grace came to a stop.

She turned towards me and I held out the dandelion keychain. "This is for you, Ace."

Grace's eyes lit up. "You didn't. Where did you find this?"

I smiled. "At one of the booths along the midway."

Without a beat of hesitation, Grace took her house keys out of the pocket of her jacket and added the keychain to the central ring. She ran her fingers over the petals, then she looked up at me, her eyes glassy. "I love it, Nicholas."

I wrapped my arms around her waist and pulled her close, pressing my lips gently to hers.

And then, not so gently.

When we eventually came up for air, I tucked a strand of hair behind her ear. In the glow of the street lanterns, she looked stunning. At that moment, I knew I wanted to spend every waking moment with her. I could barely imagine how I'd made it this long without having Grace in my life.

I leaned in close and nuzzled her neck.

Then, Grace tilted her head, and whispered, "catch me if you can."

Before I could react, she leapt up from the swing and darted across the playground. I took off after her, laughing. She ran towards the slides and hurriedly climbed the stairs, but I thought fast. I scrambled up the slide, reaching the top at the same time as she. I sat down and pulled her into my lap.

"Gotcha."

Grace giggled and circled her arms around my neck. "That, you did."

I kissed her deeply as the sky exploded into a thousand colors.

Grace's eyes were wide as she looked up. "Fireworks."

I wrapped my arms around her and she rested her head against my chest. Together, we watched the RiverSpring fireworks paint the night sky in various colors and shapes. Aside from the boom of the firecrackers, the evening felt peaceful, like the fireworks show was just for us.

Like the whole world was just for us.

The last of the fireworks exploded across the sky and the world was silent once again. In the park, there were likely crowds of people beginning to head home, but I could happily believe that Grace and I were the only ones awake in Aston Falls. Grace was still wrapped in my arms on the slide, and my chin rested on the top of her head. A cool breeze blew through the playground and Grace shivered in my arms.

"Want to go?" I asked quietly, not wanting to disturb the peaceful moment.

Grace nodded and my head bounced with hers. Slowly, she untangled herself from me and sat between my legs. We slid down the slide together, and she took my hand as we started the walk to her house.

"How're you feeling about things at Morning Bell?" I asked as we strolled the empty pathway.

"Good. Like, really good. I can't thank you enough for your help the last month and a half." She faced me, her eyes shining with sincerity. "You saved me, Nicholas."

She stood on her tiptoes and kissed me before we started walking again. My body buzzed with happiness. I was glad to hear that I'd been of some help around Morning Bell.

"I actually have an idea to get new customers," I said. "It's risky, but I think we can do it."

"When it comes to the cafe, there's nothing I wouldn't risk. What do you have in mind?"

I shot her a half-smile. "It's a surprise. Do you think you can trust me?"

Grace was silent and I wondered whether I'd over-stepped. I had a feeling she had a hard time trusting people —likely because of me—and there was nothing I wouldn't do to make it up to her. I was about to backtrack, to tell her not to worry about it, when she spoke. "Yes."

Joy radiated through my chest and I kissed her hand. I'd had this idea in the back of my mind for a long while, and I was sure she'd be thrilled with the surprise.

"What about you?" Grace asked shyly. "You've done so much for me in recent weeks. I'd love to help you with something, too."

"You've already helped me, Ace. More than you know."

She smiled. "You know what I mean."

"I do." My smile faded and I tousled my hair. "I have been thinking about something I'd love to do while I'm here in Aston Falls. But, I'm not sure how to go about it."

"Spill it."

"Well… I've been wanting to host a football day camp or something for the kids here." I shrugged, feeling a bit self-conscious. "Playing paper football with Nolan at the cafe was a lot of fun, and I was thinking—why not extend that to the whole town? I would've loved a program like that growing up, and we could get a bunch of local families involved. Plus, I think there'd be a lot of interest, Aston Falls is pretty obsessed with football."

Grace knocked me with her hip. "No thanks to you." Then, she looked at me seriously. "Honestly, though, that's a great idea, Nicholas. You're right, our town would love it, and it's so kind of you to offer to do something like this for the kids."

I grinned, touched by her praise. Feeling more confident after her words, I continued. "I could put together a series of football-related activities and lessons. I'd want it to be inclusive, to have something for every kid rather than placing them into specific roles and positions."

"And you could send invites around to local children." Grace's eyes lit up. "And perhaps some kids from out of town."

"Maybe Morning Bell could cater it?"

"Absolutely! This is going to be so much fun. The kids will *love* it."

I chuckled, appreciating her enthusiasm. "I've never run a day camp before."

"We'll figure it out." Grace swatted her hand. "Just imagine. Chicago's—soon to be Pittsburgh's—top quarterback hosting a football camp here in little ol' Aston Falls. The town will be talking about this for years to come."

Grace babbled on excitedly, but her words struck me weirdly. My mouth turned down into a grimace as a bitter taste flooded my tongue.

That's right. Chicago.

The one place I'd been trying to forget—and succeeding as of late. How much longer did Grace and I have together? What did the future have in store for us? Would we stay together when I had to return to Chicago?

Grace was still going on about the football day camp and I shook off the anxious feeling in my stomach. I didn't want to think about our future right now. We had the present moment together, and that was all that mattered.

28

GRACE

*I*t was early. Earlier than I would've cared to be awake on my day off.

But, Nicholas asked me to meet him in front of the cafe at 6am for his big surprise, and I wasn't going to say no. Curiosity nagged at me, and I wanted to see what he had in mind for today.

I hopped from foot to foot, both to keep warm and due to the nervous excitement flowing through my veins. In my hands, I held the sweet little dandelion keychain he'd given me. I couldn't wait to see him again.

It'd been a week since our carnival date and what an amazing week it had been. Nicholas and I saw each other whenever we could—sneaking kisses in the back office, cuddling and talking on the rooftop after our shifts, eating our meals together. We were inseparable, and the fact that he worked at the cafe meant that we could spend time together without arousing much suspicion.

Miraculously, it seemed that the town gossips didn't have much to say about Nicholas and me. I saw the sly gleam in Ms. Rodriguez's eyes whenever Nicholas and I shared a flirty look. I heard Mrs. Applebaum's whispers when she noticed Nicholas's fingers linger on mine a moment too long.

But, as far as I could tell, the Aston Falls rumor mill had gone suspiciously quiet.

Most surprising of all was that we'd managed to keep our relationship from Austin. Nicholas and I often talked about telling him, but neither of us knew how. Nicholas's divorce wasn't yet finalized—it seemed that Whitney changed her mind on almost a daily basis regarding what she wanted out of the divorce. And I didn't think Austin would be thrilled with the thought of my dating his best friend.

Especially because telling him about our relationship now likely meant having to share when this all started—in high school, under his nose.

It had to come from us, there was no question. And while I worried that Austin might hear about us from the gossipy ladies at Morning Bell, Nicholas insisted that, even if there were rumors, Austin never took them to heart.

The only other person who might have a clue about us was Nicholas's mother. When she came by the cafe or saw the two of us together, she normally shot us a knowing look. But, she'd never pried or directly asked either of us whether we were together. She was giving us our space and I respected that.

It wasn't altogether surprising—Eleanor King had a special place in my heart. Despite being incredibly busy with work when we were in high school, she always came to Nicholas's football games with a loving little smile and peanut butter cookies. After Mom died, Eleanor had made a special effort to let me know that I could rely on her if I needed to. Though it wasn't the same as having my own mother back, her kindness and warmth often reminded me of Mom.

The sound of rubber on concrete brought me back to the present moment. Nicholas's Jeep turned the corner and came to a stop in front of the cafe.

I ran around to the driver's side door and jumped in his arms, kissing him square on the lips. Nicholas picked me up like I was light as a sheet of paper, and brought me around to the back of the car.

"Want to help me with these?" He grabbed a couple of grocery bags from the trunk.

"Of course." The statement came out as more of a question as I picked up one of the bags and almost toppled over sideways. It was heavier than expected. "What's in here? Bricks? Are we about to build a whole new Morning Bell?"

Nicholas laughed. "Not exactly."

I stared at him, perplexed, and then proceeded to help him unload the rest of the bags. There were four reusable grocery bags in total, all filled to the brim. Despite the chill of the early morning, I was sweating by the time we had the bags lined up on the counter in Morning Bell.

I wiped my forehead and turned to Nicholas. "Now are you going to tell me what we're doing?"

His eyes sparkled, and he bit his lower lip. His very nice lower lip.

It occurred to me that I could just hop up onto the counter and make out with him a little. It would certainly be a nice way to spend this early morning. But apparently, Nicholas had other ideas.

"Okay, Ace, hear me out," he said, hauling a big sack of flour out of one of the bags. "We're going to bake pastries and brew coffee."

I blinked a few times, not understanding. "So... just like any other day at Morning Bell?"

"Almost. Except that we're going to make double the amount. And, all before noon."

My jaw dropped to the floor. "Before *noon*? How on earth are we going to manage that?"

Nicholas smiled cryptically. "Don't worry, I thought of some... reinforcements."

Like clockwork, the bell above the front door of the cafe rang as someone entered. I whirled around to see Austin coming in the door, closely followed by a familiar face.

"Ella?" I squeaked.

She laughed. "Hey, Gracie. Surp—"

Before she could finish the word, I'd already dived around the counter and practically jumped onto my best friend, tackling her with a hug.

I couldn't believe it. It had been months since I'd seen Ella in person.

"What are you doing here? Why are you here? How long are you in Aston Falls?" The questions tumbled out of my mouth one after the other.

Ella shook her head. "Slow down, Gracie. I'm here for a couple of days. I wanted to surprise you and your ridiculous brother helped me organize the whole thing."

I swiveled to face Austin, who was standing next to Nicholas at the serving counter and watching our exchange with a bewildered smile.

"You knew Els was coming to town and you didn't tell me??"

Austin put up his hands in surrender. "Don't look at me, this weirdo just showed up on my doorstep last night. No warning or anything. Demanded I let her sleep on the futon in my guest bedroom."

Ella rolled her eyes and gave Austin a swift punch to the shoulder. "Yeah, right." Then, she turned towards me and placed her hands on her hips. "We've been called to duty. What can we do to help?"

With the ticking clock weighing on us, we got down to business and, over the next few hours, Ella, Austin, Nicholas and I worked to get everything ready in time. Austin and Nicholas were in charge of brewing coffees and teas and checking on pastries in the ovens, while Ella and I did most of the baking and chatting.

It felt so good to catch up with my best friend in person. She looked good, if not exhausted. Her dark eyes featured purple circles underneath and her lips were slightly chapped. Her brown hair was pulled into a messy bun, and her fingernails were cut short to keep her from biting them. When I asked about NYC, she diverted the conversation back to me. It seemed she didn't have much to say about her life in the city.

Despite my curiosity, it didn't take long for the two of us to fall into our old patterns. We talked and laughed as we made pastries, and my heart was light from spending time with her.

"Els, I missed you," I said, wrapping her in another hug.

She giggled. "Careful, G. You're getting flour all over my favorite hoodie."

"*My* favorite hoodie," Austin hollered from the front of the cafe.

"Not anymore!" Ella shot back. Then, she lowered her voice. "Gracie, you and Nicholas are insanely cute. I see the way he looks at you—the boy is *smitten*."

My cheeks warmed and I couldn't keep a beaming smile from spreading across my face. "You think?"

"I know!" Ella said passionately. "You don't see it? Every

time he comes in here, his eyes are totally glued on you. I doubt he's even aware I'm here. I've never seen anything like it."

I bit my lip. "I'm kind of crazy about him."

"And he is clearly crazy about you."

Ella's words made my heart skip a beat and butterflies flew in my stomach. The next time Nicholas came into the kitchen, I noticed the way his eyes lingered on me. I blushed furiously and wished I could kiss him right there on the spot. But, that would certainly give us away to Austin.

When it was just Ella and me again, I swiveled towards her. "You don't think Austin knows, does he?"

Ella rolled her eyes. "The boy is as oblivious as they come. You and Nicholas could be making out by the coffee machine and he'd still have no idea."

I chuckled despite myself. Ella was right. My brother was smart, but he wasn't the most observant.

The clock struck midday and our time was up. Luckily, Ella and I were just pulling the last of the cheese scones out of the oven. We shared a high-five and I sighed, exhausted, as Nicholas and Austin carefully packed the scones and brought them out to the Jeep with the rest of the treats. I still had no idea where Nicholas wanted to take the pastries and hot drinks—or why—but I trusted the man with my life. I would've followed him wherever he was taking me.

I waved at Ella and Austin as the Jeep pulled away from the curb. We drove down Center Street, passing the colorful storefronts and bustling pedestrians, and then turned left.

"You're really not going to tell me where we're going?" I asked Nicholas for what must've been the fourth time in twenty minutes.

Nicholas just shook his head, his smile cryptic as ever.

My eyebrows drew together as the smell of the cheese

scones made my stomach grumble. I hadn't yet eaten today. I looked into the back seat, wishing I could grab just one scone. Then, I turned towards Nicholas with a teasing smile. "Is it a picnic? Are we going for a *really* big picnic?"

At this, Nicholas chuckled. "No, Ace. We're almost there."

We pulled up in front of a massive gray warehouse. My eyes were wide as saucers. "The Aston Falls Farmers Market?"

"First one of the season."

"But how?" I stuttered. "Why?"

Getting a booth at the Aston Falls Farmers Market was near impossible. And the first market of the season? Unheard of if you weren't one of the market regulars. The booths were perpetually booked, chock full of local businesses and shops. There was no way that we could get a spot. The waiting list was five years... minimum.

"For you, Ace?" Nicholas kissed me. "There's always a way."

29

NICHOLAS

"*I* can't remember the last time I was this exhausted." Grace flopped onto the stool behind the small serving counter and crossed an ankle over her knee. She gently massaged the bottom of her foot, digging her knuckles into the arch.

Without thinking twice, I pulled up a stool next to her and took her foot in my hands. I rubbed her sole in circular motions and her eyes lit up. She leaned against the counter, a blissful smile on her face.

"You're really good at that," Grace said dreamily.

I smiled. "Having a massage therapist dedicated to your team teaches you a thing or two about foot massages."

"Guess JJ was wrong then."

I tilted my head to the side. "Wrong about what?"

"Nothin'."

Grace moaned quietly and closed her eyes, and I decided not to pry.

It had been a long afternoon at the Farmers Market and we were taking a well-deserved half-hour break. Grace had been on her feet nonstop, serving the long line of customers at the till while I got the food and hot drinks together. The rush continued through lunch and for most of the afternoon, and there was a bit of a lull now before the evening rush.

I could hardly believe how busy the Morning Bell booth had been. The turnout had been better than I'd dared hoped for. Most of our pastries were gone and I'd texted Austin to see if he and Ella could brew up more tea and decaf coffee.

Grace moaned again as I massaged her other foot. Her hands were folded in her lap, and her eyelids flickered. Her face was peaceful, her expression relaxed, content.

The work I'd done to secure this spot had clearly been worth it.

I'd been after Mayor Davis for weeks about the Aston Falls Farmers Market. The booths were incredibly hard to come by, and when I'd asked whether I could get a booth for the first market of the season, Mayor Davis had all but laughed in my face.

Then, late last night, I got a call. Mayor Davis informed me that there'd been a last minute cancellation for today's market. He said that, if Grace and I could get everything together in time, the spot was ours. I'd taken the chance, confirming that we would be there. As soon as I hung up the phone, I texted both Grace and Austin to meet me in the morning. It was a happy coincidence that Ella was in town and was willing to lend a hand.

In the end, the scramble of this morning had worked out perfectly. Every single customer who'd been by the Morning Bell booth had raved about the pastries and drinks. Grace and I gave out piles of business cards, and I couldn't believe that there were so many people in Aston Falls who hadn't heard of Morning Bell Cafe.

"A lot of these customers probably come from out of town," Grace had whispered when I'd made a comment. "This farmers market is known statewide."

That was the best news I could've anticipated—if Morning Bell was known and loved across Montana, there was no way that Ross's Burgers could buy the place out.

I finished massaging the bottoms of Grace's feet and she stretched her arms, yawning. "I'm going to grab a soda from the vending machine." She stood. "Want anything?"

"A Coke would be great."

Grace nodded before sneaking around the counter and heading towards the front of the warehouse. I washed my hands in the small sink at the back of our booth and then began to arrange the pastries in the display, placing the freshest cookies in front.

"No way. Is that... Nicholas King? Lucky number 13?"

I looked up from the display to see a tall, slightly over-weight man with a shock of red hair staring at me. I bit the inside of my cheek. I recognized the guy, but couldn't place him.

My lack of response didn't seem to affect him in the least. Within seconds, he was standing right in front of me, so close that I instinctively took a step back.

His brown eyes were wide with wonder. "It *is* you. Nick King. I never thought I'd see the day." He brought both thumbs to his chest. "Jon Maybury. Remember me? Lil Jonny?"

My mouth fell open. "Jonny? Wow, you look so..." My eyes traveled over his rather sizable physique. "Different."

Jonny Maybury was the water boy for our football team in high school. He'd been a sweet kid—not very athletic, but he *knew* football. It was always fun to talk strategy with Jonny after a game. The man who stood before me looked nothing like the pale, scrawny, freckled kid from back then.

Jonny took a quick glance around the booth, his thick eyebrows drawing in. "Never in my life did I expect to see the great Nicholas King working... here. Isn't this booth for a cafe in town?"

"Morning Bell?" I smiled easily. "I'm helping out for a couple of months during the off-season."

Jonny scoffed and reached across the counter, slapping my injured shoulder. I winced as a wave of pain shot down the right side of my body and I took a step further back, out of his reach. He didn't seem to notice.

"What happened to you, dude?" Jonny boomed. "You just disappeared right after high school. Right after prom, actually. The town couldn't believe it. One moment, you're here with us, the next, you're being drafted to play pro."

Jonny guffawed good-naturedly and reached out to smack my shoulder, but I was ready this time. I clapped his hand with mine, maneuvering into a slightly awkward handshake.

He licked his lips. "I told them, though, I did. I said that a guy like Nicholas King? He's going places. He doesn't have time for little people like us."

I winced again, but this time because his words hit me funny. "That isn't really what happened."

Jonny swatted his hand and blew a raspberry, blowing spittle everywhere. "Of course it is. And I don't blame you! If I had your arm, I would've done the same. Just got outta town, no goodbye, no last words, nothing."

He stared at me with wide, excited eyes, but all I could manage was a feeble smile. Jonny's words were a painful reminder of the regret and shame that had been haunting me since high school. Though Grace and I had talked about prom night, I still felt awful for the mistakes I'd made all those years ago.

I forced myself to ignore the pit in my stomach and I exhaled in a laugh. Things were different now. I wasn't the same dumb high school kid who couldn't handle his problems. Grace and I were happy together. So happy, in fact, that she was on my mind almost all of the time. I didn't want to break up, and I was sure she didn't either.

Grace was my present, past and future. This was about more than second chances—it was about showing her that I'd changed, and that I'd never leave her like that again. That I wanted things to work between us, no matter what it took.

30

NICHOLAS

The day of the football camp, I got out of bed early and slipped on my customized number 13 jersey. I grabbed my bag of supplies, bounded down the stairs of our house, and gave Mom a quick kiss on the cheek. I popped into Grandpa's room to say hi before flying out the door.

I arrived at Morning Bell in time to see Grace opening the front door of the cafe. Though it was a Sunday, she'd insisted on closing the cafe to help me with the football camp. She justified her choice by saying that Morning Bell was catering the camp and she wanted to be present in case there were any problems with the food.

In all honesty, I was happy that she was spending the day with me. My stomach was a tangle of nerves and excitement, and Grace had an incredible way of making me feel calm.

After picking up the food at Morning Bell, we made our way to Aston Falls High and its massive football field. It was going to be a warm, sunny mid-June day, and the dewy grass squelched under our feet as we walked across the field.

I smiled as I looked around the field, and my breath hitched. I had so many wonderful memories here. It was surreal to return to this place after years of being away.

"Is this 'King's Kids?'" a voice hollered from the direction of the parking lot.

I twisted around to see a woman and two children striding briskly across the field. I pointed at my jersey, with "King's Kids" scrawled on the front alongside the number 13. "That's right!"

The children approached and Grace reached into the box of jerseys. She pulled out a couple of our smallest sizes, and the boy slipped into his easily. The girl's jersey, however, was slightly too big and she pouted.

Grace kneeled in the wet grass and smiled at the girl. "Don't worry about it, hun. All we need is a little creativity and style."

Grace grabbed the bottom of her own "King's Kids" jersey and deftly twisted it into a fashionable knot. She made a show of turning her torso and pursing her lips, giving fashion models everywhere a run for their money. The girl's face brightened and Grace showed her how to make her own knot. The girl squealed and skipped away to show her brother and mother.

"Nicely done." I threw my arm over Grace's shoulder and kissed the top of her head. I poked the knot she'd made. "This is a good look on you."

Grace shrugged. "I have been thinking about pursuing a career in football. Purely for the jerseys, of course."

"Wise choice."

Over the next few minutes, kids flooded the field and Grace checked them in with a bright smile. While several local children had signed up for the football camp, we also had a surprising amount of kids from outside of Aston Falls. Grace had used her connections to reach out across the state, and families from all over Montana were arriving to participate in the "King's Kids Football Day Camp."

I jogged in a small circle, trying to dispel some of the nervous energy. Soon, it was time to kick off the day camp. I ran my fingers through my hair, wondering where to start.

Somehow, Grace sensed my trepidation and squeezed my hand. "You've got this, Nicholas."

"I'm not sure. There's a lot of moving parts today."

Grace smiled. "Trust the process. That's why we put together a schedule."

We'd spent days brainstorming fun football-related activities for the kids and, in the end, the real struggle was trying to squeeze all of the options into a single day. It was good to know that there was no lack of activities for future football day camps.

Spurred on by a supportive nod from Grace, I took a deep breath and approached the circle of kids in the center of the field. We got started with icebreaker games, and then I introduced the football-themed scavenger hunt that Grace and I had set up around the field.

To my surprise, coaching the kids and guiding them through the various activities was the most fun I'd had with football in a very long time. Over the years, football had become my job, my career, and I hardly ever played for fun anymore.

Hearing the shouts and hiccups of children's laughter was invigorating. I began to see football the way I used to see it—as a game, a sport, a challenge I truly loved.

As the kids played, I turned my face towards the midday sun, letting the summer rays touch my skin. The air smelled like freshly-cut grass and blossoming flowers. I felt completely content.

A slender hand grasped my wrist, and a small palm pressed against mine. I opened my eyes to the beautiful woman standing next to me.

"So?" Grace asked quietly. "Is this a raging success, or is this a raging success?"

I stroked my chin pensively. "I'm going to say... it's a raging success."

She giggled and leaned her head against my shoulder.

"Thank you, Ace," I said sincerely, kissing the top of her head. "I couldn't have done this without you. You're amazing."

She looked at me, her cheeks pink. "*You're* amazing. This was your idea, Nicholas. This was all you."

"Except the scones." I laughed, gesturing towards the food tables at the side of the field. "Not even in my wildest dreams could I pull off those delicious cheese scones."

Grace swatted her hand. "Sure you could. With a little patience and practice. And cheese."

I rested my cheek on her head. Parents were scattered in clumps around the food tables, talking and laughing while their kids exhausted themselves. Almost every adult was holding a plate with varied pastries from Morning Bell. For lunch, we'd be serving a selection of sandwiches that Tommy had made.

"Wouldn't it be fun to be a kid again?" Grace asked wistfully, her eyes following the children on the field. "You have no obligations other than to run around all day and see your friends and get dirty."

"Our life right now isn't too far off," I mused. "We *have* been running around Aston Falls quite a bit. Not to mention sliding around in ketchup."

She laughed. "I wonder if one of the perks of parenting is that you get to be a kid sometimes yourself. You get to laugh, play, get muddy and no one minds because you're with your kid."

"Maybe. I guess we'll find out one day."

She stiffened and then turned her emerald eyes on me. "Will we?"

I bit my tongue. Did I go too far? Grace and I had barely talked about our immediate futures, let alone touched on the topic of children or a family.

If I was honest, though, it was something I'd been thinking about a lot lately... ever since I'd pushed Grace on the swing a couple weeks ago. What would it be like to have kids of our own? To raise a family together? To grow old together?

At that moment, there was an explosion of cheers on the field as one of the teams won this round of ultimate football. I checked my watch—it was just about lunch time.

"Good job, Team Xtreme!" I shouted, running towards the group. "And don't worry, Team Vortex, you'll have a chance to redeem yourselves after lunch. There are sandwiches and cookies set up on the food tables for you guys. Time for a break."

There were "oohs" and "ahhs" as the kids vacated the field and went straight for the food tables. Grace handed out sandwiches, cookies, and water bottles with a wide smile. She chatted and joked with the kids and their parents, friendly as ever. As soon as the children were settled in a big circle on the field, she returned to my side.

I felt inspired by the thoughts of our future, and there was something I wanted to say to her. Something I wanted to talk to her about. And what better place to do it than the location of our first kiss?

Before I could talk myself out of it, I took her hand in mine, interlacing our fingers.

"I have an idea," I whispered. "Follow me."

31

GRACE

$\mathcal{N}$icholas's hand was firm and warm as he led me towards the large brick building that was Aston Falls High. Spending time at my old high school wasn't unusual—I'd volunteered at a few school dances over the years and attended the odd high school football game. But, being here with Nicholas was bizarre. Like we were stepping into the past together.

I took off my sunglasses as we approached the front doors, and my heart skipped. Where was he taking me? What was his big idea? If I knew anything about Nicholas, it was that he was full of surprises.

Right before we entered the school, though, Nicholas veered right. I let him lead me around the corner to a place I knew very, very well. He took me straight to the bench where we'd confessed our feelings all those years ago.

I felt breathless and my cheeks were warm. Nicholas stood next to the bench and took both of my hands in his.

"What are we doing here?" I asked, my voice faint.

Nicholas's eyes searched my face and he took a deep

breath. "Ace, you know that I meant what I said on prom night, right?"

I placed a hand on his cheek. His scruff was soft beneath my fingers. "I know."

"The thing is... I still mean it. I'm crazy about you. My feelings haven't changed since the first time I saw you."

Tingles of electricity shot up my arms where Nicholas was holding my hands. I couldn't tear my eyes away from his gray gaze and I let his amazing words wash over me.

"You were this quiet, shy girl in the grade below me who played puzzles and read a lot of books." He smiled wide, seeming to remember something pleasant. "But, you were special, I could see it immediately. You were hilarious and smart and feisty, and you constantly took me by surprise. Whenever I was with you, I never wanted our time to end. And every time we were apart, I missed you."

My breath caught in my chest. He licked his lips and my stomach fluttered.

Then, his expression changed. He looked down, and the corners of his lips turned to a grimace. "When I left, I did everything I could to move on. I thought I'd moved on. I dated, got engaged, got married. And I loved Whitney, don't get me wrong. But I don't think I realized until I saw you again just how much I missed you. I think I missed you every day."

I held my hand to his cheek again, unable to say the words because my throat was closed up. Unable to say that I'd missed him too.

His eyes met mine again. "Coming back to Aston Falls this spring was the best decision I've made in a long, long time."

Nicholas took my hand from his cheek and tenderly kissed my palm. I was frozen, lightheaded with the beauty of his words. I wanted to run through the fields and shout it from the rooftops—"Nicholas King is crazy about me! ME, Grace Bell!"

Still speechless, I took a step closer to him and wound my arms around his neck. The touch of his skin sent delicious electric shocks through my body. Then, slowly, we began to sway. Like we were back at prom, dancing together.

My breath started to return to normal and I couldn't hold back my words any longer. "Nicholas King, one of my favorite things about you is that you're always surprising me, too. When we met almost thirteen years ago, I thought you were just a jock. Another overly-athletic, sports-obsessed guy on the football team. But then, I got to know you, and you were nothing like what I expected."

Nicholas's heartbeat was steady under my cheek. I'd never heard a sound so beautiful.

I took a shaky breath, overcome by emotion. "You were kind, and generous, and smart, and you always did the right thing. When you left, I was a mess. A terrible mess. It took me a long time to pick myself up again."

Nicholas stiffened and I tilted my head up to look at him. He was shaking his head, his expression pained. "I can't tell you how sorry I—"

"I know." I placed a finger on his lips to quiet him. "Your apology meant the world to me, healed some of the cracks in my heart. But, what's done is done. You can't change your past, you can only try to do better in the future."

Nicholas winced and kissed my palm again. "You were a mess, Ace? I can't believe that. You're always beautiful to me."

I blushed. "Even during the craziest rushes? When I'm sweaty and greasy and covered in various food items?"

Nicholas's eyes twinkled. "Especially then."

I chuckled shyly and wound my arms tighter behind his neck. "Sometimes, I guess, the mess is worth it."

Nicholas's lips flashed a smile as I repeated my words from our ketchup adventure. Without a word, he brought me in for a hug, cradling me close to his body. I shut my eyes and let myself melt into him.

Being wrapped in the arms of Nicholas King was as close to heaven on earth as I could've imagined.

Hand in hand, Nicholas and I returned to the Aston Falls High football field. We shared a secret smile before he returned to the center of the group of kids with his hands held up enthusiastically.

I watched him as he wrangled the children together and gave them instructions on the "Fake Out" game we had planned. He was smiling, his perfect teeth gleaming in the afternoon sun and his gray eyes sparkling silver. His biceps bulged out the short sleeves of his jersey and I realized again just how attractive he was. I'd noticed a few of the women checking out his athletic physique when they thought no one was looking.

But, as distracting as his arms were, the real joy was in watching the amusement on his face. He was a natural, born to coach these kids and share his passion for the sport he loved so much.

As the kids broke into groups for the game, I turned towards the food tables. I was delighted to see that the treats from Morning Bell were a success. A few of the parents had even asked for business cards from the cafe and inquired about whether we catered other events. Dad would be thrilled to hear that Morning Bell would soon be known across Montana.

I was putting a fresh batch of donuts when I heard a familiar voice.

"Yoohoo, Gracie!"

Mrs. Applebaum and Ms. Rodriguez were approaching from the school parking lot. Mrs. Applebaum had her hand up and was waving at me manically.

I waved back, laughing. "What're you ladies doing here on this fine afternoon?"

"Out for a stroll, of course." Ms. Rodriguez smiled. "It's such a lovely summer day, isn't it?"

Without waiting for my response, Ms. Rodriguez daintily picked up a donut, and not so daintily shoved it into her mouth. The white powder exploded around her lips as she moaned with delight. I had a feeling that the nice weather wasn't the only thing that brought them to the football field.

Mrs. Applebaum tutted and grabbed a donut for herself. She took a careful bite. "Really, Alicia. When was the last time you ate a donut? Wipe your mouth, you look *ridiculous.*"

Ms. Rodriguez pouted and grabbed a small mirror from her purse while Mrs. Applebaum faced me. "We saw your note on the door of Morning Bell, Gracie, and thought we'd come and see for ourselves. So, the rumors are true— Nicholas King has organized an entire football day camp."

"I'm not sure how much of that was a rumor, Mrs. Applebaum." I shrugged. "We did put up signs all across town."

"Of course you did, dear." Mrs. Applebaum waved a hand, clearly not caring for my answer. "How are things going between you two lovebirds, anyhow?"

Her eyes were alert and hyper-focused, and she was standing awfully close to me. Ms. Rodriguez had finished wiping her lips and she also leaned towards me eagerly. I resisted the urge to take a step back, away from their prying eyes.

"Things are good." I shifted from foot to foot awkwardly. "We're good."

"Of course you are!" Mrs. Applebaum boomed, drawing the attention of parents nearby. "I knew it. I said it all along."

"We could *both* tell." Ms. Rodriguez nodded enthusiastically. "Even when the two of you were in high school. You're destined to be together."

My cheeks flushed red and I looked towards Nicholas. He was running across the field with the children, his tanned skin glowing in the sunlight. Butterflies exploded in my stomach at the sight of him.

"And, if that's the case, what's the point in talking about it?" Mrs. Applebaum tsked and then sighed. "In a way, you and Nicholas King are old news. Ten years old news."

"That is," Ms. Rodriguez added, "until he leaves."

I froze, my hand poised above the donuts.

"He's not going to leave again, is he?" Mrs. Applebaum asked Ms. Rodriguez, like this matter didn't concern me in the slightest. "After everything that's happened between them?"

"Doesn't matter." Ms. Rodriguez shook her head. "Love conquers all, and all that. They'll figure it out."

"Well, I just don't know what Gracie's going to do." Mrs. Applebaum tutted. "If Mr. Applebaum and I were in a similar situation, I can't imagine what I'd think."

"But, Nicholas works in Chicago."

"Oh, didn't you hear? He's likely going to be traded to Pittsburgh this season. I ran into Eleanor at the grocery store yesterday. She seemed rather mopey about it all. But, it sounds like the trade is going to be finalized soon."

Mrs. Applebaum and Ms. Rodriguez continued speaking like I wasn't there. I tried not to listen to their mutterings, but their words struck a chord.

Were they right? Was Nicholas about to leave again? But then, why did he tell me all of those wonderful things by our bench? Surely, you couldn't just tell someone you were crazy about them and then leave them hanging.

A wave of nausea rolled through my stomach and my chest constricted. That was *exactly* what Nicholas had done to me in high school. Just ten years ago.

Don't go there, Grace.

I banished the thought, shaking my head adamantly.

Things were different now. Nicholas and I were no longer in high school, we weren't teenagers anymore. We were full-grown adults, and we'd both learned a lot over the years. We were both ready to commit to this relationship now, no matter the distance between us.

Right?

32

NICHOLAS

*T*oday was a big day.

Last week, after the football day camp, Grace told me that she wanted to hire another staff member to help us at Morning Bell. The cafe was busier than ever, given the returning regulars and the new customers from our outreach efforts. Not to mention it was now late June and the summer rush was starting.

Between Grace, Tommy and myself, running the cafe was more than full-time work. Plus, the extra money we had brought in at the Aston Falls Farmers Market had given Gracie a financial cushion. It was the right decision for her business, and I was so happy to see her gaining confidence in herself and her management abilities.

We got to work creating a concise but detailed presentation for her dad demonstrating the rise in business Morning Bell had seen under her management. We'd gone through the finances and showed the budget we had for an extra paycheck. And, Grace had had the wonderful idea of asking around the high school and gauging interest in working at Morning Bell.

Then, she presented the proposition to her father. I'd offered to go with her, to stand next to her, but she'd shaken her head and smiled. She had this, and we both knew it.

After she'd received her dad's approval to start the search, she was so excited that it took everything I had to keep her from bouncing through the ceiling. We'd sorted through various resumes, coming up with a shortlist that we then showed to her dad.

And today? We were making our final decision based on interviews that we'd held over the last couple of days.

"What did you think of the boy who just graduated Aston Falls High?" Grace asked, frowning at his resume. "He seemed nice. And he's Mrs. Applebaum's sister-in-law's roommate's nephew."

I raised my eyebrows teasingly. "Is that connection meant to be a good thing or a bad thing?"

Grace giggled. "Unclear."

"The good thing is he didn't have Mrs. Applebaum's penchant for chatter." Mr. Bell sighed. "It was hard enough getting him to tell us his last name." He picked up the last resume from the pile and his eyebrows shot up. "Now, Kris Murphy. She seemed like she might be a good fit."

Grace nodded as she peeked at Kris's resume over her father's shoulder. "She's intelligent and very capable. Not to mention she's got a sassy side to her."

I chuckled. "That will keep the cafe in line during the rushes."

"We need someone sturdy on her feet," Mr. Bell said. "I like her."

Grace and I shared a secret look. We'd talked about Kris a few times already and she was our top pick, too. Not that we would have mentioned it to Mr. Bell before tonight.

Mr. Bell stood from the cushy office chair I'd brought

from the back office and poured himself another cup of decaf coffee. It was late and we were all exhausted. We'd shut the cafe at 8pm tonight, and we'd been looking over resumes for the past couple of hours.

Truthfully, there were times when it felt like Mr. Bell was interviewing Grace and me. He was sitting on one side of the serving counter, perched in the tall office chair, while Grace and I sat on the other side. I kept waiting for him to segue into an intense interrogation of our relationship. But, according to Grace, Mr. Bell was as oblivious as Austin. He didn't have a clue that we'd been seeing each other for the past few weeks.

I felt the familiar gnaw of guilt deep in my belly. I didn't want to hide my relationship with Grace anymore. Especially not from my best friend and his father, who'd always been there for me.

It was getting to the point that I no longer cared whether Grace or I told them. Just as long as Austin found out from one of us.

Mr. Bell took a long sip of coffee and sighed with delight. He looked at Grace and me. "You two... I can't believe what the two of you have done with Morning Bell. I never expected that our cafe would be this busy ever again. But, clearly, you're doing something right."

I bowed my head in thanks and snuck a look at Grace. Her cheeks and the tip of her nose were pink and she was smiling proudly.

She should be proud, she'd worked so hard to get to this point.

"I remember the days when it was just Gracie's mom and me," Mr. Bell said wistfully, lips pressed together. "Morning Bell was the talk of the town then, we really had it together. Seeing it decline over the years has broken my heart. But now? It's like watching our beloved cafe come alive once again. I couldn't be happier, you make an exceptional team."

Grace bumped her shoulder into mine, and I glanced at her with a smile. "Couldn't agree more."

Her green eyes were glassy with happiness. She was adorable, and it took everything I had not to pull her close and kiss her right then. We did make a great team, the two of us. Whether in the cafe, on the football field, or in our relationship.

"It'll be hard to fill your shoes when you leave for Chicago in three weeks."

Mr. Bell's words sent a shock of ice down my spine and my skin went clammy. Grace's dreamy smile faltered and dropped. We both turned to face Mr. Bell, a sudden tension in the air.

He was shaking his head, oblivious to our reactions. "Well, I suppose you won't necessarily be in Chicago. You might be headed to Pittsburgh, I hear. Or wherever else wants a piece of the great Nicholas King."

My mouth dried and I couldn't bring myself to look at Grace. We hadn't discussed the future, what would happen in just a few weeks when I was meant to return to my career and the big city.

Mr. Bell picked at the pile of resumes on the table. His mouth formed a grimace. "It was incredibly good thinking on your parts to hire a high school student. They'll have a job for most of the summer before Ross's Burgers takes ownership."

There was a gut-wrenching silence as Grace and I digested this information. My heart was beating loudly in my ears and my limbs were frozen.

"Dad?" Grace's voice was strangled. "You're still set on selling to Ross's Burgers?"

Mr. Bell nodded sadly. "It's not a done deal yet, but Jim McNeil sent over the Letter of Intent today to get access to our operational and financial records. Things are looking good. The money they're proposing would take care of us for a long time, Gracie. You could even go to school."

Grace's lips were pressed together and she glared at the floor. I wanted nothing more than to wrap my body around her. Protect her. Shield her.

But, before I could do any of that, Mr. Bell turned to me. "Your partner in crime here is leaving soon, anyway. So, you'll be free to take off, too."

It was the final twist of the knife in the wound. His words stopped me in my tracks and my stomach flipped.

I could almost feel the chill emanating from Grace's chair. I had a feeling that the last person she wanted comforting her right now was me. Her blonde hair hid her face as she stared at the ground, her knuckles were clasped white in her lap.

Chills erupted over my skin and the world went sideways. It was like I was experiencing some terrible deja vu. We hadn't managed to save Morning Bell—the one thing I promised I'd help with. And, on top of that, I was meant to be leaving soon.

Leaving Grace. Again.

Because of me, she was hurting. Again.

What had I done?

33

GRACE

I'd done everything wrong.

Somewhere, over the past couple of months, I'd lost my way. I must've missed something... something big. And I was wracking my brain to figure out what it was.

Because, in the span of the next month, I was going to be losing Nicholas—the love of my life—and Morning Bell—my childhood dream.

My body ached with disappointment and the sting of failure. I'd put my heart and soul and energy into Morning Bell, but Dad still wanted to take the deal with Ross's Burgers. It was the end of June now, and the buyout was happening in August. What more could I have done?

Maybe I should've worked longer hours to get the cafe running smoothly sooner. Maybe I should've done more baking in the mornings. Maybe I should've focused on the cafe, instead of taking time off to go paddleboarding, stroll the carnival, or help with the football day camp.

Actually, I could confirm that that last point was a big error in judgment on my part. Because each of those events

—each of those days that I'd loved so much—were days I'd spent with Nicholas King.

The man who, once again, was going to leave me.

When Dad brought up Nicholas's departure date at the cafe a few days ago, my stomach sank to my toes. Dad was right, Nicholas was supposed to be leaving in just a couple of weeks now. But the worst part? That Nicholas didn't fight it, he didn't deny it. He'd just stood there, frozen. It was like watching one of the worst moments of my life replay in slow motion. And my recently healed heart cracked open once again.

I'd spent the last few days lying low, trying to recover from the double whammy of shock. I moved through Morning Bell and my daily tasks on auto-pilot. I served our customers with a smile, I put orders through to our suppliers, I even managed to hire Kris—with the caveat that Morning Bell may change hands in a few weeks.

But, even as I completed these tasks, my mind was elsewhere. I was thinking about Nicholas's departure date in mid-July, and the fact that my time with Morning Bell was quickly running out.

It was painful. I thought I'd proven myself. I thought I'd impressed Dad with the presentation Nicholas and I had put together. I thought I'd done a good job managing Morning Bell.

Now, I felt like I'd failed. Failed spectacularly.

Where had I gone wrong?

"Ace?"

What moment had I made the mistake that brought me here?

"Ace? Hello?"

Had I not worked hard enough over the years? Had I not done enough for Morning Bell? Or was the mistake that I'd relied on Nicholas King for help when I should've stayed far away?

"Ace!" A hand gripped my wrist and I was pulled from the depths of my thoughts.

"Sorry, what?" I asked.

Nicholas stared at me, his gray eyes flat. He gestured to the cloth in my hand. "You've been wiping that table for the past twenty minutes."

"Oh," I said absently. The cloth was now practically dry. "Whoops."

I walked to the sink behind the serving counter and ran water over the cloth before spraying disinfectant on the fabric. I returned to the tables and resumed my robotic wiping. The cafe had closed minutes ago and the room was eerily silent. Neither Nicholas nor I had bothered to turn on the radio.

"Anyway." Nicholas watched me closely. "I was curious to see if you wanted to hang out after our shift?"

Over the past few days, this question had become more of a statement. Since the double whammy, Nicholas had asked me almost every day whether I wanted to spend time together after our shift. And every time, I'd said no.

The thought of him leaving, the thought of giving up Morning Bell, was too much to bear. I couldn't handle spending any more time with him knowing that it would just hurt all the more when he eventually left.

Now, the problem was that, after days of flimsy excuses, I was beginning to run out. I fell back on a tried and true.

"Can't." I shrugged. "I'm hanging out with Austin."

Nicholas cocked an eyebrow. "I happen to know that Austin has plans tonight. His friend, Christian, is in town from LA."

There was a pregnant pause.

My foggy mind scrambled for another excuse and I forced a smile. "I could be hanging out with them, too?"

Nicholas shook his head and pinched the bridge of his nose. When he looked at me, his eyes were so sad, so exhausted. It broke my heart to see him this way, and I wished I could reach out and comfort him. But I was frozen, I couldn't move. It was like some terrible but undeniable chasm had opened up between us.

"Look, Ace. I know you're avoiding me," he said quietly. "But we need to talk about this. Talk about us."

My heart wrenched and I thought I might be sick. I knew what he meant—what "talk about us" entailed. I'd been through enough breakups to understand exactly where this was going.

Though, usually, I was the one saying the words.

I shook my head. I didn't know how to have this conversation with him, but I knew where it was going. Nicholas was leaving Aston Falls for his big city life, and I was stuck here. Soon, stuck without a job.

I could never ask him to give up his career to stay with me in Aston Falls. And, it wasn't like he'd asked me to come with him to wherever he went next.

We'd never even said we loved each other.

Ring!!

The blaring sound pierced the awkward, heavy silence in the cafe. Nicholas looked shaken as he checked the caller ID on his phone. He rubbed a hand over his face and took a deep breath.

"I'm so sorry," he muttered, his expression pained. "I have to take this. It's my lawyer."

I nodded once, stiffly, and he answered the call. I turned back towards the table I was wiping, but my shameful ears were trying to tune into Nicholas's phone conversation. Not that there was much to listen to. His side of the conversation consisted of a lot of "uh huh"s and "that's great"s.

Finally, Nicholas said goodbye and hung up. He faced me and rubbed the back of his neck. He looked… relieved.

"That was one of my divorce lawyers. It's final. The divorce is going through." He shook his head in disbelief. "Whitney miraculously agreed to all of the terms and has gone quiet. We're just waiting for her to sign the papers. It's been an uphill battle these past few months, she wasn't willing to compromise on anything and wanted to split hairs on almost every single aspect of our lives. But, she must've finally grown tired of fighting."

Nicholas stared at his phone screen, his brow slightly furrowed. Like he couldn't quite believe what had happened.

But, I believed it. He'd just divorced one of the world's most beautiful women. He had free reign now to move wherever his football career brought him. Experience the thrills of the big cities. Date the next supermodel who fell into his lap.

My throat was dry and it was suddenly hard to breathe. I used every ounce of strength I had left to force a smile.

"I'm happy for you, Nicholas." Despite my breaking heart, my words were sincere. "Now, you can move to Pittsburgh without anything or anyone holding you back."

Before he could respond, before I could see his face, I turned on my heel and disappeared into the kitchen.

34

NICHOLAS

I rolled over in bed and checked the time—2:32am. It had officially been four hours since I'd gone to bed. Four hours that I'd been rolling around, wide awake and unable to sleep. It was a sour reminder of the weeks that I'd been unable to sleep before I came to Aston Falls.

But this time? This was somehow much worse.

Every time I closed my eyes, I saw Grace's face at the cafe earlier this evening. The moment replayed like some horrible slideshow on the back of my eyelids. I couldn't forget the look in her eyes when she told me that I'd be moving to Pittsburgh without anyone holding me back.

Was this really how she felt? Was this what she wanted?

I couldn't bring myself to follow her, couldn't insist that she talk to me. Instead, I'd stood there at the front of the cafe like an idiot, staring at the kitchen door where she'd disappeared. When she eventually came back, she'd smiled at me coolly and informed me that I should head off and that I needn't worry about coming in for work over the coming days. Now that she'd hired Kris, she didn't need me.

Those words had hurt almost more than anything.

My limbs felt restless and agitated and I kicked off my blankets. I walked downstairs and grabbed a glass of water. I wasn't particularly thirsty but I had to do something. Get rid of this extra miserable energy.

I downed an entire glass and filled it again.

I couldn't ignore the problem anymore. For months, I'd blissfully cast aside all thoughts of the future, blaming the distance between the present moment and the moment I'd have to leave Aston Falls. But I couldn't get around it now, I was returning to Chicago in a couple of weeks.

That was what I was *meant* to do.

The deal with Pittsburgh should be done any day now, according to Arnie, and my new team was relying on me. My future teammates—my future coaches—they were expecting me. And I couldn't let them down without tarnishing my name.

But, even more than that? I knew I had to do this for my grandpa and Mom. Pittsburgh was a championship team— my best chance at fulfilling their dream. For as long as I could remember, my little family had depended on my football career. It was the one thing that kept us together, propelled us forward, when things fell apart after my dad left. It was the one thing that gave us hope when all hope seemed lost.

I couldn't fathom what my grandparents and mom had sacrificed over the years for this dream to come true. They'd scrounged every extra dollar for my lessons and equipment. They'd driven me to early morning practices, and missed work for my games. They'd put in effort every single day to give me the best chance at succeeding. I couldn't let them down.

But, I also couldn't let Grace down. Not again.

Her dream was to run Morning Bell, to stay in Aston Falls. I couldn't ask her to follow me, I couldn't ask her to give up everything she and *her* family had worked hard for. Her mom and dad had grown Morning Bell from scratch, and I knew Grace wasn't going to let Ross's Burgers move in without a fight.

I didn't blame her. It was one of the many things I loved about her.

Sure, according to Mr. Bell, the deal was more or less done. But, I didn't believe it, and I certainly couldn't hope for it just so that Grace might want to come with me. I believed in Grace with all my heart, and I'd seen the amount of effort and love she put into Morning Bell.

She *had* to run it. It was in her blood, like she was destined for it.

So, I was back at square one.

My stomach twisted into a painful knot and my head spun with an awful, unwelcome realization. I filled my glass with water again and chugged it quickly, hoping it would calm me down.

It didn't.

Because the reality was that I'd been here before, debating this exact same issue. Suddenly, I felt like I was 18 again, having to choose between my career and the girl I wanted to spend the rest of my life with.

What was I going to do?

I waited until the sun was shining through my window before I got up. I changed into my gray sweatpants and a navy hoodie, and I went downstairs without bothering to shave or comb my hair. It wasn't like I had anywhere to go today. Not anymore.

I put on a pot of coffee and sat at the counter, staring blankly through the picture window.

After getting water last night, I still hadn't been able to sleep. The memory of Grace's expression in the cafe—how hurt and resigned she looked—was like a waking nightmare. She'd felt so far away, her walls completely impenetrable. She wasn't the Grace Bell I was crazy about, she was a stranger. And I hated the distance between us.

"Morning, Nick," Mom said brightly as she waltzed into the kitchen. Her voice was a perfect contrast to my heavy thoughts. "How'd you sleep?"

"Fine," I lied. I couldn't bring myself to tell her the truth —that I'd been miserable all night at the thought of leaving Grace.

"Good, good." Mom bustled around the kitchen counter. She grabbed herself a coffee and passed me one too. "Grandpa's looking better this morning, have you been to see him?"

"Not yet."

"Apparently Austin received another batch of his medication. Would you mind popping over to the clinic sometime this morning to pick it up?"

"Absolutely."

Mom faced me and her eyes took in my rumpled presence. Her eyebrows drew together in concern. "Is everything okay, Nick? It looks like you didn't sleep a wink."

Instead of answering, I downed the rest of my coffee. I wasn't ready to speak to my mom about this. Not yet. I couldn't tell her that I was unsure about going to Pittsburgh, that I was doubting the dream we'd shared for years. "I'm fine. I'll head to the clinic now."

Mom frowned. "That's okay. Enjoy your coffee and—"

"Done." I forced a smile and held up my empty cup. I kissed her on the cheek before disappearing down the hallway.

Minutes later, I was walking the back streets to get to Austin's medical office. I'd changed into slacks and a black t-shirt, and I hadn't shaved so the scruff along my chin was itchy. But, it was nothing compared to the terrible headache I'd had since 5am.

The bell above the entrance signaled my arrival at the Aston Falls Medical Clinic. Becca, her dyed red hair piled on top of her head, didn't even bother lowering her phone. "Appointment?"

"No. I'm here to pick up some medication for my grandpa."

Becca popped her gum. "Who's your grandpa?"

I refrained from rolling my eyes. Everyone knew everyone in Aston Falls, and Becca must've known that my grandpa was Wayne King. But, I approached the desk anyway to give his name.

"Hey bro," a joyful voice called from the doctor's office just beyond the reception. Austin strolled out in his white doctor's coat, tucking a pen into his shirt pocket. "Didn't expect to see you here so early. And woah... looking like *that*. You okay?"

Austin took in my disheveled appearance and I shoved my hands in my pockets. Admittedly, my hair was messier than usual, and I was sure that I had deep purple circles under my eyes.

"All good," I said quickly. "Just here to pick up Grandpa's meds."

Austin raised his eyebrows. He wasn't going to leave me alone until I gave him an answer.

"And I have a headache," I muttered.

"I have something for that."

Austin nodded cordially at Becca, who still didn't look up from her phone, and I followed him into the small doctor's office. He shuffled through the drawers next to the examination table and pulled out a small container of pills.

"Advil. On the house," he said as he threw me the container. He then grabbed a full bottle of water from the vending machine outside the room.

I swallowed the Advil, wincing as the pill scratched down my throat.

"You look like crap, Nick." Austin shook his head. "Is everything okay? Is it Whitney?"

My heart twisted painfully and I took another long swig of water. Whitney wasn't the person I was upset over, but I couldn't tell Austin about Grace. So, instead, I skirted the question. "Love sucks. If only you could logic yourself out of heartbreak."

Austin chuckled dryly and slapped my left shoulder. "If only. Would make life much easier to navigate."

I nodded sourly, running my fingers through my hair. I felt queasy, but the headache was becoming more of a muted ache than a searing pain.

"Look, Nick," Austin said reasonably. "Do you love her?"

Austin's words reverberated inside my head and I thought for a long moment. Did I love Grace?

All of a sudden, I knew the answer. "Yes. Of course I love her. I've always loved her."

He shrugged. "Well, that's the only thing that matters."

"It isn't that simple, Aus. There's a lot of people counting on me. Depending on me."

"So?" Austin crossed his arms. "If they belong in your life, they'll understand."

My chest felt tight. "But, I let her down. I've let her down so many times already."

"Nobody's perfect," Austin said. "We all make mistakes. But, the good news is that, soon, you'll be back in the city. And you can dedicate all of your time and energy to making her happy. In Chicago or Pittsburgh or wherever you go next. Lucky number 13, right?"

My best friend held up a hand for a high five and I feebly smacked my palm against his. Austin clearly thought I was speaking about Whitney, and I knew he meant well.

But, unfortunately, he was right.

Chicago was my real life. Playing football was what I was meant to be doing. Aston Falls was a dream, a blissful break from reality before returning to the grind and hardship of the city. This was a vacation, a strawberry milkshake after a kale salad.

And people weren't meant to have strawberry milkshakes forever.

35

GRACE

I swirled my spoon around my small cup of Bubblegum ice cream. Normally, I would've opted for a double scoop on a waffle cone, but my appetite just wasn't there today. I watched the multi-colored gumballs streak the thick blue goop, my eyes following the circular motion.

"Planning on eating that, Gracie?"

Startled, I looked up from the hypnotizing ice cream. JJ was staring at me with her eyebrows raised, one hand resting on the counter.

I stared at my cup again and shrugged. "Probably."

"Good. Because ice cream is good for you, and you look *rough.*"

I shot JJ a glance, and she quickly covered her mouth and apologized. JJ was known for putting her foot in her mouth. She was often a little *too* honest when it wasn't warranted. But, over the years, I'd learned to appreciate her bluntness. You always knew where you stood with JJ.

"I want to eat it," I insisted. "I just... my stomach's off."

JJ nodded, her expression sympathetic. "It sounds like you've been off a lot lately."

For some reason, I found myself holding back a sob. Over the fact that I had no appetite. Ridiculous.

The truth was that ever since things had started falling apart between Nicholas and me, my stomach had been twisted into a huge, tight knot. There simply wasn't any space for food.

"When you told me you were dropping by to see me before my shift started, I assumed you were hankering for ice cream." JJ chuckled, glancing at my rapidly-melting blue puddle. "Are you sure you don't want any Rocky Road?"

I hazarded a smile. "Bubblegum's fine."

"Despite the fact that you hate it?"

"I don't *hate* it. Bubblegum's just... not my favorite. But it reminds me of Mom."

JJ patted my shoulder and puttered back behind the counter. Her hair was perfectly curled and she was wearing the absurd, frilly pink apron that Sweets n' Sundaes required all of their staff to wear. Ella and I always joked that she looked more like a candy striper than an ice cream server.

I stared out the window of Sweets n' Sundaes, wondering how things were going at Morning Bell. Dad was training Kris and had steadfastly kicked me out. His resolute and stubborn stance reminded me of someone I knew (me).

Today, I wasn't in the mood to fight with Dad. I'd been distracted at work over the past few days, and I could barely manage a smile for the customers. I had a feeling that Dad encouraging me to get out of the cafe was also his way of giving me a break. I was worried about him working the floor, but Kris was there, and I had a feeling that she would put her foot down if Dad became stressed.

JJ returned with a cup of coffee and a chocolate chip cookie. She handed me the cookie and sipped the coffee. I broke the cookie into small pieces and ate them one tiny bite at a time.

"What do you say we get Ella on the phone?" JJ asked. "I think we could all do with some girl talk."

"Don't you have to get ready for work?"

"A girl can multitask. Besides, I doubt Applebaum's going to be coming by for a visit today."

"You never know," I said as I took out my phone. "She's been hanging around Morning Bell a lot lately."

JJ wiggled her eyebrows. "That probably has more to do with gossip than anything else. I'm boring to her. It's just Ted and me. But you? There's definite drama there."

I felt a pang in my heart and I winced.

JJ's face dropped and she hurriedly drew me into a hug. "Oh gosh. Sorry, Gracie. I didn't mean it like that. I just meant—"

"It's okay," I brushed off her apology with a small smile.

With JJ's arm around my shoulder, we called Ella. She picked up on the second ring, and her appearance shocked me. Her hair was a greasy mess and her eyes were puffy. She looked like she'd been crying. A lot.

"Ella." I exhaled. "Are you okay?"

She blinked a couple of times and fiddled with her hair. She smiled wanly. "I'm fine. Why do you ask?"

"Because your face is blotchy and your eyes are red," JJ offered.

Ella raised her eyebrows and laughed, but her laugh sounded anything but genuine. "Honestly, ladies. I'm fine. I just had a really late night. I'll put on some makeup before I go into work, okay? Now, what's up?"

JJ and I looked at each other and then turned back to the

screen. Ella was adjusting her green hoodie, and there was a very obvious spaghetti sauce stain on the front. Typical Ella.

"Hang on." Ella leaned into the screen. "Are you guys at Sweets n' Sundaes?"

JJ nodded. "Gracie's here for an ice cream puddle."

"I'm not hungry," I grumbled, picking at a piece of cookie.

"How come?" Ella asked.

I hesitated for a moment, wondering if I really should burden my friends with this. Ella was obviously really busy with work, and JJ was meant to be working at this very moment. I didn't feel good dragging them into my problems.

Before I could say anything, JJ elbowed me lightly in the ribs. "Go on. Spit it out, Gracie."

Her words triggered the opening of a dam. I divulged the entire story with Nicholas, starting with the amazing Carnival date, and ending with Nicholas's probable move to Pittsburgh in a week and a half. I told Ella and JJ all about the football day camp, and his work in the cafe, and the earth-shattering kisses we'd shared. I described the moment Nicholas said he was crazy about me, and about how our relationship was so seamless, so easy.

Or so I'd thought.

"I just can't believe it." I shook my head, feeling drained. "After everything that's happened between us—all of the wonderful days we spent together—he's leaving. Again."

The ice cream parlor was completely silent, except for a couple of sniffles. My sniffles. I hadn't even realized I'd started crying.

JJ passed me a tissue and I wiped the tears from my eyes.

"Honey," Ella said gently. "I don't want you to take this the wrong way... but what did you expect? You knew Nicholas was leaving whenever football started up again."

"I know." My chest felt tight. "I guess I just... ignored it for a little while."

Ella bit her lip, her eyebrows drawn together. Then, she shrugged. "Well, do you love him?"

Her words echoed through the ice cream shop and my breath hitched. Both she and JJ stared at me expectantly. "Neither of us have said it, no."

Ella shook her head. "Doesn't matter what you've said. Do you *feel* it?"

I couldn't hide anything from my girls. I dropped my head.

"Yes," I whispered.

"What was that?" Ella asked loudly.

"Yes," I said a little louder.

"Still didn't hear it. Did you, JJ?"

JJ smiled slyly. "I didn't hear anything. I think she needs to speak up."

"Fine!" I exclaimed, chuckling at my friends' antics. "Fine, I love him. Yes."

JJ and Ella nodded smugly, looking all too satisfied with themselves.

But, apparently, I wasn't done. My body buzzed and the words spilled from my mouth, the deepest truth I'd ever known. "I love him. I love Nicholas King. He's the most amazing person I've ever met and, when I'm with him, things just feel *right*. More right than they've ever been. He's kind and smart and generous, and his smile literally makes me melt. I want to spend every single day of my life with him."

I felt breathless with the force of the revelation. Ella giggled, raising her hands to the sky in a "Hallelujah!" fashion.

But JJ? Her mouth was pressed into a thin line and her

eyes shone. She looked... almost upset. The smile dropped off my face immediately and I placed a hand on her shoulder.

"Is something the matter?" I asked gently.

She smiled, but it didn't reach her eyes. "Nothing at all. I'm— I'm just really happy for you."

"Gracie, what are you still doing here?!" Ella screeched. "You need to tell him. Go tell him."

My heart slammed against my ribcage. "But, what if it's all one-sided? What if it's just me?"

Ella licked her lips. "You're not a kid anymore. This is your *life*. And you deserve an answer, no matter what it is. You have no idea what he'll say... Maybe he does want to stay in Aston Falls. Maybe he wants you to come with him in a week and half. We just don't know."

Her words sent a spark of adrenaline through my body and warmth rose to my cheeks. She was right. I deserved to know the truth, and I deserved to speak my truth. Besides, communication was the foundation of all solid relationships, right?

I stood from my stool so quickly that it almost toppled over. Determination spread through my body like wildfire. I needed to go. Now. Take advantage of this pure, unadulterated—perhaps misguided—courage. "I'm going. I'm doing this."

JJ and Ella cheered, their hands in the air. "Finally!"

I grabbed my jacket, my mind racing as I tried to think of what to say to Nicholas. I'd go by his house first, and if he wasn't there, I'd go to the riverfront playground.

It was time I told Nicholas King exactly how I felt about him. Finally.

36

NICHOLAS

I walked slowly down the stairs. My body ached today, my shoulder in more pain than it had been in months. Of course, the fact that I was barely sleeping and spent recent nights tossing and turning didn't help.

It had been five days since I'd seen Grace. Five very long days. I missed her so much. I wanted nothing more than to speak with her. But she'd made it clear that she didn't need me back at Morning Bell, and I wanted to give her space.

Though, I was very tempted to drop by—just to see her, to hear her voice. I didn't want our relationship to end like this.

I approached Grandpa's door and opened it quietly to peer in. Grandpa was never awake at this time, but I wanted to check on him.

"Hey Nick."

Grandpa's firm voice surprised me and I pushed the door open. "Hey Gramps. You're awake."

"Couldn't sleep." He chuckled and the noise was a wheeze. But, he was alert and focused. His gray eyes were clear and his cheeks were rosy. He looked healthier than I'd seen him since I'd returned to Aston Falls.

Then, I noticed something else.

"Where's your oxygen?" I asked, rushing over. The big tank that had been a staple next to his bed was gone.

"Don't need it. Austin came by early this morning to pick it up."

I smiled and the tension in my shoulders released. "You really *are* feeling better."

Over the months that I'd been watching Grandpa, his health had been a constant stress. After my shifts at the cafe, I usually spent an hour or two in his room with him, and we'd talk or watch football together. Even when he was asleep, I'd sit in his room with him, allowing the whooshing noise of the oxygen tank to lull me to sleep in the chair next to his bed, not to be disturbed until Mom came home from her shift at the Inn.

Recently, I'd noticed that Grandpa's health was improving. The medication his doctor in Bozeman had prescribed him was clearly helping. His health had been the one bright spot in the darkness of my thoughts about my future.

"Pull up a seat." Grandpa smiled, gesturing towards the chair.

I couldn't say no to him. I sat in the plush armchair and crossed my ankle over my knee, but then winced as a searing pain shot down my leg. I planted my feet firmly on the ground.

"Nick, I've been wanting to speak with you for some time." Grandpa spoke slowly. "You seem... down these days."

"I'm not." I forced a smile. The last thing I wanted to do was burden Grandpa with my relationship problems.

"Nickyyy." Grandpa's voice was low and he shook his

head. If there was one thing Grandpa was good at, it was knowing when I was lying.

I ran my fingers through my hair. "I'm just not sure what to do." I paused, searching for the words. "I have to make a... difficult choice. But no matter what I do, I'm letting down someone I love."

Grandpa frowned, pondering my dilemma. "Coming to a crossroads in life can be challenging, especially when the choice you make affects others. But, if I've learned anything in my 80 plus years, it's that there's oftentimes no way to make everyone happy. The best thing you can do is what makes *you* happy. If the people you love also love you, that's all they want, too."

I shrugged. "I don't think it's that simple."

"I *know* it's that simple." Grandpa smiled, his gray eyes twinkling. "Just look at you."

"Me?"

"Yes. All your mother and I want is for you to be happy."

I froze, my breath caught in my chest. Was it really that simple? Would he and Mom really just *accept* that I wanted to quit football and stay in Aston Falls? But, I couldn't ask them for that. Not after all of the sacrifices they'd made for me.

I massaged my shoulder while my mind wandered. Part of me wanted desperately to tell Grandpa the truth—that I was unsure about my future in football. Another part of me found it unbelievably selfish on my part that I was even considering asking him whether I should give up my chances at a championship.

"Shoulder still bothering you?" Grandpa asked, pulling me from my thoughts.

"A bit." I shrugged and then held back a wince from the

resulting pain. "A lot of my injuries are acting up these days. It's getting worse as I'm getting older."

Grandpa rubbed the white scruff along his chin. "Maybe it's about time you considered retiring."

My eyebrows shot up and my mouth popped open. What did he say?

"After all," Grandpa continued. "Some of the greatest football players in the world are retiring at 27, 28 these days. It could be your time, too."

"I can't do that." My voice was uneven, but the words were robotic. "My winning a championship has been our goal for years. You and Mom are counting on me."

"Nickyyyy," he used that low voice again. The one that implied I was being ridiculous. "I love you because you're my grandson, not because you're a quarterback. Your mom and I are proud of you because of the strong, caring man you've become, not because you can throw a ball across a field."

I could barely breathe. I stared at my hands, locked together in my lap.

Then, Grandpa placed a frail hand on mine and I met his eyes.

"We just want you to be happy," he said again, his eyes clear and genuine.

Like he somehow knew this was exactly what I needed to hear.

"How did you know?" I asked faintly.

Grandpa laughed. "I might've been incapacitated these past few months, but I know a lovestruck boy when I see him. You've got a girl here, and if you think she's the one—if you want to stay with her—you need to do that. Besides." He gestured to my shoulder. "You have to take care of your body, or you'll end up like me."

He wheezed with laughter and I couldn't help but join in. Grandpa seemed like his old self again—his smart, sharp, funny self.

But, more than that, I knew he was right. I *did* have a girl here, a girl I loved from the bottom of my heart. And it was about time I told her.

"I have to go, Gramps." I stood from the chair and squeezed his hand lightly. "I'll be back soon."

Grandpa chuckled as I ran out the door. "Go get her."

This was it. I was going to tell Grace I loved her.

Nothing could stop me. Even if she no longer wanted to be with me, I wanted her to understand just how much I cared about her. As long as the truth was out, I was sure that Grace and I could make something work—as a couple, as friends, or even just connected by Austin, as we'd always been.

I wanted her in my life—in whatever way she felt comfortable with.

But first, I had to put on proper pants.

And shave.

And at least make it *look* like I hadn't been living in sweatpants the last five days.

I ran to my childhood bedroom and hurriedly changed into the one nice button-down I had that wasn't in my dirty laundry pile. I threw on my blue jeans and put the smallest amount of gel in my hair. I trimmed down my stubble—I knew how much Grace loved the scruff along my chin—and then I sprayed on a bit of cologne.

I brushed my teeth and flashed a smile at the mirror. A heady mix of adrenaline and happiness were coursing through my veins. I couldn't wait to see Grace—to tell her the truth.

I darted out my bedroom door and down the stairs. My body was sore, but I was too pumped to be bothered. As I reached the bottom stair, I heard voices coming from the kitchen. It sounded like Mom and another woman.

Grace?

My heart leapt and I jogged towards the kitchen.

I turned the corner and stopped dead in my tracks.

Mom was standing at the counter, a cup of coffee held awkwardly in front of her. But, the person sitting across from her wasn't Grace.

"Whitney?"

37

NICHOLAS

hitney was sitting in my kitchen.
                    With my mother. In Aston Falls.

It took a few moments for me to wrap my head around just what was happening. I blinked a couple of times, but that didn't change anything. Whitney was still there, staring back at me.

She stood from her chair and batted her long eyelashes sultrily. "Hey, baby."

Whitney teetered towards me, her stilettos clacking on the hardwood floor. She was wearing a tight white dress that hugged her curves, and her long blonde hair was perfectly flat-ironed. She smiled flirtatiously, and then stood in front of me, a little too close, and air-kissed me on both cheeks.

She placed her hands lightly on my shoulders. "I missed you."

I stared at her dumbly, my mouth wide open. It was absolutely surreal to see Whitney here in my childhood home.

Mom cleared her throat and I snapped to attention,

looking her way. Whitney crossed her arms before facing Mom, clearly annoyed with the interruption.

"I'm uh..." Mom started, leaving her coffee mug in the sink. "I'm going to check on Grandpa. There's coffee for you in the pot, Nick."

"Oh, Nicky doesn't need coffee." Whitney shook her head, not bothering to disguise the disgust in her tone. "We only drink tea at home."

I smiled at her thinly and placed myself between her and Mom. They'd never gotten along. We'd been married for two years, and her opinion of my mom had never changed. And Whitney clearly made Mom uncomfortable. I'd always pegged their frosty relationship on extenuating circumstances—Mom was tired from traveling to Chicago, Whitney was on a diet that week, I was busy with football and couldn't spend enough time with either of them...

Now, I wasn't sure what to think.

Mom put her head down and left the kitchen. But, before she turned the corner, she placed a reassuring hand on my shoulder.

As soon as Mom disappeared, Whitney turned her piercing blue eyes on me.

There was no denying it. Whitney Cade was a model for a reason—she was beautiful. Her wide eyes were like drops of turquoise ocean water, and her lips were plump and smiling. Her face was angular but youthful, and her teeth were perfectly straight and white.

When we'd first met, I was taken aback by Whitney's beauty. But, I fell for her because of her spark. Her ambition and determination. She wanted to be a model, so she went for it. Then, more recently, she decided she wanted to be an actress. So she went for that, too.

It wasn't until much later that I'd learned that her

methods weren't always clean and squeaky. In recent months, I'd found myself wondering just how many people Whitney had walked over to get to where she was today.

"It's so good to see you." She looped her tanned arms behind my neck and drew me into a hug, pressing her body against mine.

I stood stiffly in her arms, trying to breathe through the cloud of perfume. "Hi Whitney. What are you doing here?"

She ran her fingers down my arms and took my hands. Then, she looked up at me and pouted prettily. "The truth? I miss you, Nicky. I want to get back together."

My head jerked back. "You want *us* to get back together?"

"Yes," she said with a hint of an Australian accent. It was something she'd picked up in her acting classes and came out at the weirdest of times. "I... lost my way. But I want to put our past behind us."

"Why?"

"Because I love you, stupid," she huffed, crossing her arms. "I've always loved you. And I want to be there for you on this next step of your journey. You'll need someone to support you, to cook and clean for you."

I couldn't help but snort. "When have you ever done either of those things?"

"So we'll order takeout," she answered sharply. "Pittsburgh has good restaurants."

Pricks of discomfort ran the length of my spine and my blood went cold. I narrowed my eyes. "How do you know about Pittsburgh?"

According to Arnie, the deal with Pittsburgh was in the final stages and would close in the next couple of days. But the information wasn't public, and it wouldn't be until the deal was finalized. There was no way Whitney could know that Pittsburgh was looking to trade for me.

Whitney shrugged. "I heard the news around Chicago. You know, people talk. And they're saying that you're about to be traded to Pittsburgh. I want to be there for you... as your wife."

She grabbed her purse and took out a thick manila folder. She held the folder out to me, her eyes wide and innocent.

I cocked an eyebrow and then opened the folder. "Our divorce papers."

"That's right. I don't want to sign these, Nicky. I want us to get back together."

She reached for my hand and tried to pull me close, but I turned away. My body felt hot and cold, my chest tight. This wasn't happening. This wasn't possible. How was Whitney in my kitchen right now? After months of ugly divorce proceedings?

"Why would I consider getting back with someone who refused to fight for our relationship when we had one?" I murmured, walking to the other side of the kitchen counter. "Besides, aren't you seeing a basketball player in Chicago?"

At this, Whitney's pretty facade began to crumble. Her eyebrows drew in and her nose wrinkled into a sneer. "That's neither here nor there."

"I bet he doesn't feel that way."

Her nostrils flared and she exploded. "What did you expect me to do, Nicholas? Huh? You were never home! It was boring and I wanted my old, fun life back."

I shook my head, my fingernails digging into the sides of the counter. We'd had this argument so many times before.

"I was playing *football*. For my *job*. To build a life for the both of us." I forced myself to slow down, to take a breath. "Look, I'm tired of fighting about this."

Whitney's eyes flashed with anger, but then, her face

changed again. She pouted her bottom lip and blinked her eyelashes. She walked towards me slowly, never breaking eye contact.

"I'm tired, too. So let's just... put it in the past. Let's move on." She ran her fingers slowly down my bicep, and then interlaced her fingers with mine. I recognized this tactic—the final sting before the kill.

"I want to be with you, Nicholas." Her voice was husky and her eyes bore into mine. "Don't you want to be with me?"

38

GRACE

I closed my eyes and took a deep breath of the summer air. It was hard to believe it was already July, that things had changed so quickly over the spring.

It was amazing how much change a few months could bring.

I patted my flowy skirt self-consciously. My stomach was a mess of nerves and anxiety, but I was also beyond excited. I was about to tell Nicholas how I felt about him, and I couldn't wait another moment.

After speaking with Ella and JJ at the ice cream parlor, I'd gone home and changed into my cute coral skirt and a light blouse. I'd opted to wear my white sneakers instead of my usual work shoes, and I'd even done my hair in a half-ponytail as I knew Nicholas loved it that way.

Now, I was standing in front of Nicholas's house, carrying a full container of freshly-baked cheese scones from Morning Bell—his favorite treat. I'd stuck a post-it on top with a drawing of a dandelion.

All I had to do now was walk up the driveway, knock, and spill my guts.

I took another deep breath, letting the scent of flowers and pine trees calm me down. Then, I threw my shoulders back and walked up Nicholas's driveway. In my head, I was rehearsing the little speech I'd put together for him. I knew exactly what I was going to say.

I raised my hand to knock on his door when a bright flash through the window caught my eye. Curious, I peered through into the kitchen.

My heart stopped and I almost dropped the scones.

Nicholas was leaning against the kitchen counter. He looked gorgeous, as usual—his hair was gelled, his jaw lined with a hint of stubble. He was wearing the blue jeans I loved, and his button-down shirt hugged his muscles.

But, what shocked me was the woman pressed against him. She was turned away, and her long, blonde hair hung straight down her back. She ran her long-taloned fingers down Nicholas's bicep comfortably, flirtatiously.

Nicholas was staring at her intently, his gray eyes focused on hers. He said something and she laughed loudly but prettily, flipping her bleached blonde hair to the side. Another flash.

I recognized the woman's profile immediately.

Whitney Cade. Top ranking model. Aspiring actress. And Nicholas's ex-wife.

I froze. I'd never seen a model in person before—and especially not wrapped around the man I loved.

Whitney was exactly what I would've expected a model to look like. She was so drop-dead gorgeous that it was hard *not* to look at her. Her long, thick blonde hair fell down her back like a waterfall. Her little nose and angular cheekbones made her blue eyes look huge... Captivatingly so. She wore a stunning, couture cream-colored dress—a style that I'd only seen in fashion magazines and TV shows. And was that a Louis Vuitton handbag on the counter?

But worst of all? Whitney was tall, slim and toned, but with a perfect hourglass figure. In other words, she was everything I wasn't. I looked down at myself—at my short and curveless body. My outfit was almost embarrassingly childish compared to hers.

Whitney was like Grace 2.0. The better version of whatever I thought I had to offer.

Before my eyes, Whitney looped both arms around Nicholas's neck and stepped even closer to him, if that were possible. Nicholas didn't back away. He didn't seem the least bit bothered. He tilted his head and it looked like he might... kiss her?

The container of scones crashed to the ground as I leapt away from the window. Waves of hot and cold coursed through my body and my legs turned to jello. I wasn't about to watch that—watch Nicholas kiss another woman.

I had to get out here.

I was picking up the container of scones when the front door opened. Eleanor King popped her head out. Before I could gesture for her to keep quiet, she frowned. "Grace?"

Through the kitchen window, I saw Nicholas's head snap up. We made awkward, desperate eye contact and his face went white.

I couldn't stand here a moment longer. I ran.

39

NICHOLAS

G race disappeared down the driveway, holding a container in one hand and the side of her pink skirt in the other. Whitney was still pressed against me, her perfume almost nauseating.

Grace saw us through the window. I knew how it must've looked to her.

I had to go after her.

I sidestepped around Whitney to run after Grace. But, sharp fingernails grasped my wrists, cutting into my skin.

"Where do you think you're going?" Whitney asked, her voice shrill. She pulled me back towards her. "We're in the middle of a conversation."

"We're in the middle of me telling you to leave," I said impatiently, my eyes lingering on the now empty driveway. "I have to go."

Whitney released me and placed her hands on her hips. When she spoke, her words were biting and sarcastic. "So, you have somewhere *better* to be?"

I didn't have to think. "Yes."

Her eyes flashed with anger and her mouth popped

open and closed like a fish. Whitney wasn't used to rejection. "What's *that* supposed to mean?"

I tore my gaze from the driveway to look at my ex-wife. Really look at her.

Her cheeks were patchy, her mouth was pulled up in a sneer, and her arms were crossed. I suddenly felt unbelievably sad. I felt sad for the couple we used to be, back when we believed we were happy.

But, Whitney was still my ex-wife. She'd still had a huge impact on my life and I used to love her in the not-so-distant past. So, I faced her and asked a question I already knew the answer to.

"Whitney, why do you want to get back together with me?"

She scoffed. "Because I love you. We're supposed to be together." She poked a finger to my chest. "Model and quarterback. Actress and pro football player. That's what's *meant* to happen."

I shook my head sadly. "Love doesn't happen because it's supposed to. In fact, love often happens when it's *not* supposed to."

Whitney stared at me blankly for a moment, and then threw her hands in the air in exasperation. "Nicholas, *grow up!* Who cares about love. For people like us, love just doesn't matter."

There it was. The truth.

I paused, my eyes searching hers. She didn't seem particularly sad or angry or upset. She mostly seemed bored.

I turned away. "I need to go."

Whitney gritted her teeth so loud I could hear. When she spoke, her voice was like the threatening rumble of a storm cloud. "No. You need to stay. Because I always get what I want, and I *want* you to stay."

I faced my ex-wife again and she glared at me.

And I felt... nothing. Just tired and resigned.

"Not this time, Whitney," I said quietly, opening my palms. "I'm sorry. We're split up now and I think it's better for the both of us."

"You don't know what you want, Nicholas. You never have," she spat.

I shook my head sadly, holding my hands up in surrender. I couldn't fight like this anymore. "I'm sorry, but I really have to go. I can help you book the Aston Falls Express later, if you want."

Whitney's mouth curled into another sneer. She cackled. "The Express? You think I came on the *Express*? Oh, honey, I flew here. In a helicopter *you* paid for."

A whisper of a smile crossed my lips. "Of course." I turned away for the last time. "Good luck, Whitney. I wish you the best."

I left her in the kitchen, open-mouthed. As I passed Mom by the front door, I opened my mouth to apologize, to tell her I'd be back soon and I'd deal with Whitney.

But, Mom cut me off. "Go, Nick. Go get her."

She didn't need to tell me twice.

I dived out the door and raced down our street. I ran to Grace's house as fast as I could, but no one was home. I ran to the cafe, to the river, to our playground. My heart was in my throat and my chest was tight. Where was she? Where'd she go?

I needed to find Grace.

40

GRACE

*R*ight now, there were two things I knew to be true —I couldn't go home, and I couldn't go to Morning Bell.

Because, knowing Nicholas—knowing the sweet, caring side of him that made me so confused in the first place— he'd want to find me. Explain why he and Whitney were basically making out in the kitchen. Explain why he was breaking up with me.

I couldn't stand to hear the note of pity in his voice, the way his heartbreakingly beautiful gray eyes would be wide and worried as he confessed that he and his model wife were getting back together. That would tear me apart.

So, I simply made sure I couldn't be found.

I turned off my phone and I debated running to Austin's house, or to Sweets n' Sundaes, or to the playground by the riverfront. But Nicholas would find me at one of those places eventually. After all these years, he still knew all of my favorite spots.

I had to go somewhere he wouldn't think to look. Which was how I ended up at the Aston Falls church.

My body felt numb as I stepped through the huge mahogany doors of the church. It was a stunning structure —with high, arched ceilings and plenty of windows. The atmosphere inside was usually light and welcoming, and even the pews felt more comfortable than they did at other churches I'd visited. It was no surprise that the church was often booked for weddings months in advance.

I ambled through the vestibule and, upon realizing the church was empty, I deflated completely. No one was here, not even Pastor MacLean. Which meant that I could collapse in relative quiet and solitude.

I barely made it across the back pew when I broke down. I rested my head on the cold, stone wall of the church and let the tears flow freely down my face. My limbs felt impossibly heavy and my heart squeezed with pain. Everything hurt.

I had made a mistake, in the end. A terrible mistake.

I'd fallen for Nicholas King. And, once again, he hadn't caught me.

How could I have been so stupid ? How could I have done this all over again?

Awful memories of a too-familiar past raked through my mind. I remembered that fateful moment all those years ago when I'd learned that Nicholas King had left town without saying goodbye. Mere hours after confessing his feelings for me.

What had followed were days of silent tears, the ache of a private heartbreak. The one thing I knew for certain was that Austin could never find out about the blip that was Nicholas and me. So, I cried and healed all by myself.

And, it was happening again. I'd done the very thing I'd expressly set out *not* to do—I'd fallen in love with him all over again.

My hand in my pocket ran over the dandelion keychain he'd given me. What was I thinking? How did I let it get this far? There'd been a reason that Nicholas and I had never said "I love you." That we'd never told Austin the truth.

I'd somehow convinced myself that Nicholas King—one of the world's top football players, Chicago's starting quarterback—wanted to be with me. Me—Grace Bell, a quiet, short, and rather overwhelmed small-town cafe worker. Why on earth would he choose to be with me when he could be with Whitney Cade?

I was clearly delusional. That was the only explanation.

Eventually, my breathing slowed and I blinked my swollen eyes as I gazed numbly around the empty church.

I hadn't been here in a long, long time—Sunday mornings were often spent at Morning Bell. And, as nice as this church was, I couldn't go near it without thinking of Mom.

I missed her more than ever. And the thought of her now was a bittersweet twist in the wound.

When I was little, Mom and I would have special "girls' days" just for us. I always looked forward to those days because Austin and Dad—the boys—wouldn't be with us and I'd have Mom all to myself. In the mornings, we'd dress up and leave the house looking our best. We'd stroll through town and get some ice cream—she'd order Bubblegum, and I'd get Rocky Road—and then we'd go to the river. We usually ended up here, at the Aston Falls church. We'd sit in the gardens out back and talk and play.

As I got older, I appreciated our girls' days less and less. By the time I was thirteen, I almost always bailed to hang out with my friends. Mom never seemed to mind, and she let me go with a wistful smile.

After she'd passed away, I wished that I could've gone

back and redone every single girls' day with her a hundred times over.

Now, it felt like, on top of everything else, I was losing the last little sliver I had of her. In just a few weeks, less than a month, Morning Bell would be sold to Ross's Burgers. As much as I loved our cafe for everything that it was, I also loved it because it was Mom's. It was the last piece I had of her and I wasn't ready to let it go.

In a very real way, the fact that I couldn't save Morning Bell felt like I'd failed her.

Dizzy, I leaned my head against the wall and let my body break into sobs once again.

What I wouldn't do to speak to her now. When it came to heartache, there was no one who knew what to say quite like a mom. What would she say? What would she do? I tried to imagine her arms circling around me, resting my head on her warm, comforting shoulder instead of the hard stone of the church wall.

Forgive me? I prayed, but I didn't know who I was speaking to. Mom, God, or the future me who now had to pick up the pieces of my life.

Rules of the heart weren't meant to be broken, and I'd broken my one cardinal rule—I'd given Nicholas a second chance. What a huge mistake that had been. And, like all mistakes, I was facing the consequences.

The sky outside the church windows was dark when I finally decided to leave. Pastor MacLean had come through to light the candles, and a few churchgoers were scattered around the pews, their hands raised in prayer.

The last thing I wanted was to face people with my

swollen eyes, red nose and puffy lips. So, every time someone entered the church, I simply bowed my head and murmured under my breath. I hoped I looked more like a focused devotee than a maniac who talked to herself in the back corner.

Now, I rose to a stand, my legs shaky. I was exhausted and emotionally drained. I literally had no tears left to cry.

I moved along the back pew, my head bowed, and then quietly left the church. I was right in thinking that Nicholas wouldn't find me here. That was the one ray of light in this otherwise dismal situation.

Unless, he didn't find me because he wasn't looking.

My head pounded and I felt sick all over again. Perhaps Nicholas had decided that I wasn't worth chasing and he'd simply left town with Whitney. After all, that was a much easier, less messy option. He'd just disappear into his big city life and I'd return to guiltily scanning the tabloids for news about him.

All I wanted to do was go home and lie in my dark bedroom, but I couldn't face Dad. What would I even say? I also couldn't collapse on JJ's couch given that she and Ted were painting their apartment and they barely had space for themselves. And, I wasn't about to knock down the door of just anyone in my current state.

There was only one other place I could think to stay— Austin's penthouse above his medical office. It was risky, but I doubted Nicholas would have the gall to go there right now. And chances were that Austin was already getting ready for bed and wouldn't push me for details as to why I looked like such a wreck.

Before I could talk myself out of it, I set off along Center Street towards the medical clinic. When I reached the clinic, I went around the side to his lovely pinewood front door.

Austin had renovated the entire penthouse all by himself when he'd moved back to Aston Falls. The pinewood door was a modern yet simple touch.

I took a deep breath and raised my fist to knock. Hesitated.

This was a stupid idea. Nicholas might be here.

Please let it only be Austin. Please let it only be Austin.

I whispered the words under my breath as I knocked once. Twice.

I stepped back into the shadows, my stomach somersaulting. I realized that I didn't have an excuse for why I'd shown up in a skirt and blouse, makeup running down my face and my hair a mess.

My muddled brain scrambled and struggled to think of something.

Nothing.

I was about to turn on my heel and run away when the front door flew open, revealing a mess of curly hair backlit by the stairway light.

"Gracie?"

The familiar voice washed over me like warm water on a cold day, and my breath hitched. I took a step forward and fell into Ella's arms.

"Grace," she said, worried. "Grace, what's wrong? Are you okay? What's happened?"

I exhaled a hiccuping breath as I hugged my best friend closer. I didn't know why she'd answered Austin's door or what she was doing here in Aston Falls again so soon after her last visit, but she was exactly who I needed to see right now. Finally, I pulled back and wiped my eyes.

"Long story," I croaked, my voice raw. "Is Austin home?"

"No." Ella gently led me into Austin's sleek and spacious vestibule, and I took off my shoes. Together, we climbed the modern steel steps up to his penthouse. "Nicholas called him about something and he went out a little while ago. What's going on?"

Keeping her arm firmly around me, Ella and I turned the corner into Austin's gorgeous, renovated living room. It was a large, open-plan space with black leather sofas, a flatscreen TV, and big windows all around. The ceilings were tall and featured classic wood beams. The living room opened onto a modern and spacious kitchen with everything you could ever need to make a meal.

By the kitchen counter, I spotted a small, black suitcase. "You staying awhile?"

Ella glanced at the suitcase and then back at me. "I was hoping to stay with you at your dad's, but he said you'd been gone all day so I came here and dropped my stuff. After talking earlier, I tried calling you a few times but the calls kept going straight to voicemail. I managed to find a flight and caught the last train to Aston Falls."

"Els, you didn't have to do that," I said automatically, swatting my hand. Then, I realized what a mess I must look like, and I bit my lip.

"Of course I did. And I'm glad I did because here we are. Besides, my family was getting antsy. I was here a few weeks ago, but apparently I didn't spend enough time with them on my last visit." Ella rolled her eyes. "Now, are you okay?"

The sympathy in her tone, the sweet way she asked the question, made tears rush to my eyes all over again.

"No," I whispered, my voice tearful.

Without another word, Ella grabbed her suitcase, pulled out a pair of sweats and a hoodie, and shooed me towards the bathroom. When I emerged, changed out of my outfit, she'd set out a couple of granola bars, a jar of pure cocoa, and a bowl of small date squares.

She gestured towards the food apologetically. "Sorry, your brother has the *worst* taste in junk food."

Ella brought the "junk food" over to the custom coffee table in the middle of the living room, and patted the spot next to her on the leather sofa. Her brown eyes were wide, and she'd whipped her curly hair into a bun.

"Now, spill," she said.

And I did. I told her about my excitement to see Nicholas and confess my feelings to him, and how sure and confident I felt when I approached his house. And then, when I peered through the kitchen window... the heartbreaking moment I saw Whitney and Nicholas pressed together and leaning in.

Ella's jaw dropped further and further with every detail.

"So," she said quietly when I'd finished. "Do you think they kissed?"

My stomach flipped nauseatingly. "I don't know. I wasn't about to stick around and find out."

"Of course not," Ella said quickly. She bit the inside of her cheek. "This is just... not what I expected. At all. He seems like such a good guy."

"I thought so, too." I exhaled a deep breath. "But you should have seen them, Els. They were so beautiful together, it hurt. Plus, she was his wife for two years—how can I compete with that? They clearly belong together."

Ella wrinkled her nose. "That doesn't mean anything."

"It was so obvious, though. He even shaved for her, made his hair nice for her. He must've known she was coming."

"You don't know that, Grace."

"Don't I? It's like a rule of nature, Els. A girl like me just doesn't belong with a guy like Nicholas King."

Ella simply shook her head while a bitter taste filled my mouth. I grimaced and popped a date square onto my tongue only to grimace further. Man, healthy food just didn't cut it when all you wanted was ice cream and cookie dough.

I fell back onto the couch. "Honestly, with the way things are going, maybe I'll just move away from Aston Falls. Dad still wants to sell Morning Bell in a month, and I can't seem to get my love life in order. I think it's time to call it quits. Get a cat and a tiny apartment in Miami or Paris. Or come to live in New York with you."

Ella's smile faltered, just slightly, when the front door opened downstairs. Loud footsteps entered the vestibule and Ella and I froze on the couch, eyes wide. A man's voice murmured from downstairs, but the words were muffled.

"Austin?" Ella called tentatively, standing from the couch.

"Just saying bye to Nicholas," he shouted. "He's trying to find Grace but refuses to tell me why."

"Grace?" Ella squeaked and I hoped I was the only one who could hear the shrill tone in her voice.

The door closed downstairs and Austin's heavy footsteps clambered up to the penthouse. When he entered the room and saw me on the couch, his face dropped. Confusion spread across his features.

"Gracie?" he asked. "What are you doing here? Nicholas was just looking for you."

My heart slammed and I opened my mouth, but nothing came out.

"Grace and I are having a girl's night. Duh." Ella stepped in, saving my butt. She stood in front of me. "Didn't I tell you that? We're hijacking your place tonight."

Austin cocked an eyebrow and he smiled as he squared up with Ella. "I think I'd remember that, Els. You trying to pull a fast one on me?"

"It's not like it's hard to do," Ella shot back.

Austin opened his mouth to retort, but I held up my hands. "It's okay, Austin. I'm exhausted, so I'm going to head to bed. You're fine if I stay with Ella in the guest room?"

Without waiting for an answer, I blew past him down the hallway, trying to hide my face. But, Austin reached out and touched my arm. "Gracie, have you been crying?"

The concern in his voice made me teary all over again and I floundered for a moment.

Luckily, Ella was on top of this one, too.

"We were watching a Nicholas Sparks movie. *The Best of Me.* You know, a classic for waterworks," she said swiftly.

Shooting me a final glance, Austin let me go. A dull relief filled my body as I padded down the hall towards the two bedrooms, Ella and Austin's quiet murmurs following me from the living room. Though Ella and Austin were best friends, I trusted Ella to keep my secret with every ounce of my being.

I went to the guest room and didn't even bother turning on the light before I collapsed on the futon and fell into a restless sleep.

41

NICHOLAS

My feet hit the pavement, hard and fast, as I sprinted forward. My knees ached, but I did what I always did and ignored the pain, pushing through to the end. My chest rose with every breath and my exhales were a noisy, regular rhythm.

I was in the zone and nothing could stop me. Not the dense warmth of the summer day, not the noise of children on the playground nearby. Not even the shattered pieces of my heart. I was too used to this, too familiar with pushing down any ounce of pain or regret or sadness, channeling it instead to my muscles and limbs.

I'd sometimes wondered whether the guilt and shame I'd carried around for years after what happened on prom night had propelled me this far into my football career.

I finished the sprint and checked my time, frowning at the numbers on my smartwatch. I was clocking in slower than I would've liked, though I shouldn't have been surprised. Between working at Morning Bell and caring for Grandpa, my off-season workout regime had taken a serious backseat.

There was also a certain someone I had wanted to prioritize more than my training these past few months.

I approached the small copse of trees next to the river pathway where I'd dropped my things. I grabbed a bottle of Gatorade and downed the whole thing, wiping beads of sweat off my forehead. An elderly couple strolled by, hand in hand, and gave me a wave as they passed. I waved back, my public persona in play, and watched them for a few moments before realizing that I was picturing Grace and me doing the same thing one day.

But Grace and I would never be that happy, loving elderly couple.

I huffed out a breath and grabbed the set of weights I'd brought to the park. I lifted one and then the other, barely registering the flirtatious smile of a woman jogging past. I continued my rhythmic exhales as I lifted the weights, but soon, it was apparent that my thoughts would no longer be subdued.

Grace flooded my senses.

After what happened with Whitney last week, I hadn't managed to speak to Grace. I'd spent the rest of that day searching for her. I'd visited every single place we'd been to together, every nook and cranny of Aston Falls that she'd ever spoken about or alluded to. I'd even risked Austin finding out about us the hard way and asked him for help. I needed to tell her that things with Whitney and me weren't how I was sure they looked through the kitchen window.

By the time night had fallen, it was obvious that Grace had no desire to be found.

I'd spent that whole night wide awake, wondering where she was and whether she was okay. The next day, I'd called Austin and he'd confirmed that Grace had spent the night at his place.

That phone conversation had woken me up to a lot of things. For weeks now, I'd been urging her to speak about us —about our relationship—but she'd always made up excuses to get out of the conversation.

Grace clearly didn't want to see me. She clearly didn't want to speak to me.

It was about time I respected her wishes.

I didn't blame Grace for wanting to avoid talking to me. I'd hurt her so many times before, it was only fair that she called the shots during our breakup. She deserved better than this anyway, better than someone who kept loving her then leaving her.

I dropped the weights and placed both hands on the massive tree branch above my head. I pulled myself up and down, pushing past the ache in my injured shoulder.

My mind wanted to draw parallels between Grace's avoidant behavior and Whitney's. And though I didn't want to compare the two women, the differences were night and day. While Whitney had seemed bored and even disdainful when I had attempted to fight for our marriage, Grace seemed agitated and upset. And I didn't know how to help if she wouldn't talk to me.

So, I'd decided to give her space. I hadn't been by the cafe, I hadn't been by her house. On the rare occasion that I'd seen her through the windows of Morning Bell, she'd turned away quickly and I'd crossed to the other side of the street. Our relationship, as we knew it, was over.

And the only logical next step was for me to leave and get out of her way for good. The timing was perfect anyway —as of five days ago, the deal with Pittsburgh had been finalized.

In two days, I'd be leaving Aston Falls. Leaving the woman I loved. Again.

Two miserable truths, two realities that tore my heart apart. I was reminded of Mom's expression and I idly wondered about the third bad thing. I needed to get ice cream. ASAP.

I dropped from the tree branch, and a familiar aching pain tore through my shoulder.

There was the third bad thing.

Mom was always right.

"Hey, Nick!" I turned and saw Austin running towards me. His eyes registered my hand where it clutched my shoulder, and his smile dropped off his face. "You okay?"

I stood straight. "Been better."

Austin stopped in front of me. He was wearing an old jersey from our high school days. "Take it easy. You don't want to injure yourself again before the season starts."

Instead of replying, I grabbed a bottle of water and took a huge drink.

Austin noticed my silence and I could feel his eyes on me. "You don't seem particularly happy about that. That *is* what you want, isn't it?"

I ran my fingers through my hair, strangely frustrated. "What I want?" I grumbled. "Who even cares what I want?"

Austin crossed his arms, clearly surprised at my tone. "I do. We do. Your friends and family care."

"If only it was so simple."

"It *is* that simple. If you don't want to play football anymore, then quit. Retire your number."

I grimaced. "I don't think Mom and Grandpa would be so understanding."

To my surprise, Austin burst into laughter. "Have you tried actually *talking* to them about it? You might be surprised what they say."

I shook my head, but my conversation with Grandpa a

few days ago tugged at my memory. I'd never considered having such an honest conversation with my family before. I'd always just run on the assumption that they needed me to play football, and that was that.

"Look, Nick." Austin squared up to me. "You're not in high school anymore. You *can* make active choices in your life to go after what you want, what makes you happy. It really is *that* simple."

I nodded slowly, letting Austin's words wash over me.

"Anyway, want to run for a bit?" Austin asked brightly, oblivious to the thoughts whirling in my mind. "It's been awhile since I had a running buddy and it seems like you could use some endorphins."

"Ah, I should head home. Mom wanted me to pick stuff up for dinner."

Austin shrugged. "Suit yourself. We're having a family dinner tonight, too. Though the jury's out on how that's going to go."

My heart skipped a beat at the thought of Grace with her family tonight. I missed her. "What do you mean?"

"Gracie has been down in the dumps for, like, a week now. I can practically see the cloud hanging over her head wherever she goes. I don't know what's gotten into her."

A pang of misery ripped through my body.

I knew what was making Grace so upset. I just wished I knew how to fix it.

42

GRACE

"*A*re you sure you have everything under control?" I asked earnestly, hands on my hips. "Because if you're nervous, I can stay."

Kris rolled her eyes. "Yes, Grace. I've got it."

"And you feel good about closing?"

"Absolutely. Your dad trained me, you trained me, and we've done, like, three trial runs. I think I'm good."

I stared at her a moment longer and she raised her eyebrows, her mouth quirked into a smile. She sure *looked* confident, like she knew what she was doing.

But wasn't that just the trademark look of a sixteen year old girl?

Still, I'd been impressed with Kris's work since she'd started at the cafe. As expected, she was intelligent, capable, and amazing with the customers. She managed to strike the perfect balance of directness and humor, and her sassy side was a godsend during rushes.

Though some customers might have initially been thrown off by her thick black eyeliner, ruby red lipstick, and hair cut into a sharp bob, I'd come to appreciate her semi-gothic appearance. Besides, her hair was still a sweet strawberry blonde—apparently her mom refused to let her dye it black. It was an argument she'd recounted to me a number of times during slow moments at the cafe.

Kris and I were locked into a staring contest, and I was the first to blink. I hesitantly removed my apron and hung it behind the door.

"Okay, Kris. I know you've got this," I said slowly. "Tommy is here for the next hour, and if you guys need anything—and I mean *anything*, like the pens at the serving counter run out or there's no more tissues—all you have to do is call me or run next door. I'll be here in a flash."

"Thanks, Grace." Kris laughed and handed me my jean jacket. "But I think we're good. Tommy and I can do this."

"Honestly, I don't mind coming back whenever—"

"We'll call you if we need you. I promise."

While talking, she'd gently nudged me towards the back entrance. Now, she was standing with her arms crossed, a smile on her lips, waiting for me to go. I nodded slightly before turning on my heel and walking out the back door.

As soon as the door slammed behind me, I was overcome by the silence. No more bubbling sauces on the stove, no more clanking as Tommy moved about the kitchen, no more laughter and conversations from the front of the restaurant.

It was just… quiet.

I took a breath and shook off the intense desire to run back into Morning Bell. Was this what it was like to have a child? Constantly worried and anxious and wanting to be sure that everything was okay?

But, I had to trust Tommy and Kris to run the cafe in my absence. That was what good bosses did, right? They trusted the people they hired and didn't micromanage.

Loosening the reins was hard given the amount of time and energy I'd put into Morning Bell the last few days. I was throwing a hail mary, making a last ditch, desperate attempt to show Dad—and myself—that I could run Morning Bell. But, I was at the end of my rope.

Time was quickly running out. It was mid-July and, in a couple of short weeks, Dad would sign Morning Bell over to Ross's Burgers.

I couldn't process the thought without risking a total fold on my part.

Of course, it didn't hurt that part of the reason I'd been able to be so dedicated and hardworking lately was to keep the heartache at bay.

Nicholas and I were no longer on speaking terms. Though I'd seen him around Aston Falls a few times, I always made sure to avert my gaze. I wasn't sure whether Whitney was still in town, and I wasn't about to risk seeing her hanging off his arm, or pressed against him. Or worse, seeing him kiss her. The mere thought made my stomach curdle.

So, I'd done my best to avoid him completely. Anytime Austin brought him up, I quickly diverted the subject. Anytime anyone in town spoke of Nicholas, I made sure to bow out of the conversation. My heart was too fragile, too broken. I was damaged goods and all I wanted was to return to how things were before he came back. Before I gave him that second chance.

Even if my existence before was rather boring and miserable at times.

Despite my resolution to avoid all things Nicholas King, the worst moments were when I forgot that we were broken up. At times, I would surface from the back office after a pile of paperwork, looking for his smile and a cup of coffee, only to realize that he was gone and would never return. Or, I'd be serving a customer and would reflexively look for him, only to find that he wasn't there and a pang of sadness would shock my body.

The truth was that I missed him. There, I said it.

I was wrong for feeling that way and I knew it. Despite wanting to cry myself to sleep every night, I tried to put on a brave face and hold back the tears.

Ella and JJ would've told me that I was ridiculous for missing him, and I needed to move on ASAP. They would've handed me a pile of headshots of "eligible bachelors" around Aston Falls and downloaded dating apps onto my phone.

But, there was no escaping the reality that Nicholas King had somehow implanted himself into my heart the moment I first laid eyes on him. And his hold on me had never left.

"Gracie? What are you doing out there?" Austin was staring at me from the front porch of our house, his head tilted. It occurred to me that I probably did look a little nuts, hiding in the shadows of Morning Bell with my head down and my jean jacket lopsided over my shoulders.

"I was just... thinking." I scrambled for a subject change. "You're early for family dinner!"

Austin raised his eyebrows. "As are you. What're you thinking about?"

I opened my mouth to answer, but didn't trust myself to say anything that didn't involve the word "Nicholas." So, instead, I pasted a big, fake smile on my face and strode towards him.

I approached the porch and climbed the stairs but Austin stood in my way, blocking me from walking through the front door.

"Excuse me, weirdo," I said impatiently. "We might be early, but we might as well help Dad."

Austin's eyes scanned my face and I immediately cast my head down. Dang it, I'd forgotten about his annoying twinny sixth sense thing. How did he always know when something was bothering me? And was it a switch that I could turn off?

"Grace, I think it's time we had a chat. Big brother to little sister."

"Erm." I cleared my throat. "Big brother by twenty minutes and sixteen seconds. Barely counts."

"Oh, it counts. Because I'll always be twenty minutes and sixteen seconds older and wiser than you."

I rolled my eyes. It had been awhile since he'd used *that* argument. "That's ridiculous and we both know it."

"Maybe." Austin shrugged. "But I think it's about time we cleared the air. Grace, what is going on with you?"

"Me? What do you mean?"

"You've been this sad, mopey person for days now. It's like there's something in the water—both you and Nicholas are like these sad potatoes that refuse to be happy about..."

Austin trailed off, frozen. Because at the mention of Nicholas's name, my eyes stung with tears. I turned away, trying to hurriedly brush away the droplets.

Not here. Not now. He couldn't see me cry.

I started to walk down the steps, but Austin grabbed my arm, holding me back.

"Gracie," Austin said my name like a question, his voice low. "Are you and Nicholas upset over the same thing?"

My heart skittered and I looked around wildly. How could I get out of this conversation? But, my vision blurred and I held back a hiccuping sob. Despite trying to free myself from his grasp, Austin placed his hands on my shoulders and gently swiveled me around.

Having an athletic brother was the literal pits sometimes.

"Gracie?" Austin asked, trying to meet my eyes. "Did something... happen between you two?"

I bit my lip so hard I almost drew blood, but I couldn't keep a straight face anymore. I broke down. My shoulders crumpled and the tears I'd been holding back for days escaped down my cheeks. Austin drew me in for a hug, letting me wipe my nose on his shoulder like any good big brother would.

Eventually, he pulled away and sat on the top step of the porch stairs. "Tell me everything."

43

GRACE

*a*nd I did tell him everything.

While Austin and I sat on the front steps of our house and the sky turned dark, I spilled my guts. I told him the truth—my truth. I explained how I'd been feeling, careful to leave out anything that directly implicated Nicholas—they were still best friends and I didn't want to inflict unnecessary damage on their friendship.

I told him that I'd had a crush on Nicholas for as long as I could remember, and that I'd hoped we might be together after prom. I told him about our beautiful relationship over the summer, and the spectacularly awful "non-breakup" breakup we'd had.

"And now, Dad is selling Morning Bell," I finished quietly. My head rested on Austin's shoulder and I used the sleeve of his shirt to blow my nose. "I just... I miss Mom so much these days, Aus. Morning Bell is a part of our family. Part of her legacy. I can't bear the thought of selling it."

Austin was silent for a long time and my body stiffened. Maybe I'd said way too much. Maybe I sounded insane and he was considering putting me in a mental hospital.

"I miss her too," Austin eventually said, his shoulders drooping. "Every single day, every single second."

His voice broke my heart and I held tight onto his arm. We sat in silence for a long, long time, and I took comfort in the fact that Austin Bell was my brother.

"Are you mad about Nicholas and me?" I finally asked quietly. "Please don't be mad."

Austin was chewing his lip, his arm loose around my shoulders, which I took to be a good sign.

"I'm not mad," he said. "Just processing. This is a lot."

"I know. I never, ever would've wanted things to go this way."

Austin shook his head. "Me neither."

So, he was mad. Not that blamed him.

I looked at my hands clasped in my lap. I felt terrible. I'd lied to my twin brother for years.

"Don't get me wrong, I'm not mad that you didn't tell me," Austin added, reading my mind. This twin sixth sense thing was out of hand. "We all have secrets. I'm just mad at the part I played in it."

I sat straight and stared at him. "The part you played?"

"Well, yeah. If what you're saying is true, then *I'm* part of the reason you guys broke up in the first place."

"No, Austin." I shook my head. "This had nothing to do with you. Nicholas and I just aren't... meant to be."

I went to lean my head on his shoulder again, but I didn't get the chance. In a flash, Austin was standing at the bottom of the steps, pacing back and forth. He was frowning at the ground, like he was working something out.

Eventually, he came to stand directly in front of me. To my surprise, instead of seeming confused like he had moments before, his blue eyes were fiery with frustration.

I leaned away from him, bewildered. "What's wrong?"

"What's *wrong*?" Austin exploded. "You. Him. This. This whole self-pitying, we-aren't-meant-to-be thing. How can you both be so stubborn? Just because you have a history doesn't mean the past needs to repeat itself."

I blinked a couple of times. "What are you talking about? Nicholas is back with Whitney, isn't he?"

"No. Why would you think that?"

My stomach fell to the floor. "You know," I muttered. "She was here. In Aston Falls. I assumed because they were getting back together."

Austin gave me a look. His perfect "I'm a doctor and I'm smarter than you" look. It used to drive me nuts as a kid and I couldn't say I was a big fan of it now either.

"Did you ever confirm this wild assumption?" Austin asked.

Mute, I shook my head.

"You two, I swear," Austin muttered under his breath, pinching the bridge of his nose. "Gracie, you're the best sister I could've ever asked for. You're intelligent, and generous, and almost annoyingly nice to everyone you meet. But, have you ever stopped to consider that you have more to offer the world than keeping small and quiet?"

I frowned in confusion and opened my mouth to defend myself.

"See?" Austin smiled. "You have so much spark and ambition, and you should wear it confidently. Wear it bravely. Maybe it's time you stop discounting yourself and start asking for what you truly want. You and Nicholas both. I just don't understand why the two of you are *choosing* to leave behind someone you lo—"

Austin cut himself off and pressed his lips together. His eyes darted around, his tell that he'd said something he shouldn't have.

"I'm sorry," I whispered. "What were you about to say?"

Austin opened and closed his mouth, looking remarkably like a giraffe mid-meal. Then, he set his jaw. "Nothing. But, I would urge you to really, properly think about what you're doing right now."

I frowned, irritated by the riddle in his statement. "And just *what* am I doing right now?"

At this, Austin smiled. Cryptically. Annoyingly. "Beats me. But, remember what Mom used to say, Gracie—to love and be loved is the bravest thing you'll ever do."

Before I could respond, he blew past me and opened the front door of the house.

Right before he stepped inside, he looked back. "And Gracie? Talk to Dad. Level with him. I'd bet you good money that he would want you to run Morning Bell if he believed that was what you truly wanted. He knows that Morning Bell is Mom's legacy, too."

With a wink, Austin disappeared through the front door.

I sat frozen on the porch steps, my heart racing a mile a minute and my skin patchy and hot. It was like Austin's words had slapped me to wakefulness. Like I'd just been given the biggest reality check of my life.

He was right. I'd been beyond foolish, beyond cowardly. I'd been hiding behind fear for so, so long, using it as an excuse to protect myself from feeling any more pain. But, had I also been preventing myself from feeling love?

Because that's what this was all about, wasn't it? I loved Nicholas King with every fiber of my being. And it scared the pants off of me.

My chest felt tight as my gaze rose to the sky. Aston Falls was just small enough not to give off too much light pollution and, above my head, I saw the smallest sprinkling of stars. I searched the heavens for a moment, wishing I could see Mom there.

Then, a breeze washed over my skin. Warm and comforting and tender. I closed my eyes and breathed it in, relishing the smell of fresh flowers. As the breeze dissipated, so too did my anxieties and worries.

I knew what I had to do. Something I should've done long ago.

44

NICHOLAS

I stood on the corner of Center Street and stared at the entrance of Morning Bell Cafe. It was a quiet Monday morning and very few people were on the street. Morning Bell's windows were dark and the antique wooden sign in the window read "Closed."

I took a few moments to commit the building to memory. The sweet, butter yellow of the exterior and the white trim around the windows and door. The flower pots out front that contained blooming flowers in every color. The wooden stairs leading to the front door that always creaked when you stepped on them.

There wasn't a single thing about Morning Bell that didn't perfectly encapsulate Aston Falls—its friendliness, warmth, and community. And I loved the cafe for that.

I loved it for other reasons too, of course.

The thought that Morning Bell might be gone when I next came back to Aston Falls made my chest ache. Because I would be back, I could never let another ten years pass before coming home. And Aston Falls was my home. This summer showed me just how much I loved my small, quirky hometown and everyone in it.

The time had come for me to leave again. I was booked on the first Aston Falls Express tomorrow morning, and my bags were packed. Tomorrow evening, I would be back in Chicago to pack up the small, cluttered apartment I'd moved into after splitting from Whitney.

If I was being honest, though, the thought of returning to the city was completely unappealing. I was already homesick knowing I was leaving Aston Falls.

Ridiculous. A pro football player feeling homesick.

But, here we were.

There was just one final thing I had to do before I left. And, lucky for me, Mr. Bell had given me the perfect opportunity to do it.

I awkwardly clasped the sheets of paper in my hand, wishing I'd put them in an envelope, or tied them with a ribbon or something. How did people hand-deliver letters these days? Or should I have commissioned a carrier pigeon? Maybe an email was the better way to go?

I shook my head. I had to stop doubting myself. The words on the paper were meant for Grace's eyes first and foremost—it was my way of showing her how much I'd changed, how much she'd changed me. That she made me want to be a better man. A more honest, braver man.

The thought of never seeing her again, never hearing her voice or her laugh filled me with so much dread and heartache, it took my breath away. All I could do was hope that we could find some way to be in each others' lives—even if it was just the odd phone call or group chat with Austin.

I took a deep breath, steeled myself against a wave of uncertainty, and strode forward. For some reason, Mr. Bell had been very vocal about the fact that Grace wouldn't be at Morning Bell this morning, but I hoped she was. If not, I was planning on going next door to deliver the letter anyway. I needed to see her one more time before I left.

I opened the front door of Morning Bell and the familiar tinkle of the bell announced my arrival.

I paused in the doorway, confused. The cafe's chairs were set up around the serving counter as they had been when we were conducting interviews for Morning Bell's next hire. I remembered Kris sitting on that side of the counter, while Mr. Bell, Grace and I sat on the other. The plush office chair was even pushed up to the counter, facing away from the door.

The room was deserted. There wasn't a single noise from the kitchen.

"Mr. Bell?" I called, wondering if he was in the back office.

Suddenly, the office chair whipped around, nearly giving me a heart attack.

My heart then slammed twice when I saw who was sitting in the chair.

"Hello, Mr. King." Grace's quiet, sweet voice had a formal lilt.

I blinked a couple of times, my lips twitching. The office chair basically swallowed her whole, but with her chin tilted up, her smile confident and certain, she took up space. Her blonde hair was slicked back into a neat ponytail and she was wearing a prim white blouse with a navy blazer. Long, silver earrings dangled from her ears. She looked good... different, but good.

Grace stood and leaned across the counter, offering her hand for me to shake.

I stared at her hand for a moment, confused. Then, she

raised an eyebrow and I realized how rude I was being. I sprung to life, striding forward to shake it. She gestured for me to sit in the chair across from her—the chair where the interviewees sat.

"What's going on?" I asked when I found my voice.

"Well, Mr. King." Grace clasped her hands on top of the counter and glanced at the sheet of paper in front of her. "I've spent the last couple of days reviewing your credentials and your experience."

This was unmistakably a job interview. But for what job, I had no idea.

And I'd never noticed just how gorgeous Grace looked when she was being her professional, business self. I bit my lip to keep from smiling.

Grace pushed the paper aside and looked at me. Really looked at me. And I was plunged back into the beautiful emerald depths of her eyes.

"I've been incredibly impressed with your work over the past couple of months. Despite having no experience, you've been a big help around here and I think it's time I was honest with you."

Her words hung in the silence and it was like time slowed. Grace paused, and her brow flinched just the tiniest bit. A swell of emotions passed through her eyes and I wished I could reach out and grab her hand. I had a feeling that her next words would be important. I listened closely.

"I've loved having you here at Morning Bell," she started and her voice barely wavered. "I know that you have an exciting career ahead of you. You're headed to Pittsburgh, and you're joining what could be a championship team. Not to mention the appeal of the big city life. But, I wanted to extend this offer to you, should you ever want to take it. I'd like to offer you to… stay."

I couldn't breathe, couldn't speak. I pinched the skin of my hand under the counter to be sure that this wasn't a dream.

It wasn't.

"I know that Morning Bell is nothing compared to your amazing football career, and I know Aston Falls could never compare to Chicago or Pittsburgh. But, if you want it, you will always have a place here. You will always have a place with me, and with Morning Bell. Because it's official now, Morning Bell isn't going anywhere, and I couldn't have done it without you."

My chest lifted with joy at the news. Morning Bell wasn't being sold?

"The bottom line is..." Grace squeezed her eyes shut to center herself. When she opened them, her gaze was strong and sure. "Nicholas King, I want to be with you. I've always wanted to be with you. I've spent my life being afraid and hiding from my feelings. I was a coward, and I don't want to be anymore."

I reached for her hand, wanting to touch her, put my arms around her, something. But, she continued talking.

"You're my person, the one I want to be with forever. If you want to stay here with me and run Morning Bell, that's great. And, if you want to go to Chicago or Pittsburgh and play football, that's great, too. We'll do long distance. At the end of the day, I want to be with you. And if, by some miracle, you want to be with me too, I want to make this work."

45

GRACE

I was so grateful that words had come out of my mouth because I was so nervous I could be sick.

My confession, my truth, hung in the air between Nicholas and me, and I suddenly wondered whether I'd been shouting, the words felt so loud. My heart was threatening to beat out of my chest and my stomach was twisted into a terrified knot. I'd never felt so vulnerable, so exposed.

So totally and completely open.

My eyes were locked on Nicholas's face, scanning his beautiful features—his jaw that could cut glass, the sharpness of his silver eyes, the full pout of his lips. I even noticed the slight dip in his cheek where his dimple lived. What I wouldn't do to see him smile like that again.

I just hoped that I hadn't ruined everything or crossed a line with my confession.

A myriad of emotions danced through my chest—I was afraid, uneasy, exhilarated and excited all at once.

In all honesty, I was a mess of emotions these days. After my talk with Austin a few days ago, I'd finally had the courage to sit down with dad and have a good, long conversation about Morning Bell. I confessed that I'd been working so hard to prove to him that I could run our beloved cafe.

To my surprise, Dad almost collapsed with happiness. He'd said that he wanted nothing more than for me to take over the cafe. He believed in me, he'd always believed in me, but he didn't want to hold me back. He knew that I'd stayed in Aston Falls after high school to help him after Mom died, and he felt guilt for that every day. He felt he couldn't ask me to take over the family business after all that I'd sacrificed for him.

Imagine his relief to hear that my dream *was* to run Morning Bell. Together, we'd made a plan. A plan to keep Morning Bell, and Mom's legacy, intact.

After that, I knew there was one thing I still had to do.

I had to find the courage to tell Nicholas how I felt. I had to be brave enough to tell him I loved him, even if that meant doing long distance while he was in Pittsburgh. Or breaking up for good.

Now, I'd played all my cards, I'd showed my hand. It was up to Nicholas to make his move.

I watched as his face set into an unreadable, deadpan expression. Without a word, he stood from the serving counter and walked towards the front door.

My stomach hit the floor and a wave of devastation threatened to pull me under. What had gone wrong?

I stared after Nicholas, wide-eyed and speechless, as he left through the front door. I stood shakily and opened my mouth to say something, to call after him, but what could I possibly say? That was it.

But, right before I could die from embarrassment and shame, Nicholas popped his head back into Morning Bell. His mouth quirked into that adorable half-smile that always made my heart skip a beat, and he lifted a single finger. He gestured for me to follow him before disappearing out the door again.

There were a million choice words I had for him, but my brain had since stopped communicating with my mouth.

I hobbled around the counter and through the front door—I'd put on my one pair of tan heels for this "interview" and I was now kicking myself for making that decision. It was soon apparent that there was no way I could keep up with Nicholas's long strides while hobbling.

I ditched the heels on the front lawn of Morning Bell, and I stood tall and proud as I buttoned up my blazer, smoothed down my dress skirt, and went after Nicholas with my bare feet.

I followed him down Center Street and towards the river, ignoring the stares and whispers of the townspeople as they noticed my bizarre fashion choices. We strolled all the way to the river pathway, and then took a left.

My heart picked up speed. I knew where we were going.

Nicholas stepped into the playground—our playground—and turned to face me. He handed me the papers he held in his hand.

"Read it," he said quietly, his silver eyes melting into mine.

I turned my gaze to the paper and did as he asked. It took me a few moments to register just what this letter was, but then, my breath caught. "It's a resignation letter. You're... retiring? From football?"

Nicholas was smiling down at me. He'd moved closer and I felt the magnetic pull between us stronger than ever.

"I'm retiring," he confirmed.

Before I could say or do anything, Nicholas turned on his heel and ran to the edge of the playground. He picked the one, lone dandelion poking through the cement and tied the stem in a loop. When he approached me again, his eyes were tender and sweet.

"What's going on?" I asked, breathless.

Nicholas smiled and took my hand. "This is a promise ring, Ace. Before you said anything today, I'd already made my decision. I finally got up the courage to speak to Mom and Grandpa, and they're incredibly supportive of my decision to retire. They want me to move back home as much as I want to be here. I *want* to stay, I want to live in Aston Falls, I want to run football camps for kids and work at Morning Bell. And I want to be with you because... I love you."

My entire body was shaking and I thought I might collapse. "But, you're giving up your football career. Are you sure this is what you want?"

Nicholas nodded and then frowned thoughtfully. His silver eyes glowed as they met mine. "I'm not giving it up. I'm making a choice. A better choice. I'm choosing to do what will make me happy. And these last few months? They've meant everything to me, they've been the best moments of my life. The only rival is prom night, when we danced together and shared our first kiss."

My skin tingled, and I was pretty sure the only thing holding me up was Nicholas's firm but gentle grip on my hand. Like he was giving me strength.

"You were my first love, Grace," he said. "And I love you more every second that I'm with you. I'm sorry for the years that I spent being a coward. See, you called yourself a coward, but you've never seemed that way to me. You give me strength, you make me want to be a braver man. And, if you could trust me, I promise to do everything I can to make you happy. That's my promise to you, Ace. Forever and always."

I was speechless, I couldn't even breathe. All I knew was the heat traveling through my limbs, the sparks where Nicholas's hand met mine, the way my heart was healing, mending with his words, beating strong and whole.

"I love you, too," I whispered, my breath almost lost to the gentle summer breeze.

But Nicholas heard. A beaming, beautiful smile spread across his face, his dimple on full display. His eyes didn't leave mine as he slipped the dandelion ring onto my finger. He placed a hand on my cheek and then onto my neck, seemingly memorizing my features. I looped my arms behind his neck.

"Does this mean you're taking the job?" I whispered, my hands running down his firm chest.

His fingers grazed my chin and he tilted my head up to look at him. "Forever."

My heart almost exploded as he slowly, wonderfully, cupped the back of my head and leaned in. When our lips met, it was like the first taste of a strawberry milkshake after years of dieting, the first time you ever see a shooting star, the first whisper of warm ocean water after a cold winter.

Nicholas King was never my biggest mistake. He was my greatest challenge, my greatest memory, my greatest love. He was my soul mate, and there was no escaping the fact that, after everything we'd been through, we were meant to be.

Our second chance was meant to be.

46

GRACE

Three Months Later...

"Order up!" I hollered from the kitchen, where Tommy and I were putting the finishing touches on twelve eggs benedicts.

Kris came whirling into the kitchen, her blonde hair tied back into a severe low bun and her lipstick somehow flawless. She effortlessly grabbed three plates. "On it! I'll let 13 know."

"Don't call him that," I sang, grabbing another three plates and following her out of the kitchen. "The number's old news now."

Kris shot me a smug smile. "We have an understanding. He's letting me call him 13 today in exchange for me closing this evening."

"You're closing?" I asked out the side of my mouth as we approached the table. "Since when?"

Kris pressed her lips shut. "I really shouldn't have said that. Ignore me."

I wanted to ask her to elaborate on what she allegedly shouldn't have said, but she hurried ahead to the huge table by the window. She dropped off the eggs benedicts and ran back to the kitchen for more.

I deposited my three plates, smiling and chatting with the group. This was my favorite part of the job now—spending time with the customers, having conversations while they enjoyed their meals. It turned out that this large group consisted of three families who were visiting Aston Falls from out of state to do some hiking and late-season paddleboarding.

"Oh, did you go through Sam's?" I asked.

"We did," one of the women answered, her black hair bobbing as she nodded. "He was wonderful, so charming and helpful. We've been talking about coming back to Aston Falls this winter for sled tours."

"I can't speak for the sled tours myself, but the paddleboarding here is pretty legendary." I winked, and then grabbed a full bottle of ketchup from an empty table nearby to give to one of the young boys who was looking for some.

"I'll say." The woman's husband chuckled. "We also heard that we *had* to stop by this little place, and we're so glad we did. We have friends in Texas who raved about their trip to Morning Bell Cafe this past summer. And now that we're here, I can see why."

I blushed at their compliments. "Well, Morning Bell wouldn't be here if it wasn't for my parents."

A warm, firm arm slid around my waist. "Not to mention her amazing boyfriend."

I turned to Nicholas and couldn't keep a dopey smile from spreading across my face. The group of twelve laughed as Nicholas kissed me lightly on the cheek.

We left them to enjoy their meals and walked back to the serving counter together, hand in hand.

I'd been at the helm of Morning Bell for a few months now, and the cafe was flourishing, if I dared say so myself. Of course, there was no way I could take all the credit. Kris and Tommy were the best workers I could've ever asked for.

And, Nicholas... Well, I couldn't have done this—any of this—without him. Now, he ran the day-to-day operations of the cafe while I took care of the overall management. He'd also started running regular football day camps for the kids, and I loved to see how happy it made him. We worked together flawlessly. Like we were two cogs of the same machine.

Aston Falls, and in particular, Mayor Bob Davis, seemed pretty happy that Morning Bell wasn't going anywhere. Though it was fall now, the summer rush had never ended. We were busy as ever. And, with Nicholas by my side, there was nothing I couldn't face.

The front door of the cafe opened and a portly man I recognized strode in.

Speaking of things I didn't want to face...

Jim McNeil, the representative from Ross's Burgers, removed his heavy brown jacket—which seemed way too warm for this lovely fall day anyway—and took off his hat. He cast a perfunctory glance around the cafe before very obviously turning his nose up at the patrons. He approached the counter and I dropped Nicholas's hand.

"Want me to kick him out, babe?" Nicholas murmured.

I pressed my lips together. "No thanks, hun. I got it."

Nicholas placed his hand on my lower back—even after months of being together, his touch still sent chills down my spine—and then he disappeared into the kitchen.

"Welcome to the Morning Bell Cafe," I said, my voice frosty but formal. "How can I help you?"

I hadn't had the pleasure of seeing Jim McNeil since the summer, and I'd counted my blessings. He'd proven himself to be as bad, if not worse, than his first impression suggested. Over the summer, when Dad called him to reject his offer to buy Morning Bell, Jim turned into an absolute nightmare. He'd come by the cafe in person to yell at Dad, but luckily, Nicholas and I were here to kick him out.

And now, he was back. I dreaded to think why.

"You again," he said snottily, lowering his eyes to glance at my face. "I'm back to make this miserable hole another offer. And you'd be smart to take it."

"Would I?" I asked, my voice sugary sweet. "Somehow, I doubt that."

Jim's beady eyes narrowed. "You'd better tread lightly, girl. These kinds of offers don't come around every day."

"Maybe, maybe not. But I doubt you can offer us anything we'd want. You're simply... not what we're looking for."

I smiled at him flimsily and pointed towards the front door. Jim's nostrils flared and I thought he might spit out a few insults, until I saw his eyes glance over my shoulder. I peeked back and Nicholas was leaning against the wall, his jaw set and his arms crossed. Even in an apron, his bulging biceps spoke for themselves.

With a final glare in my direction, Jim put on his hat and winter jacket and left the cafe.

"That was great!" I squealed, running into Nicholas's arms. He pulled me close and placed a tender kiss on my lips.

"Okay, you two," a familiar voice chuckled from down the counter. "No PDA at work!"

I pulled away from Nicholas and blushed. "Sorry, Dad. Won't happen again, I promise."

Dad chuckled and rolled his eyes jokingly before returning to his newspaper.

Though he'd technically retired this past summer when he'd handed Nicholas and me the keys to Morning Bell, Dad visited the cafe almost every day. He liked being surrounded by the laughter and conversations of the customers. Every once in a while, he'd sign up for a shift to help us out—he said it "kept him young."

"Oh, Nicholas, before I forget." I grabbed a paper bag filled with scones from the display case. "This is for your mom. She called earlier and asked if you could drop some treats by her house."

Nicholas laughed. "She didn't ask me to get her anything when I went by her house to see her and Grandpa this morning."

In July, when Nicholas returned to Aston Falls after packing up his apartment in Chicago, he'd moved into a lovely, spacious house on the edge of town. He was currently renovating the interior and he'd been incredibly curious as to my tastes on the decor.

I was trying not to get ahead of myself and assume anything. It was sweet that he wanted my opinion.

"Ah." I smiled. "We did also have a chat, too."

"I swear, she talks to you more than she talks to me."

I winked. "It's just because she likes me better."

Nicholas wrapped his arms around my waist and pulled me close. His silver eyes smoldered. "Who could blame her?"

I could no longer breathe and it took everything I had not to fall into kissing Nicholas here and now. But, we had time. We had all the time in the world to spend together and grow our relationship.

That was one of the best parts about him and me. Knowing that, no matter what, loving each other made us braver.

And our relationship had only grown stronger and better with every day. Sometimes, when I woke up in the mornings, it was hard to believe that I wasn't living in a fairy tale. Nicholas was my prince, the love of my life, and I couldn't imagine my future without him. As for Whitney? She'd signed the divorce papers months ago, and was apparently dating another pro athlete in Chicago.

Nicholas kissed me on the forehead just as the front door burst open. Austin bound into the cafe and made a beeline straight for Dad. He slid into the stool next to him. "Sorry I'm late! Was on the phone with Ella."

He reached across the counter and gave Nicholas a fist bump before Nicholas went back to the kitchen. Despite all of our worries and fears, Austin was extremely supportive of our relationship. He and Nicholas had had a long talk over the summer, and they were now closer than ever.

Almost annoyingly so. Like when they both teased me about the ridiculous barefoot-chase incident.

"Ella?" I asked Austin. "How's she doing?"

"She's good… Except that Carly is getting married."

My jaw hit the floor. "Carly? Like baby Carly?"

"The very same. Except that she's 22 now. No longer a baby."

"Guess Ella's going to be coming back to town," I mused and a slow smile spread across my face. "At least for a little while."

Which meant that I'd have my best friend back for

longer than a couple days. After the tumultuous few months I'd had, I couldn't think of better news.

"It also means that she'll need help managing her crazy relatives." Austin chuckled darkly and took a long pull of a bottle of water. "It's going to be an interesting few weeks."

I smiled absentmindedly as I slipped into a daydream about Ella, JJ and I strolling the riverfront, going to the farmer's market, hitting up the fall festival together... Nicholas and Ted could join us too. I couldn't wait.

I was about to ask Austin when she was coming back to town when I noticed the dark expression on his face. He was staring at his phone, his mouth pressed into a thin line and his eyes stormy.

I'd seen that same look on his face a few times over the past few months. But, every time I'd pried, he'd brushed me off.

Now, I tried to tap into my twinny sixth sense, but I got nothing. What was on his mind?

I supposed that was another thing Ella and I could do together—wear down Austin so he'd finally tell us what was sending him into these strange spirals.

The hours flew past, as they so often did these days. The cafe was bustling and busy all day, and as we approached closing time, my face hurt from smiling.

I emerged from the back office after getting some paperwork done and I tapped Kris on the shoulder. "Hey, hun, your shift's up. Thanks for the help today, we can take it from here."

Kris raised an eyebrow, a cryptic smile on her lips. "No... I'm closing tonight. Don't you remember?"

I blinked a few times. With all of the drama with Jim McNeil, and the daily goings on around the cafe, I'd completely forgotten what Kris had said to me earlier.

"That's right." I bit the inside of my cheek. "I didn't update the schedule, though, so you're free to head home. It's a school night, I'm sure you have homework or something. Plus, I doubt your parents would be thrilled with me keeping you late."

I placed a friendly hand on her shoulder but she shook her head. "Don't you worry. I think *you're* the one with the plans tonight."

Before I could ask her what she meant, she raised her eyebrows and very obviously nodded to a point over my shoulder.

I turned to see Nicholas standing in the doorway and my heart ached with how gorgeous he was. He had changed out of his jeans and into a blue button-down shirt and black slacks that fit him perfectly. In his hand, he held a single yellow flower.

"What's this?" I asked, approaching him.

Nicholas held out the flower. "It's a dahlia. According to my mom, it symbolizes everlasting commitment and love. Plus, it's a little nicer than a dandelion."

I touched the delicate petals. "I love it."

Nicholas smiled and gently took my hand. "Want to get out of here?"

Like he'd ever have to convince me.

But, instead of leaving through the front door of Morning Bell, Nicholas pulled me up the stairs towards the rooftop patio. We'd closed the patio a couple of days ago after a beautiful summer season, and I hadn't been back there since.

The patio looked nothing like I remembered.

The fairy lights twinkled overhead and garlands of flowers and ivy hung from the strands of light. Candles flickered and danced around the exterior railing of the patio, and soft, soothing music played from the patio speakers. All of the furniture had been cleared away and, in the center, a cozy blanket was laid out. A picnic basket and two flutes of what appeared to be champagne were set next to the blanket.

Nicholas knelt to grab the flutes and held one out to me, his eyes dancing.

"What's going on?" My voice was breathy and uneven.

"We're here to celebrate," Nicholas said. He clinked his glass against mine and the noise echoed through the night.

"Celebrate what?"

Nicholas bit his lip and looked at me earnestly. He took our flutes and placed them on the railing behind him. Then, he wound his hands around my hips and we began to sway.

"Celebrate the lucky number 13." Nicholas smiled. "Because, thirteen years ago today, I knew that I had an unmistakable, undeniable, insurmountable crush on you."

I frowned as I counted back in my head. "But, thirteen years ago, you would've just met me."

Nicholas was silent and he nodded once. A slow, sexy smile spread across his features and my knees went weak.

"Oh," I breathed.

"Ace, I know that we've had a bumpy road getting here," Nicholas said, kissing my palm. "But, there is literally no one else I would've done this journey for. Everything that brought us here, all of the pain, the suffering, the struggles... to me, it's all been worth it. If it means that I get to see you everyday—work with you, laugh with you, kiss you—it was all worth it."

Butterflies fluttered in my stomach and a warm glow

spread through my limbs. I pressed my cheek against Nicholas's warm, comforting chest. "I don't think I've ever been so happy."

Nicholas chuckled and then, slowly, he stepped away from me. Without dropping my hand, he got down on one knee, his silver eyes boring into mine.

"What are you doing?" I whispered.

"Something I've wanted to do for a long while now." Nicholas reached into his back pocket and pulled out a tiny black box.

He popped the top and a gorgeous, sparkling round diamond ring fringed with emerald accents blinked up at me.

I gasped, absolutely speechless.

"Grace Bell," Nicholas murmured and his husky voice sent tingles over my skin. "I love you more with every breath, and with every moment that passes, I know I'll never stop. Will you marry me?"

My breath had left me completely, so when I spoke, I knew that it was with my entire body, mind and soul.

"Yes."

Nicholas's face lit up and he leapt to his feet, taking me in his arms and spinning me around. With his touch, I could breathe again and I burst into ridiculous, ecstatic, overjoyed laughter. His lips met mine, and fireworks and flickering candles exploded behind my eyelids.

When we finally came up for air, I leaned away, just slightly. I smiled cheekily, my body buzzing with happiness. "You do realize that, technically, we've gotten together three times now?"

At this, Nicholas smiled an achingly beautiful smile. In his eyes, I saw our future—our children, our house, our family. I couldn't wait to spend forever with the man I loved.

"Guess Mom was wrong about one thing," he whispered, pressing his forehead to mine. "Good things come in threes too."

Thank you for reading!

If you enjoyed the story, I'd appreciate if you were able to leave a review! As a new author, reviews mean everything to me, and I'm so grateful for each and every one of them.